Murder in Copper

WITHDRAWN

by

Virgil Alexander

Aakenbaaken & Kent

Murder in Copper

ISBN: 978-1-938436-64-2

Dedication

To my fellow miners. After working 42 years in mining and metals processing all over the US, in Canada, South American, and Europe, I met thousands of highly-intelligent, decent, hardworking men and women, from CEOs to laborers, almost all of whom I'm proud to call friend.

Several of my characters in my series of mysteries, both recurring and cameo characters, are based in part on real people I have known. Sheriff Bitters has the physical features and the good characteristics of Robert Reed, mechanical engineer. Lee Gallo is based on Leonard Vanell, chief chemist. George Simmons is a mix of several mining characters I've known, especially George Sites, maintenance supervisor, who did have lode fever and his own mine. Several geologists, including Chief Exploration Geologist Hugh Olmstead and my pal Robert Shank contributed to character Hugh Holcomb. I've previously mentioned that Al Victor has much of the personality of Harold Victor, journeyman instrumentman and San Carlos Apache, and the physical appearance of Peter Curley, Arizona Highway Patrolman, retired, a Navajo. All of these good men, mentors, coworkers, and friends—except for Pete Curley and Robert Shank who are still hale and hearty— are now deceased, but I remember them all fondly.

Delvan Hayward, Miami Library, is retiring this year; she and Mrs. Cheves are accurately represented in this story. They and several other librarians and archivists who have inspired and assisted me through the decades are the objects of Manny Sanchez's salute.

Chapter 1

Mergen Abdulov came to the University of Arizona in October as a EurMino visiting supervisor from Turkmenistan. A large, impressively-fit sixty- year-old, Mergen was pleased that he had been selected for this assignment, which was for him a six-month vacation in America. His background as a former Soviet Elite Spetnaz GRU officer was known to the bureaucrat to whom he reported in Tucson, Meret Mulikow, and it amused Abdulov greatly that the man was terrified of him.

Abdulov drove from the small but comfortable apartment provided by EurMino just off the university campus to Mulikow's casita grande at the Hacienda del Sol north of Tucson. He had checked Mulikow's office by phone, and as he expected, the bureaucrat was "working from home". He decided to drop by unexpectedly to watch his boss's discomfort at his presence. There was a doorbell on the casita, but Abdulov pounded hard on the door, then stepped slightly to the side so Mulikow couldn't see who was there.

The door opened part way and Mulikow said, "Who's there?"

"Good morning Fourth Deputy Director of Foreign Programs Mulikow. It is I, your humble servant Mergen Abdulov." He pushed the door open and entered without an invitation.

"Mergen, as I've told you before, the use of that title is inappropriate here since I am working as the program coordinator on this assignment. Americans prefer less formality."

"True, Americans are rude and undisciplined, but we are among Turkmen who respect station and prominence, Excellency." Mergen knew that his sarcasm was fully felt by Meret and grinned even more menacingly. "However, I do have some business with you. I wish to spend a week at Miami. I'll tour the mine and interview Diana and the department heads and then spend two weeks at the large mines near Safford. I will spend a day with Guch at the big lab and the rest of the time touring the operations and interviewing the various department heads. Could you authorize this so Helen Dane could arrange it?"

"Of course. Be sure to complete an evaluation card on the two students when you finish," Meret replied. "The dates will have to be agreed upon by the host companies. As soon as Ms. Dane has them arranged, I'll e-mail the information."

"Good. Do you still have Russian Standard Gold Reserve in your bar? I would like a glass of *real* vodka."

"The bottle still has some drinks in it. Here, take it with you and you can enjoy more than one drink of the nectar of the steppes."

~

Graham County Sheriff's Sergeant Brendan Allred had just finished the daily command conference call with the undersheriff and the other sergeants. He was reviewing his notes from that call and his earlier roll call with deputies reporting to him, when his cell phone rang with the caller ID of DEA Phoenix.

"Good morning, Special Agent in Charge John Scott," Bren said. "Isn't this kind of early for you to be at work?"

"Nah, I'm calling from my swimming pool. Just another lazy winter day in tropical Phoenix."

"You know that I can see you're calling from the office, right?"

"Ah, you got me. Do you remember Guillermo Benson, a guy we put away for dealing, attempted murder, assault, and a few other charges?"

"I'm not likely to ever forget Billy Boy. I was one of the attempts and assaults—the only time I've been wounded in the line of duty. He got three twenty-year sentences."

"That's only technically true," John said. "He somehow got a presidential pardon for the drug charges in 2010, and he served the other charges concurrently, so he came up for parole last month. I was notified of his hearing before the parole board and spoke against releasing him. But he has maintained perfect behavior, earned a degree, in sociology of all things, and was a trustee librarian. They have paroled him."

"That's not right. The guy is a psychopath."

"The parole board let him respond to their decision. He was brilliant. He pointed out that he was seventeen when he became involved in the criminal enterprise and almost nineteen when arrested and that he has become wiser with age and serving his time. He thanked them and assured them he would make the most of his life now. Then he turned to me and said he didn't hold any ill will and that he knew I was just doing my job. Then he said, 'Give Deputy Allred my regards.' Bren, the look in his eyes gave me chills. Your testimony of his callous shooting of Officer Phillips when he was already hit and on the ground got him the long sentence. I'm pretty sure he's blaming you. Also, he knows you are no longer with Mesa PD, so he's kept track of you."

"Well, I was happy he was going away for a long time, though obviously not as long as we thought. It won't be easy for him to find me. When I relocated, I took extreme privacy measures. My address and personal information don't appear on ownership, tax records, credit cards, billing, or legal personal transactions. I don't use social media, and Monica uses a pseudonym and is very careful who she friends and what she posts. I imagine what Benson knows about me came from news stories."

"I've sent you a couple of photos of what he looks like now and of his work truck. You should know he was offered a choice of several jobs that hire rehabilitated convicts. He chose to be a parts runner for an industrial supplier out of Apache Junction. A big part of their business is serving the mines, so he will be driving right through your area on a regular basis. I'm sure that's not coincidental."

"Thanks for the warning and the pictures."

Bren knew that his privacy was well protected. His business and ownership transactions were sent to Leo Foundation through a mail-receiving company, and his brother-in-law lawyer acted as an agent for all his personal business. But he also knew that as people in the area became comfortable with Benson, they would likely unthinkingly tell him where Bren lived.

~

When Mergen Abdulov was provided with his itinerary for the next three weeks, he pulled the files on the two Turkmen students and reviewed their backgrounds. As he expected, they were both excellent students with good behavior, fine personal habits, and unblemished records.

Diana Niyazov was from an educated, well-off family living in a fine home in Ashgabat. She had a brother just finishing high school. There was a note that the family was not closely related to the past President Niyazov. Diana's EurMino assignment was as an assayer and research chemist at SWI Miami.

Guch Babayev was from a poor herding family in rural Ahal Province, and he attended university on scholarships. Abdulov noted with approval that Guch had completed military cadet reserve training while at the university. Guch was assigned as an assay technologist in a large automated lab in Safford.

Abdulov studied the different routes to the mines he would visit and decided to eventually try them all during this and future roundtrips from Tucson. He was quite intrigued with the Sonoran Desert that covered southern Arizona; being from the Karakum desert, he found the contrast remarkable.

This American desert was full of plants and was much more mountainous than his native land. The prickly pear cactus and some of the shrubs and bushes resembled the cacti and shrubs of home, but Arizona was much more verdant, had a large variety of plants and animals, and apparently had no sand dunes. From his view, this was not a desert at all.

He arrived at the SWI operations a few miles north of Miami and was disappointed at the small size of the operation; the older mines around it were many times larger. He had interviews with their chief mining engineer, most of the other leaders in the mine, and the processing plant. He was supposed to have an interview with their executive, but he was not available the week Abdulov was there. However, he had been cleared to tour all the production facilities. He ended up having three days with nothing planned, so he elected to shadow Diana for a day and spend two days exploring the surrounding area.

Observing Diana turned out to be interesting because she was working on leach column research in which different combinations of acids, temperatures, granularity, enzymes, and bacteria were compared for efficiency with different ore types; some of this was completely new to him. In addition to the tall leach columns and a small analytical area, this lab was really more of a barn with pads of crushed ore and several very large unbroken boulders of ore with various types of electrodes connected to them.

Abdulov stood and took in the contents of the building. Then he said, "I understand the leach columns and the test ore pads, but why are those boulders connected to electricity?"

She explained, "We are recovering copper directly from native ore by electrolysis."

"You mean no added chemicals, just current through the rocks?"

"Yes. In most cases there is enough conductive metal, ambient moisture, and natural salt that the copper migrates to the cathode. We are trying different moisture contents, fracturing, and different voltages and amperages, but it does work.

"However, it takes a great deal of electricity, so is cost prohibitive. If we can figure out how to do this economically, it will revolutionize metal mining. No more leaching required, no—or at least fewer—chemicals, and only environmental improvement as heavy metals are removed from the undisturbed native ground."

"I must have copies of this research."

"I can't give it to you. It is confidential. I can't even remove files I'm working on from this building. I would be fired, if not arrested. And everything is recorded on video surveillance."

"You don't understand. I'm authorized by the Ministry of Minerals to remove any secrets we find. It is your duty as a citizen to cooperate. I do not like this, but if you do not cooperate, your family will be put in jail. So how are you going to do it?"

Diana drew in her breath and grew visibly pale. This type of coercion was routine in her country: families were arrested, jailed, and even tortured and killed for less than refusing an order. "I can't get anything out of here this week without being caught. We could arrange to meet to transfer the files at a location away from the mine."

"That's a good plan. Call me to arrange a rendezvous when your copy is in hand. I prefer it in a file envelope."

Abdulov spent the next two days traveling to the mountains and the two large nearby reservoirs. He thought there was a time these reservoirs and power lines would be of interest to the Russians, but satellites now provided that without agents.

~

Bren called Pinal County Deputy Dan Tomkin and explained that he had a favor to ask.

"Sure, Sergeant Allred. I'll help any way I can."

Bren explained the situation with Billy Benson, then added, "Guillermo Benson is a dangerous man no matter what anybody says, and I don't feel at all comfortable that he has specifically mentioned me, or that he has coincidently taken a job that will frequently have him driving past my home and office. I believe that sometime, somehow, he plans to get revenge."

"I sure don't disagree with you," Dan said. Sometimes both the court and corrections board seem to sit on their brains."

"Benson is staying in a halfway house and has a GPS ankle bracelet, which I would very much like to monitor, but I don't want to get permission from the court because he would be more likely to find out; that wouldn't be good. Would you be willing to access his movements and share the access with me?"

"Yes. In fact, the system is actually based in our office, so I already have access. I'll just add your smart phone as a blind copy to mine. So anytime you want, you'll be able to both see his live position and access his movement history. I'll be the only one that knows you are monitoring him."

"Thanks, Dan. I'll feel a lot better knowing where he is."

"My pleasure. The GPS binocular icon will appear on your phone in about a half hour. Just click and you'll have a choice of live or search history. It's self-explanatory."

Bren was happy when the icon appeared. He selected *Live*, and it showed Benson's location as the halfway house in Apache Junction, 127 miles away from Bren's home in Central. Bren did not want to involve anyone else in his concerns about a psycho criminal possibly seeking revenge against him, especially not Monica. She was stressed enough worrying about the viability of her pregnancy without that. He wanted to insulate everyone else from the situation, so he needed extreme vigilance and preparation.

Dan sent a message that the connection was made and added, "Benson is supposed to be in the halfway house every night at ten. Before he travels, he must call the house to inform them when and where he's going and call his probation officer with the same information. When he stays overnight, he notifies his parole officer where he's staying. He calls the house by 9:30 p.m., telling them where he is staying and when he expects to be home, and he must answer the parole officer's call to his room phone at 10:00 p.m.

"Occasionally customers ask him to return the next day to haul a repair item or a stack of their freight pallets back to Apache Junction. In such cases he ends up having to stay overnight, but normally except for Morenci, he goes home every night. So, they are keeping tabs on him besides just his GPS travels."

Bren pondered the situation with some anxiety. Then he thought, "I have the alarm and monitoring on the house, and an alarm on the office. I'll add video monitoring to the office and include a camera that focuses on the street and my house. Mom and Monica are licensed for concealed carry and are capable of effective defense, but I don't want to alarm them so will only mention the threat if it becomes tangible. Vigilance and normalcy are the order of the day."

Bren realized he was trying to convince himself.

~

Diana had previous short visits with Mergen Abdulov, about once a month, when he would interview her and fill out an evaluation card. Each time he had called her and arranged to meet her for a dinner meeting, and much to her relief, he had left immediately after. Even then, she did not trust or like Abdulov; he obviously knew little about mining and metallurgy, and he seemed more like a government thug than a scientist.

This visit had firmed up her opinion of him, and she was truly horrified by the threat. She decided now would be the best time to get the confidential files. Her boss was occupied in meetings in Phoenix, and Mr. Peralta, who was very interested in the research and often popped in, was out of state for the week.

On Thursday afternoon, Diana was entering results into the computer. She had deliberately left a bottle of Gatorade on the edge of the desk. She started transcribing her notes into the computer when she reached for a tablet and knocked the Gatorade to the floor. She moved the large barrel cleaning cart and cleaned the spill, leaving the cart blocking the view of the camera as she resumed entering the data.

The confidential accordion file was already out. She printed a copy of the spreadsheet and placed it in a previously used accordion file, which she then put in the two-handled crate she used for transporting samples. She covered it with empty sample envelopes and bottles. Every Friday she took the crate home for her trip to the field office near Safford, which she visited every Monday morning.

She did her normal cleaning routine and pushed the cart back to its spot. Then, for the camera, she made a show of placing an adhesive seal on the original file, returned it to the cabinet, and locked it securely inside. She secured the windows and doors, turned off all but the night lights, took her sample box, and headed home.

She was apprehensive about being caught; it would ruin her. But worse, she had no doubt Abdulov would see that her family suffered for her failure. When she was off the property, she called Abdulov and said she would bring the file to the field office near Safford on Monday. He told her to call when she was nearing Safford, and they would decide on a meeting place to hand off the file. Diana was shaky and felt that she might throw up. She drove home and took sleeping pills and went to bed without eating.

~

On Monday, Abdulov returned to Safford. He had hardly gotten into his hotel room when he got a call from Diana saying she was near Pima and asking if he wanted to meet her. He was having a pretty serious stomach upset, so he told Diana that he was in an important meeting and that he'd call her to arrange the rendezvous afterward.

Diana came to the Pima field office primarily to run spot assays on liquid samples from a small field leaching plant, in order to give immediate feedback to the geologist in charge of the drilling contractors. She then carried the bulk of these samples back to the main lab in Miami. The regular core samples were picked up by the mail courier for delivery to Miami three times a week.

At the SWI field office, Diana unlocked the door and carried the box inside. She was lining up her sample bottles on a table when she heard a vehicle approaching the building. The confidential file lay uncovered in the box. Diana hurried to the door and looked out the window. Mr. Peralta closed the door on his pickup and walked towards the building.

Chapter 2

Diana tried not to panic. Breathe, she told herself. She saw that quite a bit of mail had been left in a white USPS mail carton, so she grabbed the accordion file and quickly put it in the bottom of the mail basket, returning the jumble of mail on top of it. She got back to her business just as the door opened.

"Mr. Peralta! I'm surprised you are here." She tried to keep her voice steady. "I normally don't see anybody here but drillers."

"I forgot that you would be here today," he said. "I will be working here until late tonight, and I'm going to need all the desk and table space. It usually only takes you about an hour to get your stuff done, doesn't it?"

"Yes, sir."

"Ok, get it finished up as soon as you can, and I'll work on some correspondence; leave the tables clear when you finish."

Fighting the panic she was feeling, Diana got to work on the samples. Her mind was racing to find a solution to this dilemma. There was no way she could possibly retrieve that file without being caught. Finally, she quietly unlatched the window, gathered her work and equipment, told Mr. Peralta goodbye, and left.

As soon as she'd driven out of sight of the building, she pulled over and called Abdulov about having to leave the stolen file. He was furious, but she explained that she had left the window unlocked and that when Mr. Peralta was gone, Abdulov could get the files. He calmed down and said it was good improvising. Diana gave him directions to the building and told him Peralta would be working late.

At six p.m., Abdulov drove almost to the field office and parked so the car was hidden from the road and office. Being careful to stay out of sight in the mesquites, he circled the building, then climbed a small knoll a short distance away. Using binoculars, he could clearly see the man working. It was getting dark with no sign that the man was finishing his work. Abdulov had two more episodes of stomach upset. He realized he needed daylight to negotiate his way back to the car, so he abandoned his vigil and would come back early in the morning to get the file. Diana had told him the office was unused most days.

Abdulov was up early and returned to his hidden parking spot. He passed a car coming from the direction of the building. He had caught on that in America everybody on dirt roads acknowledges each other with a wave, so he honored the custom. He decided to scout the vicinity to make sure no one was around before he broke into the office. He climbed the knoll and surveyed the area carefully with binoculars.

He heard the sound of a vehicle coming from behind him, an area he thought had no roads. He took cover, what there was of it, behind a sparse palo verde tree and focused his binoculars on the driver. It appeared to be a genuine cowboy with a big Stetson driving a pickup truck with a horse trailer. The cowboy parked to the north near a good-sized cattle tank less than a kilometer from Abdulov and began to open the trailer.

Abdulov decided to use that distraction to get off the knoll unseen. However, a big bull quickly got out and walked toward the pond as the cowboy closed the tailgate and got in the truck. The cowboy reacted as if sensing movement and looked directly toward Abdulov. He turned the truck around and drove closer.

The cowboy shouted out the window, asking Abdulov if he needed anything. Abdulov walked a bit closer, but not close enough to be seen clearly, and answered that he was alright. The cowboy warned him that this was reservation and he could be fined for not having a hiking permit, then made a U-turn and left the way he had come. Abdulov thought, "That cowboy was an Indian; I thought they were enemies."

He cursed himself for a major breach of camouflage; his movement had given him away. Knowing he must act quickly, Abdulov circled around the knoll and climbed in the office window. He quickly found the white US Post Office mail basket, but it was empty. In near panic, he left the building. Closing the window behind him, he drove off.

His call to Diana left her at first dumbfounded, then shaken. She said, "The mailman must have taken it."

He asked, "Who picks up the mail? The government post?"

"No. It's an Apache man who has a courier service; his name is Norbert Cassa."

Abdulov heard the tension in her voice and regretted that; a certain amount of fear in this kind of operation was good, but too much could cause mistakes.

He told Diana, "Recopy the information, and we will make other arrangements."

Abdulov was angry enough to kill, but he realized it was his fault for not getting the package as planned. *I failed to maintain my self-discipline; that always causes mistakes.*

~

Bren had carefully studied the snapshots provided by John Scott. Twenty years in prison had not been kind to Billy Benson; he was not in bad shape, but not a physical specimen either—probably fifty pounds heavier, showing mostly around his waist and neck. The handsome face was gone, replaced by a pasty, deeply-lined complexion. His dark, wavy hair was mostly gone and what was left was a fuzzy-looking off-white. At thirty-eight, he looked closer to sixty. *If I had just run into him, I would never have recognized him.*

He also reviewed Benson's prison history and the parole hearing minutes. The guy had remained free of any rules violations, and for the last ten years had been an "inside" trustee. For years he worked in the prison industries, running the supply room and delivering tools and materials to the various shops, and then he became a librarian. All his reviews were positive, and the Warden fully supported his release.

That figures. He could always turn on the charm and kiss up. That guy can endear himself to most anyone.

The delivery truck Benson drove was a late model F450 Super Duty stake-side flatbed with a lift gate. It was painted orange with the company name Just-N-Time Industrial Supply in bright yellow on the doors.

That's good. It will be easy to spot.

Bren found himself almost obsessively checking Benson's location. So far, the closest he had gotten to the Gila Valley was a delivery to Superior for Resolution Copper Company. It looked like most of his work was in Mesa and the eastern metro area of Phoenix; a lot of the customers were electrical, air conditioning, or pump businesses.

I should feel relieved about that, but I know that a psychopath with eighteen years to plan revenge will be patient and will have a well thought out plan.

~

Five years earlier, Francisco "Kiko" Peralta, Southwest-International Mining and Minerals Corporation (SWI) Executive Vice-President, had ordered his company's Research Geology Department to quietly stake claims and buy old mines and existing claims in the area northwest of Sleeping Beauty Mountain.

They managed to get the claims adjacent to both the defunct Sleeping Beauty Mine and the Freeport-McMoRan Miami mine and a scattering of claims in the rugged Myberg, Ruin, and Granite Basins. However, with the passing of two years they had not made headway on the Money Metal and Giacomo mines, which were key to the company plan for future development. Peralta met with the chief geologist on the (then-secret) project, Hugh Holcomb.

Pointing to a patchwork of holdings on the plat map of the area, Kiko said, "Hugh, we've made good progress on acquiring claims or options, but we really need to fill in the gaps—especially the Money Metal and Giacomo properties. What is the holdup on those?"

"In both cases, they are patented claims, which is great because we could buy them outright. But the problem is finding who to buy them from; the ownership is clouded as parts of estates, by claimants who hold some stock in them, and even a couple of old liens."

Kiko asked, "What do we need to do to cut through the red tape and get ownership?"

"I was recently told by the Gila County Recorder that a miner by the name of George Simmons has a better handle on the ownership history and current status of those properties than anyone; in fact, he owns a share in them. I've met him once and, while he is a bit of a character, he does know what he's talking about. I think we should hire him as a consultant. He can probably facilitate a settlement with the claimants."

"Let's do it then."

"Another way he will be of value to us is that in the 1950s he was part of the re-exploration of these and other properties in the area, so he knows the extent of the underground workings. That will save us time when we start our exploratory core drilling."

"How much do you know about the man?"

"Only what I was told, and my impression from meeting with him."

"You said somewhat of a character. What do you mean by that?"

"His appearance, for one thing. He's almost a caricature of an old–west prospector: a wiry, fit man with a gray beard and hair. Probably in his late seventies. But he is clean and neat enough . . . doesn't look like a derelict. I was very impressed with his grasp of geology and mining. On the other hand, he has a silver mine, the Tiger Lily, in the Pinal Mountains that he works by himself, and he sells ore to the local smelter. A one-man operation is odd, and he's been doing it for decades."

"Go ahead and pay him for a two-week consult on the mines and their history. While working with him, try to get a sub-rosa feel for how much he would take for his claims. We can offer both direct funds and stock, but we don't want to give away the house by overpaying. Don't tip your hand until we know more about him."

"Will do," Hugh said.

"Let's have our legal department do a deep background check on Simmons. Have them copy me on the report. If he's trustworthy, put him on a retainer as a consultant for a year, renewable as needed."

~

Graham County Deputy Manny Sanchez patrolled with the windows on the SUV down, enjoying the late October 70 degrees and the clear blue sky contrasted against the deep purple of the Santa Teresa Mountains and Mt. Graham. He found an apparently abandoned car where it had attempted to pull off North Klondyke Road to a trace road heading west. The driver had turned too wide and gotten stuck in the loose sand. The passenger door was left open and the keys were in the ignition. Manny could see three sets of footprints leaving the car heading west on the two-rut trace. There were no return tracks.

The inside of the car smelled strongly of spilled beer, and Manny noticed a beer can on the ground fifteen feet from the car. He called for a status on the car and found that it was reported stolen that morning from its owner's home in Bylas.

Since Bylas was on the San Carlos Apache Reservation, Manny called Sergeant Al Victor of the Tribal Police.

"Hey, Al," Manny said. "I found your missing car."

Chapter 3

Manny noticed that the tracks had been run over by a car or cars travelling east on the trace. Most likely the thieves caught a ride home with somebody who was leaving a party in those cottonwoods at the end of the ruts.

Al arrived within fifteen minutes. Manny explained what he had seen, pointing out where the car obliterated the footprints. Al walked a short distance further, studying the prints, then returned.

"You're right, Manny. It looks like they were planning to join a drinking party at Coors Grove. Have you searched the car?"

"I just did a quick look over of the inside and found the registration in the glove compartment; didn't do a thorough search."

"Let's take a closer look." As Manny had seen, there was nothing of interest in the car. They opened the trunk, which contained a small tool box and an official-looking accordion file with a broken stick-on seal that said: "Confidential and Proprietary Information of the Southwestern International Mining Company. Do not remove from mine property." It contained some technical drawings and notes, spreadsheets, and what looked like a memo in the Cyrillic alphabet.

Al handed the file to Manny. "What do you make of this?"

"I'm sure it should not be in the trunk of an abandoned car. This stuff seems to be pretty important to SWI; and the memo with it looks like Russian or some Slavic language, except for the SWI URL, which was automatically stamped at the bottom by the printer. Since the car is off the reservation and SWI has no presence there, I think the sheriff will want to check this out before he returns it to them."

"I don't have a problem with that," Al said, "but we should question the vehicle owner to find out what it's doing in there. Why don't you call the sheriff and see how he wants to handle this?"

Manny explained what they found to the sheriff, who said, "This is something I will personally handle. I would like to talk with you and Al about this. I'll be in Pima in an hour, could you meet me there?"

Manny replied, "Al and I will be meeting with Sergeant Allred at the Taylor Freeze in Pima for lunch and our weekly coordinating meeting at 11:30. Would that work for you?"

The sheriff agreed. Manny called Bren and explained what was happening. Nodding to Al, Manny said, "We're all set up."

"Good. Lock the file in your car, and let's ride down and check out the Grove." Al radioed the Bylas police substation to have the stolen car towed.

Manny and Al found the remains of a bonfire, a fine collection of beer cans, and miscellaneous litter scattered through the stand of cottonwoods. Harvey Richards would stop by sometime this week and pick up all the litter. Mr. Richards rented trailer space at the old Johnson Place, and for something to do, he kept the entire twenty miles along North Klondyke Road clean and sold the aluminum cans.

The tow truck arrived from Pima, and the officers, each in their own patrol car, left for their weekly lunch meeting at the Taylor Freeze in Pima.

The sheriff contacted Sergeant Bren Allred and, on finding he was working in his office in Central, offered to pick Bren up for their Pima meeting. He then tried to call Southwest International Mining and Minerals Corporation (SWI) Executive Vice-President Kiko Peralta but left a message on his voice mail.

The Pima meeting was brief. Beyond the stolen car and the mystery file, nothing much was going on in the western area of the county. The sheriff picked up the tab for lunch. It was decided that until more was known, the less said about the mystery documents, the better. The sheriff would secure the file at his office, and Manny would assist Al in questioning the car's owner.

~

Bren was startled on Tuesday afternoon upon seeing that Billy Benson was past Miami on US 60 and had turned north on the Apache trail. The truck took the turn to the SWI Miami property and was there about one hour. He then drove into Globe and stopped at a refrigeration supply business. Bren's jaw clenched as he wondered if Benson would continue east.

Bren anxiously stared at the tracking monitor, his gut told him Benson was on his way to Safford. The stop in Globe lasted fifteen minutes, then the truck continued east.

Bren drove to his office near his house, parking out of sight in the rear. He took care of paperwork, checking Benson's location frequently. Benson continued on US 70 east-bound through Safford without stopping and continued to the Freeport-McMoRan mine at Morenci. He was there only about half an hour, then drove to the Quality Inn in Safford. Bren was angry that this bad guy could even be in his town.

As she often did at dinner time, Lizzie knocked on the door and came in. "Daddy, Grandma went home, and Momma says dinner is almost ready. Come and eat, and if you need to, you can work later."

"That's a good idea. First, I think I'll park my car here in the office garage. You want to ride with me?" They got in his sheriff department SUV and drove from behind the old store he used as an office and parked the car in the attached warehouse. Holding hands, they walked diagonally across the street to the house.

Bren thought, "Just in case Billy drives around looking, he won't spot my cruiser; no sense in making it easy to find me."

~

Hugh Holcomb met at Dick's Broasted Chicken with George Simmons for lunch. "George," he said, "I'd like to hire you for a week or two, if you're available right away."

"I don't have anything I can't do later. For assessment work, I normally charge $25 an hour plus expenses, such as use of my equipment, fuel, blasting materials, and such."

"How about if I pay $50 an hour for you to consult with me on some mining claims? If we need any work done in the process, our employees will do it under your direction."

Hugh confirmed that George's MSHA Miner Certificate was current and explained that George would be required to enter a formal confidentiality agreement and keep what he did completely to himself. Hugh produced a standard confidentiality form, which George was happy to sign.

Hugh then said, "I need you to help me produce a comprehensive file on the mines and claims in the Myberg, Ruin, and Granite Basins including the history, extent of mining, description of the workings, and ownership of claims."

"Most of that stuff I can tell you from memory, and I have drawings and a description of all the actual mining that has been done in that whole Granite Basin area. My records go back almost a hundred years, because I have all of Dad's original stuff."

"That's great, George, but I also want you to physically show me where each of the significant works are located, so I can GPS mark them on my topo map. I also want to mark all the water sources. I will need a formal report on each of the claims in the Basin. So, my administrative assistant will help you with the report and do all the typing for it."

The rest of the afternoon was spent getting George contractor access to the property and putting him through the mine site orientation and safety training. After a week of working every day with George, Hugh was convinced that contracting him was a good decision.

~

Shortly after Sheriff Bobby "Bear" Bitters arrived back at his office he received the call-back from Kiko Peralta. "Hey, Bear, good to hear from you. Your message sounded urgent, so as soon as I got out of my meeting I called."

"Thanks, Kiko. We've found something that might be important to you, and before I do anything with it, I want to discuss it with you." The sheriff described the documents in detail and how they came into his possession.

Kiko's tone of voice reflected concern and tension, "Yes, that is highly sensitive and can't be discussed over the phone; but I want to get together with you to discuss this."

"Metallurgy is a bit out of my field, don't you think?"

"Yes, but multimillion-dollar theft is not, and that's what I'm worried about. There is almost no one in the company that I can trust to share my suspicions with. I want to meet with you and if nothing else get your advice, but it needs to be done in a way that only you and I will know about it."

"I understand."

"I've scheduled some time in my cabin near Flagstaff. If I arrange to have you picked up by air charter at the Globe airport tomorrow, could you spend the day discussing this with me?"

"Yes. I'll take a personal day and let my undersheriff handle things."

"Good. I'll text you the particulars when the flight plan is scheduled. Drive your civilian car to Globe, try to not look like a policeman, and keep your gun out of sight. I'm booking you as Don Evans. Do you have a device that could scan for electronic bugs?"

"Yes, we have a couple of them."

"Bring one with you, I want to make sure my car and cabin are clear before we say anything."

~

As he drove to work, Guillermo "Billy" Benson decided to drop into his boss's office. Chapo Garcia was, as his name implied, not much over five feet tall, but he was muscular and, according to the other delivery guys, had been a successful professional boxer a decade ago. There's no question he was a tough guy, but he was also a pleasant and upbeat man, and all his employees liked him.

As Billy approached the door, Chapo said, "Hey Billy! Got a question on today's route?"

"No, I haven't punched in yet. I was just wondering about something. The other guys hate to make the long run up to Morenci because it makes a really long day or an overnight stay, and they all have families. I really enjoy the drive, just seeing that much "outside" is great for me. I would be happy to make that my regular route, rather than making the other guys take a turn."

"Let me call a short meet before we dispatch, and I'll poll the guys." Chapo picked up the PA paging system to the loading dock. "Light drivers, hold up for a five-minute discussion. You heavy haulers can get going. I'll be right there." He told Billy to go on out and punch in.

Chapo had the drivers gather around him and explained Billy's offer. The other five light drivers all said they would be happy not to have that route.

"Okay," Chapo said. "Billy will get the sixty and seventy assignment as much as possible, but when Billy is off or when we need more than one truck, you'll still have to drive it. Phil, you can trade trucks with Billy today, and he'll take the long run."

Billy's first stop was at the Pinto Valley Mine, west of Miami, and the second was at a solar pump dealer in Safford. In both cases they were for a single item. At Morenci, he unloaded the material for that giant copper mine, then returned to Safford and his usual hotel for the night. He had already become friends with Stella at the front desk. Tonight, he asked if he could take her to dinner sometime.

"I never date guests. That's a set rule with me. Besides that, I'm dating a guy I'm happy with."

"Gee, maybe I better stay somewhere else, so I can ask you out."

"You conveniently ignored that last thing I told you," she laughed. "You can continue to stay here, but I guarantee hitting on me will be a waste of time."

"Okay, we'll remain buddies then. If you ever change your mind, let me know."

Billy had never been, and was not now, interested in any kind of a romantic relationship. He enjoyed the many brief encounters he found in bars and was happy they were brief. But his plan was to create many friends who could testify as to what a pleasant and helpful person he was. He also planned to mine information from them.

He had been frustrated in finding helpful information on Allred. All the online search services found no address or phone number for him. He knew Detective Allred had left Mesa PD several years ago and had seen his name all over the news stories about the discovery of an army treasure; in fact, that was how he found out Allred was a Graham County deputy. He was still coming up dry on personal information about the man. The more people in Safford that he had conversations with, the more likely he would be to get information on the cop—information to use against him.

Billy had grown a beard and now dressed in Levis and running shoes and took to wearing a cap. Since he had always been a snappy dresser, dressing like a hillbilly would greatly reduce Allred's chances of recognizing him.

Billy often sat reading at a picnic table in Firth Park, where he could watch the traffic in and out of the sheriff's office, in hopes of spotting Allred and possibly tailing him to his home.

"It's a good thing I learned patience in Florence," he thought. "This slow psychological attack on Allred can't be rushed; and it can't begin until I know how to contact him.

Chapter 4

Manny followed Al to the Bylas substation of the San Carlos Police and went inside with Al as he checked on the status of the towed car. Al contacted the owner, who was overjoyed and eager to recover his car. Al personally knew almost everyone in Bylas, so when Norbert Cassa came in to claim his car, they greeted as friends.

Al introduced Manny to Cassa. Cassa looked about forty and seemed fit at about five-feet-ten inches tall. Al led them to an interview room and handed out bottles of water as they sat down.

"So, Norbert," Al asked. "When did you notice your car was missing?"

"This morning when I was going to start my route; it was gone from my driveway."

"Do you always leave your keys in the car?"

"No. I couldn't find them on the dresser. I must've left them by mistake. So, when the car was gone, I was pretty sure someone took it. That's when I called the police. Then I borrowed my brother's truck to go to work."

Manny asked, "What kind of work do you do?"

"My business is Cassa Courier Service. I pick up and deliver things like mail to the post office and drill samples to the assayer in Safford."

"Do you deliver samples for the Freeport Mines?"

"No. They do their own stuff. I don't deliver nothing for them. The ones I pick up are mostly for core drillers working on the SWI San Carlos claims and a few small businesses in the area."

Al said, "We found a file folder belonging to SWI in your car. Where is that to be delivered?"

"I don't know. On Tuesday, Wednesday, and Friday I pick up a plastic crate of mail at the SWI field office at McKinney Wash and drop it at the Pima Post Office. It's always ready for mailing, but that file was in the box I picked up yesterday. It didn't have no address, and the sticker says it should stay there, so I think it got in the crate accidently. I'm going to take it back today."

Al said, "We're going to take the file back to SWI, so you don't have to worry about that.

Manny asked, "Did you open the file?"

"No. I thought I shouldn't because the sticker said it was confidential."

"So, you didn't break the seal on the file?"

"No, it was like that when I found it. I don't mess around with the stuff I handle; I want to keep my customers."

Al said, "It's possible that somebody was trying to steal it; if so, they may ask you about it. Tell them it wasn't in the car when it was found. Don't say anything about the police at all, just that nothing was in the car."

"I hope SWI doesn't get mad at me. They are my best customer. Sometimes they have me deliver stuff to Globe, and I do pretty good on that."

"I don't think there will be any problem with them." Al handed the keys to Norbert." It's parked behind the building."

Manny called the sheriff and told him about the interview with Norbert, then headed back to his patrol area.

~

Kiko carefully read George Simmons background report provided by HR: *George Simmons was born in Globe, attended Miami Schools, and graduated from Eastern Arizona College with a two-year certificate in Mining Technology. As a youth and later as a partner, George had routinely worked with his father, Tracy Simmons. They originally did assessment work on their own claims and later worked as a contractor on the claims of others; plus, they regularly worked their own Tiger Lily Mine in the Pinal Mountains.*

George is respected by mining professionals for his knowledge and abilities, but he does not fit comfortably into large-scale mining or the disciplined professionalism of a corporation.

George worked as an employee for all the major mining companies in Arizona from one to ten years each, which is an unusually spotty employment history. He was referred to by acquaintances as a "tramp miner." However, the investigator found in talking to former employers and coworkers that he always left on good terms and would likely be rehired by any of them.

George's wife of forty years died in 2010. He has one son, also named George, who is a Coast Guard Commander in New London, Connecticut.

His income consists of Social Security, a six-hundred dollar per month Inspiration retirement, and receipts from ore sells. He has no debt and owns a small home in Miami, a pickup truck, the Tiger Lily Mine with its plant and equipment, several mining claims in Arizona and New Mexico, and an idle metals recycling plant in Miami.

George's character seems impeccable; he has no criminal history, pays his taxes, and lives within his means. He is an infrequent light drinker, does not gamble, and town officials and businessmen all speak highly of him.

Kiko called Hugh Holcomb and after confirming that Hugh had also received the report, asked, "Where do we stand on George Simmons' holdings in our mine area?

Hugh explained, "Within our project area George has twelve claims that he has kept current. We can't be sure without core drilling, but most of them don't hold much promise for having recoverable copper; however, three of them have great value to the project. Routing our solution lines across two of them will save a lot in construction and pumping costs. The third claim is patented and has water rights; it looks promising since it has natural springs on it and would help with our water supply."

"According to the background report on him," Kiko said, "He seems to have a bad case of 'lode fever'. He has many mining claims all over the southwest. And still at almost eighty, he is hand working his mine. Do you think he would be willing to sell twelve of his claims?"

"I can't say for sure, but he was upfront with the fact that he figures most of his claims only have value as mill sites, not mines. We have visited all the claims, including his, and have an accurate location on the assessment work of all of them. Those claims which belong to others that he feels have potential are the same ones our geologists have named. I think he will sell, and I don't think he will try to rob us on the price."

Kiko asked, "What about his interest in the Money Metal Group?"

"He is emotionally invested in that mine; family ties and all. He holds interest in the Giacomo as well, and we need it. I suggest that we offer him cash and stock in SWI for his interest in the two mines. I think he will be overjoyed to be part of developing the property into a paying proposition."

Kiko said, "I'm thinking of tying both mines and his twelve claims into a single cash and stock deal, so it's all his holdings or nothing; but he ends up owning part of SWI. I'd like to meet him right away."

~

Sergeant Bren Allred carefully monitored Billy Benson's movements each time he was in Safford. On trips in which Benson returned from Morenci by 3:00 pm, he usually would stop in Safford long enough to eat, fuel his truck, and return to Apache Junction. On trips that took longer, he would stay at the Quality Inn, drive around in Safford and Thatcher, eat at different restaurants, stop in at a store, or spend a few hours in one of the local bars. He also frequently sat at the park across from the sheriff's office.

Bren had avoided letting Billy see him, for obvious reasons; but he needed to see what exactly Billy was doing hanging out by the sheriff's office. He slipped on an Arizona Cardinals windbreaker and cap and wore sunglasses just in case Billy noticed him. He took his personal Explorer and pulled into the rest area between Highway 70 and Firth Park.

The man sat at the concrete table with a book open on the table and a backpack next to him on the bench. Bren pulled out his camera and took some telephoto shots. He could see nothing about him that resembled the man in the orange jumpsuit in the photos Agent Scott had sent, and he sure didn't look like the Billy of old. The ordinary working man's clothes and cap and the bushy salt and pepper beard made him unrecognizable. Every time a car moved on Tenth Avenue, Billy paid attention to it. He was also watching the foot traffic in and out of the building.

Bren was confused that there was no sign of the big orange truck Billy drove. The GPS tracked him to the motorcycle dealer and from there to Tenth Street, where he parked. Bren looked at the GPS tracking satellite view and saw Billy had parked at about the fifth parking spot from the highway. He looked at the street and counted to the fifth spot. There was a Polaris ATV in that spot. He took a photo of it, then drove to the cycle dealership, and there sat the Just-N-Time delivery truck parked in the lot. He took a photo of that as well.

I'm not sure how he plans to attack me, but it won't be a simple assassination attempt. This is a psych op.

~

George Simmons liked working with Anna Mae Bozovich, Hugh Holcomb's administrative assistant. She understood mine location and mining jargon. She rarely had to ask for clarification of anything as she edited his field notes and typed them into a professional report. She was also energetic and pleasant.

George said, "Annie, this is very good work. I really appreciate your doing this for me. How long have you been working in mining?"

"A little over two years. I started working for Mr. Holcomb before we even had an office, and before he had any of his geologists assigned here; I worked from home. I was issued a laptop computer and smart phone and that was my office. I grew up in Miami, so understood some things about mining; but Mr. Holcomb taught me everything technical I know. He is a great boss, very patient, but he won't settle for mediocre work, either."

"I agree," George commented, "I've quite enjoyed working with him on these claims. He's a true miner." In George's mind that was the highest compliment. "So how long have you had this office? Years ago, it was a small grocery store."

"He asked me to find a building of this approximate size that had functioning electrical and water supply and lease it for four years. I found it about a month after I started working. He looked it over and sketched how he wanted it organized and had me hire a contractor and expedite getting the work done. We moved in almost two years ago. That's when the first two field geologists came on."

"He must trust you to give you that much authority."

Annie remarked, "That's his philosophy. He says he hires good people, gives them direction, and lets them do their job. If they can't do it without continual guidance, he doesn't want them."

They continued working through the notes, drawings, maps, and old files provided by George, creating a file in the same format for each mine or claim in the project area.

Kiko Peralta came into the office greeted them, and said, "I'd like to meet with George in the office. Annie, bring your recorder and make notes."

They all took seats in Hugh's office.

Kiko said, "George, SWI wants to acquire your claims in our project area. We have an offer for you, but it will be contingent on our acquiring the rights to all the property needed to actually mine. Are you interested in this?"

"Sure am," George said with a deadpan face. "But we have to talk turkey before I agree."

"Okay. First, the retainer," Kiko said. "We will pay you two thousand dollars a month retainer for up to thirty hours of work. For work above thirty hours in a month, we will pay you seventy-five dollars per hour. Plus, we will pay normal expenses involved in your consulting. Is this offer acceptable to you?"

"Yes."

"Second, we will pay twenty-five thousand dollars for the twelve claims. Third, we will trade fifty thousand shares of SWI stock, currently worth $1.57 per share, for your one-tenth interest in Money Metal and your one-eighth interest in Giacomo. But the stocks will only be finalized when SWI gets full ownership of the two properties. Are these two terms agreeable to you?"

"Yes, they are."

"Good." Kiko shook George's hand and said, "Welcome aboard. My first assignment to you as a consultant is to identify all the owners or, if deceased, their heirs and other claimants in the two mines and advise me on a practical offer for each."

"That won't take me very long; I'll get started as soon as we finish the work for Hugh."

"Your work for Hugh can wait until Wednesday. Annie will get your contracts written and processed so you can sign them. I'd like you to start on the mine offers right away."

George wanted to share his good fortune. As he left he thought, "Rumors of a mine start-up could put a kink in getting the property settled. I better keep it to myself until the Money Metal deal is sewn up. Well, at least I can call Georgy about it."

~

Manny Sanchez called in and reported off shift at six p.m. It was already dark enough that the yard light by his trailer had come on. As he got out of the car, Jenny waved at him through the open kitchen window. He caught the aroma of dinner and realized he was really hungry.

Jenny opened the door and they greeted with a kiss.

"I love the fragrance you are wearing. Is it steak?"

Laughing, Jenny punched him on the shoulder. "It is Eau du Pork Chops."

"Umm, that sounds great. I'm starving."

"Wash up fast; I'll get it all on the table."

After they settled at the table and said grace, Manny dug in with gusto, putting away one pork chop and a serving of mashed potatoes and gravy. Then he slowed down enough to talk.

Jenny asked about his day and spooned a serving of the vegetable medley onto his plate. Manny told her about having lunch with the sheriff and said everything else was just the normal routine.

"So," he asked, "Did you get your application put in at the Pima school this morning?"

"Yes, and the assistant principal Mr. Goucher interviewed me. He said that Mr. Willard, the principal, would review it and probably call me tomorrow. It might take a few days to actually get me on staff, but he felt I was the best candidate. From the reaction of the secretary when I came in, I think I'm the only applicant. Mr. Goucher asked if I would be willing to start right away as a substitute teacher until all the administrative stuff gets done. I agreed, so I'll be a substitute second grade teacher starting day after tomorrow."

"Well, congratulations, Mrs. Sanchez! Those are some lucky second graders."

They finished dinner with Pillsbury cherry turnovers, cleaned up the kitchen, and settled down to watch Hawaii Five-0, with the standard warning from Jenny that he couldn't point out all the stupid things in the show. The phone rang. Jenny saw it was Mr. Willard, so she took it in the kitchen as Manny turned down the volume on the TV.

Jenny returned with a puzzled look on her face, "That was interesting. I'm hired and will start full time day after tomorrow."

"That was fast."

"The only thing is, I may only be teaching in Pima a few weeks. He said they have fifteen elementary students on the Klondyke bus route, and he's going to see if the district will let him reactivate the Klondyke School. I would teach there and would be teaching three sixth graders, seven third graders, two second graders, and three first graders."

"Why?"

"Because they could discontinue the twice daily bus run for the elementary school and could run a smaller bus for high school students. One of their teaching assistants just moved out here, so I would have some help. He said the school is in good shape and just needs the butane tank filled and the power turned on, so the total cost would be less than the bus."

"Wow. How do you feel about that?"

"I don't know. It came out of the blue. I've only done my student teaching and don't even know if I can teach a regular class, much less four grades. He did say that if they are able to do this I will be paid as a part-time assistant principal, so I'd make a little more and my expenses would be reimbursed."

"What expenses?"

"He mentioned use of my car. I would have to attend faculty and in-service training meetings in Pima. He said that the smaller high school bus would continue to run this route, so it would bring mail and supplies and pick up my reports."

"You must have really impressed them. How long will you be teaching a second-grade class in Pima?"

"He said he hoped I could be out here in as soon as two weeks, but it depends on what the district administration says."

Jenny's phone rang. She didn't recognize the name Candy Dosela but answered anyway.

"Mrs. Sanchez? This is Candy Dosela. I just talked to Mr. Goucher and I'm going to be your teaching assistant at Klondyke School. I'm so excited! I would like to come down and meet you."

"Do you live at Klondyke?"

"Yes, kind of. We have just moved up west of Aravaipa ghost town near the edge of the reservation; my husband is the tribal ranch overseer in this corner of the rez. We will be teaching my two children; that's good because Benny can be a handful. Iris is much easier."

"I would like to meet you. When could you come?"

"I have to have the kids at the school to catch the bus at twenty to seven every morning, so as soon as they are off I could come to your house."

"Good. I'll see you about seven in the morning."

Jenny had the same stunned look as earlier." That was my new teaching assistant, Candy Dosela. She's coming over to meet me tomorrow morning. She lives up by the ghost town someplace."

"Dosela? That's got to be Cowboy Dosela's wife. He's a tribal ranch hand who was recently assigned to take care of the cattle on this side of the Santa Teresas. He's a nice guy. They live in a trailer out in the middle of nowhere. There are no utilities at all. They have some solar panels, a Kohler plant, and butane. There is no well, so he hauls water, and they have an outdoor toilet until the septic tank system is finished."

"I wonder how she called me…"

"Cell phones work fine at their house. They hit the same tower we do, just further away. They also have a satellite dish so probably have TV and internet."

"That's good, at least we can communicate. Let's go for a walk; my head is about to explode."

Chapter 5

As time passed, the SWI geology department was moved from the old Claypool store to the office building at the mine and Annie was Hugh's office manager. The building in Claypool was repurposed as the hiring office for Human Resources, and the conference room was sometimes used for vendor or other meetings that needed a venue more convenient than the mine.

Since actual mining had started Kiko Peralta was more pleased than ever to have George Simmons as a consultant. George had worked out a package with the other property owners, which was much less than Kiko expected but very agreeable to the claim holders. In fact, he was using George to discuss not only claims, but mining and refining processes. Kiko was astounded to find that George was very familiar with high-tech copper stripping machines and had been able to troubleshoot and resolve problems with the new SWI machines.

George had pointed out that he could offer scrap copper services at a much lower rate than others because of his local scrap plant. Kiko forwarded George's proposal to engineering and procurement for analysis, which resulted in a contract for that service being offered and given to George.

After acquiring a new truck and bins and updating his plant in Miami, George was ready when the new tankhouse at SWI started.

~

Sheriff 'Bear' Bitters drove his personal car to the San Carlos/Globe airport, where he found the pilot of the SWI Corporate Aerostar 650 Twin waiting. The pilot welcomed Bear aboard as Mr. Don Evans, and confirmed he was going to Flagstaff. He said they would be on the ground in forty minutes and that the temperature was 33 degrees under clear skies with a slight westerly breeze. They took off to the west, turned north over Globe, passed over Roosevelt Lake, Payson, the Mogollon Rim, and taxied to a stop at the Flagstaff terminal thirty-three minutes later.

Kiko was waiting with the engine running to keep warm. He greeted Mr. Evans and told the pilot that they would be leaving about two-thirty, so he could go into town if he wanted. Bear took out a hand-held electronic device and scanned the inside of the car, finding nothing. They engaged in small talk as Kiko headed for Flagstaff.

There were a couple of inches of snow in the shadows, but the streets, sidewalks, and all sunny areas were dry. They drove to the cabin, a six-bedroom-with-loft A-frame just north of town at the foot of the San Francisco Peaks. There the roads were clear and dry, but there was a solid light snow covering everything else.

Bear was not a fan of cold or snow, so he was happy to be inside the warmth of the cabin; he took off his Stetson and sheepskin coat and took the little bug detector out of his brief case. He did a thorough scan of the building and its contents.

"We are all clear to talk." Bear handed a cell phone to Kiko." I bought a couple of burner phones. That will give us better control of our privacy."

Kiko placed a couple of logs in the fire, then turned off the gas burner and let the logs crackle along. "Would you like a drink?"

"Some coffee?"

"Yes, I started a fresh brew when I left to pick you up," he said indicating the Bunn brewer on the counter.

Bear mixed half-and-half and sugar into a cup and took a sip, as he watched Kiko draw hot water and mixed up a packet of Swiss Miss hot chocolate. They sat in easy chairs in front of the fire." So, what's with all the intrigue?"

"I'm being super cautious because a new process and its equipment are secrets we don't want to leak out before we're ready. For one thing, we want to get patents in place before we announce. I've explained a little about that to you already, but I will avoid telling even you technical details, simply because the fewer people who know, the safer it is. But before we get into that, I have another problem that I want your help with.

"I think I've uncovered a theft scheme in our Arizona works. We have a bunch of relatively small operations here, nothing at all to compare with Phelps Dodge when we worked for them. One of them is a leaching operation on our Lost Gulch, Webster, and Ruin Basin claims. They sort of wrap around between properties of the old Inspiration, now Freeport, and the old Miami, now BHP, and a couple of other operators. We have a variety of things going-on—some underground collection of in-situ leachate and pad leaching in several nearby locations, all of which we pipe to a solvent extraction and electro-winning plant."

Bear indicated with a nod that he was understanding everything.

"We track a metallurgical balance based on assays of the ore body, the material placed on pads, and the copper-impregnated water leaching from them. We have a very good idea of how much copper we are dealing with and from experience, and we know the rate of recovery to expect as it is leached by the acid water. We measure the volume of copper solution going into the solvent extraction plant and the cleaned and concentrated copper solution going to the tankhouse.

"I know this is probably old hat with you, but bear with me for a bit." Kiko continued, "The copper is plated as a cathode in the tankhouse and we know both the amount of copper being plated and the amount remaining in the tail solution. We weigh the cathodes being shipped, so it's a closed formula; the whole process is like a black box. We put X amount of copper into the box and will get the same amount out."

"I'm still with you," Bear said.

"On the whole process our cumulative margin of error is three-tenths percent, but we are routinely recovering about eight-tenths percent less than we should. So that means we are routinely losing at least five-tenths. It doesn't sound like much, but we are producing forty thousand pounds a day. It averages a loss of about two cathodes per day. So even at our current low price of copper, that's at least one-thousand dollars per day lost. The best I can tell, it has been going on for three or four months; somebody is pocketing over 365,000 dollars a year off this fraud. Almost as bad, our stockholders are very savvy about the business and will soon be questioning our efficiency."

Bear said, "At first I thought it was small potatoes, but that is *very* grand larceny."

"And, depending on where our actual margin of error is, it could easily be 900,000 or more," Kiko added. "When you are trying to justify a small operation to shareholders, that much can make a difference. Besides, I don't like somebody getting away with that kind of theft, and I resent our trust being betrayed by people we pay to return full value to the company."

"Couldn't you just order a deep audit and call in the state investigators to find the criminals?"

"We could do that, but the minute auditors show up, the theft would suddenly stop. We could prove there was theft, but we couldn't prove how it was done or who was doing it. I figure it may involve at least three of my employees: someone to make minute adjustments to the feed rate or the assay of the pregnant copper solution going to the tank house; someone to boost the cathode shipping weights; and someone to physically remove the stolen cathodes from the property, which may mean one or more of our weighmasters may be in on it. Possibly three people in the ring or more."

"Okay, extrapolating from that, what you want is an undercover operation to figure what, how, and who and to build a case, and arrest them?"

"Yes."

"You know that Miami is out of my jurisdiction, right? It's in Gila County."

"I do. The situation is complicated by the fact that I have the other, bigger problem I want investigated: finding out who is trying to steal our process. That is mostly in Graham County but also at our Miami Operation. Additionally, most of our employees at Miami are from that area and would likely recognize any investigators from there. I want you to head the investigation with your people because I trust you and your judgment. I will reimburse every penny, including pay for fill-ins for people on the case. I knew it was probably politically thorny before I mentioned it to you, but I believe you can figure out a way to do this."

Bear thought for a while. "Tell me how you visualize getting operatives planted at your locations in a way that would not arouse suspicion."

"We have an assay lab at Miami. One of the techs is scheduled to begin maternity leave week after next. I will hire and train one of your people at our McKinney Wash project site and temporarily transfer them to Miami as a replacement."

Bear said, "I have a couple of deputies that could pull that off; they've both had lab sciences at college and exposure to crime scene and forensic lab work. One is even a female."

Kiko nodded and said, "Gender isn't important. On the other hand, two-thirds of the lab staff are female. It might let her socialize better using the same change room and toilet facilities."

"That's a good point," Bear said, nodding.

"I'd like to also have an operative with free access to the tankhouse and responsibilities that would allow them to cover the rest of the property as needed. You will need to provide them both with good cover documentation."

Bear said, "We'll need samples of your employee forms and a list of required papers, tests, and such, so it will be authentic to anyone checking their files."

"The assay tech needs to be an SWI employee, but the others could be contracted, giving them freer movement without restraints of department or shift schedules."

A light blinked on in Bear's mind. "Do your operations have any Indian ruins or historic sites on or near them?"

"Yes, both. Also, old mines, ranch sites, and such at both Miami and McKinney wash."

"It will cost you, but I know a pre-project survey company that would work with us to provide cover. It would give me an in for working in another jurisdiction; my people are on the Artifact Task Force. I can legitimately assign them to the project to look into possible antiquities violations. The owner has worked with us on investigations, and he's completely trustworthy."

"One other potential political problem," Kiko added. "The Apache tribe is a partner on the copper claims on McKinney Wash, where about half the orebody is actually on the reservation. Will that be a jurisdictional problem for you?"

"Technically, no. It's still in Graham County. But politically there can be tension with the tribe over actions we take on the rez. However, we have a great working relationship with the Bylas Substation. We'll watch our Ps and Qs and work in cooperation with them."

Kiko said, "I've heard horror stories about business deals with the tribe, but SWI has developed a good relationship with them. However, with an eye to possible changes from tribal elections, we're building the infrastructure off the reservation on patented claims we own. Our surface work on the reservation is limited to surveys, drill holes, and water improvements. The shafts and plant will be on our property and only subsurface work on the reservation."

"Let me work on putting this together," Bear said. "I'll provide the technician. When would you want to start training her?"

"I would like to start tomorrow, if that's possible."

"Plan on it. This is a card for Mike Fulton at EcoAnthro. You can check out his web page. I suggest inviting him to a proposal meeting, and I'll attend with you to work out the arrangement."

"If he can do it, I'll set it up early next week. Time is important."

~

Manny took his shower and then he and Jenny had breakfast; they cleaned up the kitchen together, and as he headed out to the car he kissed her and said, "I'm patrolling down to Pima this morning, would you like me to bring lunch?"

"Yes, that'll be a nice change. I'll have a green burro and a small enchilada fries. We could use bread and milk, too."

"Okay. I'll see you at noon. Enjoy getting to know your new assistant."

Jenny fretted a bit over what to wear. She wanted to appear professional, so she toned down her make-up and put her hair back in a roll and wore simple silver stud earrings. She wore grey slacks, "practical" heels, and a plain white shirtwaist blouse. She thought, "I look like a teenager. Some impression I'm going to make!"

She walked the short distance from their house to the school and sat on the yard wall in front, at the large turn-around for dropping off children. She and Manny had walked around the school house before and looked in the windows. It looked like a pretty good classroom with normal enough furnishings—older, but adequate. She had no idea at that time that it would ever be used again. She caught a glimpse of a pickup truck coming down the mountain on Aravaipa Town Road and thought it must be the Dosela family. The truck dropped from view as it drove down into Stowe Gulch. Jenny checked her watch; it was twenty-five before seven.

Candy Dosela drove in and parked. Two children bailed out of the truck and ran to Jenny.

Benny asked, "Are you going to be our teacher?"

"Well, not for a little while. You must be Benny. And you are Iris, right?"

"Yes!" they shouted in unison.

"Well, I'm Mrs. Sanchez. It's nice to meet you both. I will enjoy teaching you."

Candy Dosela came over and in a gently-scolding way said, "*Tishnay*. You kids calm down and don't be so rude." Offering her hand to Jenny she said, "I'm Candy Dosela. I'm so happy to meet you."

"I'm happy to meet you, and so glad to have your help!"

Benny stepped in front of his mom and asked, "Did you really shoot a bad guy?"

Candy gently smacked him on the mouth and said something menacing in Apache, then looked embarrassed "I'm so sorry. I told their dad not to tell them."

Jenny smiled at her, then looked seriously at Benny. "I'm very nice, but I don't put up with people who do bad things. Remember that."

Benny's eyes grew wide, and he had no more to say. As other parents delivered kids, Jenny knew all of them as neighbors. The parents all got out and chatted for a minute then took off, leaving the kids to wait for the bus.

The boys and girls each gathered in their own groups and chattered. The boys were strangely silent as Benny whispered to them, then an argument ensued as to whether he was lying or not. Candy again scolded Benny.

"Oh, let them go," Jenny said. "There is no way to get that cat back in the bag. I wonder how long it will be before I get called into the office to explain it to the principal." She chuckled. "We will just have to use it to our advantage; we may have some very well-behaved kids."

The bus arrived, and the driver greeted Candy. He introduced himself to Jenny as Lyman Crockett.

"I'm going to be running the high school bus once you get going out here. I'll also be your deliveryman, janitor, and handyman. If you need anything or have any problems, let me know."

The kids loaded on the bus, and Lyman headed for school. Candy and Jenny talked about how they might handle a multi-grade classroom. Jenny was thinking about seating them by grades and having a "home room" session with all of them each morning, then breaking into classes for grade-level studies.

Candy said that was what they did when she was a student at the Sawmill school. She explained some of the things the teacher did there. They agreed to have a planning and preparation session the night before the first day of Klondyke School. Jenny was glad to have Candy's experience, but she was still apprehensive about both teaching at Pima and running a one-room school later.

Chapter 6

Sergeant Bren Allred had patrolled up Fry Mesa to the reservoir and was dropping through switchbacks coming off the mesa when his cell phone rang. He pulled to the edge on the straightaway and took the call.

"Sergeant Allred, Alf Hesse here. There was just a heck of an explosion up the canyon from my place. I walked up on the ridge to the east and there was a lot of dust or smoke a couple miles further up. You may want to check it out. There's no mine up there, and I can't think of another reason for a big blast like that."

"Okay, Alf, I'm heading over there now. I'll go straight to the scene, rather than come to your place. I'll let you know what I find." Bren was on the flat in less than a minute and turned on his siren and lights. He drove as fast as he safely could. Dispatch called him on the radio and said they had numerous reports of an explosion in the Gila foothills. The explosion was felt in homes from Eden to Lizard Bump.

Bren answered that he was in route with an ETA of fifteen minutes. He drove to his brother Ray's house on Lizard Bump Road and borrowed his four-wheel ATV. He moved his emergency pack to the ATV, drove down the road to the turnoff, and headed up the ridge.

There was still visible dust in the air as he approached the area Alf had described, so he sped to that point and scanned the area with his binoculars. He found nothing. A hundred yards further up the trail he noticed ATV tracks heading down to the canyon. He found the ATV, damaged by debris from the blast, parked near the edge of a fifteen-foot arroyo. There was a good-sized cave in the opposite wall about three feet deep, where no cave had been before.

Bren heard voices coming from a distance up the canyon and called out, "Is everybody okay down there?"

"No. We're both hurt. We need help."

"Okay, I will get there as soon as I can."

Bren grabbed his first aid pack, worked his way down a little side arroyo into the main channel, and trotted up the wash where he found two teenagers. Quickly checking them, he found they had numerous small wounds from falling rocks. One kid had been hit below the knee and had a broken leg. The other was hit on the side of his head and had a large knot and an open wound. The kid with the head wound was disoriented and too dizzy to sit up.

Bren helped them to lie a bit more comfortably and covered them with heat reflective blankets to reduce shock. He called dispatch on the handheld radio and reported that he was at the scene of the explosion and explained how to access the scene.

"There are two adolescent males with serious injuries. One victim has a broken left fibula and the other has a head injury; the head injury is disoriented and unable to stand. Both victims have several other contusions and abrasions that appear to be minor."

Bren went back and checked the kids. They were both complaining of cold, but at least they were complaining. That was probably a good sign. It was sixty-five degrees up on the sunny ridge but noticeably cooler in the permanently-shadowed canyon.

Bren asked the head injury, 'What is your name?"

"I don't know."

The other kid said, "I'm Donny Hawkins, and my friend is Max Gustafson."

Max said, "Yeah, Max."

"Donny, what were you guys doing here?"

"Just messing around for fun. We found four sticks of dynamite and some fuse in his grandpa's barn, so we thought it would be fun to blow up. We thought this place was easy to get to and far away from anything, so we decided to light the dynamite and throw it in one of the little holes in the cliff and run up the creek. It went off sooner than we thought, and it made sort of a landslide from both sides of the canyon and hit us with rocks."

Max mumbled, "Dumb idea."

"Is Grandpa Cleat Gustafson?"

Donny answered, "Yes."

"Donny, was the Dynamite paper dry or oily?"

"It was soaked in oil."

"That means it was old. You guys are lucky it didn't blow up on the ATV when you hit a bump."

"I didn't know that."

Bren chuckled, "You know a lot more about dynamite than you did yesterday, don't you?"

"I'll say. Look, sheriff, can you give me anything for pain? My leg is killing me!"

"No, but the EMTs are coming. I'm going to leave you guys here for a while, so I can lead them to you. Stay still and talk to each other. Help will be here soon."

Bren explained what he knew as he guided the two EMTs and some firemen and rescue squad volunteers, including his brother Ray, to the scene.

"The dynamite was old and oily, so they no doubt have absorbed nitroglycerin through their skin. Watch for runaway hearts."

With four men on each basket, they carried the kids to the bed of the Rhino and placed them side by side and eased down the trail to the ambulance. Each time the Rhino hit a hole or a rock, Donny cried out in pain. Bren watched as they loaded the boys into the ambulance, then drove to the Gustafson place.

He explained to Mr. Gustafson what had happened and waited while he called Max and Donny's parents and got them on the way to the hospital. He radioed in that the families had been notified. Bren turned to "Grandpa".

"Cleat, do you know where the dynamite box they found is stored?"

"I forgot it was even there. I used it decades ago for clearing stumps. I have a storage shed attached to the barn. It was in there someplace."

"The boys said the sticks were really oily, so the box is probably saturated with nitroglycerin. You don't want to handle it because it can bring on a heart attack. As long as it doesn't have powder or crystals on it, we can safely burn it. Would you like me to help you dispose of it?"

"I sure would."

"I'll get some latex gloves."

They found the box, and Bren found an open spot a hundred feet from any structures. They laid a well-ventilated scrap-lumber fire, placed the box on the wood, and saturated the wood and box with kerosene. Before they lit it, they removed the gloves and dropped them in the box. Bren dropped a match on the fire, and they stood a good distance away watching the smoke rise straight up and dissipate.

"Put a half-inch layer of kitty litter on the concrete where the box was stored and leave it there for about a week," Bren said. "Then scoop it out and dispose of it by burning it off in the same way we did the box to remove the nitro. Then dispose of the residue."

In his car, Bren called Alf Hesse and thanked him for the call and explained what had happened.

Bren drove back to his office in Central and worked on his report of the incident. He finished the report and was preparing to go off duty when Sheriff Bitters called and asked him to meet for a couple of hours the next day. Of course, Bren agreed. It was unusual for Bear to schedule a one on one meeting; Bren wondered what it was that couldn't be handled on the phone.

~

Jenny Sanchez didn't sleep well the night before her first day as a school teacher. In fact, she slept in short naps until an hour before the alarm went off, when she gave up and decided to get ready early. During the night she figured out exactly how she was going to dress and ran through multiple scenarios about what her day would be like, preparing a response for all possible occurrences. Manny had slept irritatingly well, as if he wasn't concerned about her big step at all.

She was completely prepared to go when the alarm heralded the beginning a new work day. Manny was instantly awake and surprised to see her dressed.

"Well, Mrs. Sanchez, you are the finest looking teacher I've ever seen!"

"I'm a nervous wreck."

Manny smiled, cradled her face in his hands, and kissed her on the forehead. Looking straight into her eyes, he said, "No need for that. You know your stuff, and you have a gift with kids. You're going to have a wonderful day."

"I obviously don't want to be late. Get yourself ready, while I fix us some breakfast."

After breakfast, Jenny handed Manny a sack lunch she had made. "So, you are planning to be out until I get home today?"

"I'll be patrolling around the Cedar Springs area this morning, so I'll probably eat at Cobre Negro picnic ground, then check out Cottonwood Canyon in the afternoon."

"Ah, yes. Eating to the sound of the trickling stream and the whispering pines as you contemplate the natural beauty of our purple mountain majesty. Except, this is winter; the spring is probably frozen, and the wind will be cold. Take your jacket."

They embraced and kissed, and each headed out in their own car. Jenny arrived at Pima with half an hour to spare.

At the school she was greeted by Mr. Willard and one of her fellow teachers. The two of them gave her an orientation on the daily routine and emergency procedures. Then they toured the school, ending in her second-grade classroom. To her surprise, Candy Dosela walked in.

Mr. Willard said, "I've invited Candy to assist in Pima until you relocate to Klondyke."

"That's wonderful!" Jenny said. She suddenly felt a lot less anxious. "Candy, did you drive in this morning?"

"No, I rode in on the bus with the kids."

"Well, unless you really want to ride with the kids, why don't you ride with me each day?"

"I will like that. Thank you."

Jenny placed the teaching plan and roll book she had been given on the desk and printed "Mrs. Sanchez" and "Mrs. Dosela" on the whiteboard. She then reviewed with Candy the pages in each text book they were supposed to cover. Children began to show up, playing in the school yard, and school buses began to deliver their precious payloads.

The bell rang, and Jenny found herself facing nineteen second graders. Mr. Goucher came in and introduced her to them; they already knew Mrs. Dosela. The class listened to Mr. Willard give the daily PA announcements, when, among other news, he welcomed Mrs. Sanchez and invited the other teachers to introduce themselves during the day.

After the ending bell the two administrators came to her classroom and asked if there were any questions and instructed her to immediately notify them of needs or problems.

Throughout the day she had met the other teachers and staff and felt welcome. Jenny was happy and felt that she had pulled off the bluff of knowing what she was doing rather well and that she and Candy had become friends.

At home she recounted her day to Manny, who smiled and said, "I told you so. Everything's coming up roses and clover; nothing could possibly go wrong now!"

"Now you've done it! I told you to never say that!"

Chapter 7

Bren walked into the sheriff's department and greeted Jessica, the office dispatcher and receptionist. She directed him into Bear Bitter's office as the Sheriff rose and came to shake hands. Bren sat in one of three comfortable visitor chairs. Bear turned one of the others to face Bren rather than sitting behind the desk.

"We are going to conduct covert investigations into those confidential SWI papers Manny and Al found," Bear said, "and a suspected embezzlement and copper theft ring. We are talking about two high-dollar crimes, so the undercover work needs to be flawless. I want to keep the details away from even the operatives we use. They are to know only what they need to know for their specific assignment. I will stay closely involved in this investigation, and you will be in charge of the field operations.

"When I finish going over everything with you, we'll bring Pat Haley and Manny Sanchez in and get them started on their cover. I figure it will take me about an hour to go over the plans with you. Then we need to get Manny and Pat started. I have already gotten the cover documents started for Pat, because she needs to start this afternoon. Manny will have a week or so to change his look. Phone them and have them come in at 11:10."

Bren did as instructed. Then Bear related all but the SWI project details to Bren. They agreed on a plan by which they could best conduct surveillance and provide monitoring and back-up protection for the two undercover officers.

Bren was surprised at how much of the plan Bear had already set into action. In addition to the preparation for IDs, he had arranged for EcoAnthro to conduct a complete environmental and historic preconstruction survey of the SWI properties near Miami and Safford. The survey would provide the needed cover for surveillance. The Sheriff had already assigned reserve deputies as temporary replacements for the two regular deputies.

They decided not to even mention the SWI confidential project to the operatives, since the work they would be doing on the theft ring would simultaneously provide the needed intelligence concerning the project.

Deputies Haley and Sanchez arrived at eleven. The Sheriff and Bren had finished their planning, so the deputies were asked to come in early. The Sheriff had instructed Bren to make the assignments.

Bren said, "We're going undercover at the SWI Mines in Safford and Miami to catch a theft ring that is fraudulently changing the books to hide copper theft amounting to a half-million dollars or more per year. This is going to be disruptive to your lives for a while. The first thing to do is take off your uniform as soon as you get home and stay in civvies until further notice."

Turning to Manny, he said, "You will be Marco Olvera. Your assignment is as an industrial hygiene technician contractor in the mine and plant where the copper is produced. You will be an employee of EcoAnthro. This packet contains an explanation of mine processes and safety policies and practices. The book on industrial health and hygiene will familiarize you with your area of specialty. Study them thoroughly. You probably won't be at the mine for a couple of weeks, so you should have this memorized by then."

"Pat, you will begin training today as an analytical lab technician. I've given you the same packet that I gave to Manny. Study it well, but feign ignorance of copper mining on the job. You need to dye your hair dark as soon as we finish here. You will get plain brown contact lenses. Pick them up at Family Eye Center then return here to get a new photo ID, before you go for your lab training. You will be training for a week at the SWI Field Engineering office off Hot Springs Road. A map is in your packet. Meet Kiko Peralta there at two this afternoon."

Bren paused for a moment. "Peralta is the only person at SWI who knows about either of you, but even with him, stay in character at all times. We don't want anyone overhearing something inconsistent with your cover. Starting today, you each will be given a car registered to your alias.

"This assignment could last for months. You each have a place rented in the Miami area in your name. You are not to socialize or have any contact with each other beyond that which will naturally occur in the course of your jobs. As for Jenny and Andy, tell them you are going to be doing Homeland Security training. Part of it will be practicing an undercover identity."

Sheriff Bitters leaned forward on his desk and said, "Because there is a lot of money involved, having your cover blown could be deadly; don't let that happen. Pay attention to everything, without seeming nosey; being new gives you reason to ask a lot of questions. Keep track of, but don't seem to notice, little violations of policy by those around you.

"Your identity package includes a driver's license, a birth certificate, and a debit card with a two-thousand-dollar balance. Set your SWI paycheck to auto-deposit to that account. Save your receipts, but don't do anything with them until the investigation is over. Any money besides the rent, utilities, fuel, and food and household items that isn't receipted and appropriate to the investigation will have to be given to the department. Your sheriff office paycheck will continue to be issued as it now is; you both have auto-deposit, so your department pay will accumulate in your regular account."

"If you do any personal business, do it by mailed check. Don't let anybody see your cover persona associated with your real name. I know this will be hard for you Manny, but don't go to church; you both need to be recluses when you are home. If you go out with your significant other, do it out of Gila or Graham Counties. This is serious, serious business. Any questions?"

Stunned silence prevailed.

~

Cowboy Dosela started working cattle with the tribal herd when he was thirteen, and by sixteen he was considered a journeyman cowboy, doing anything that the others could do, and in many cases doing it better. He would have been happy to drop out of school and cowboy fulltime, but his parents insisted that he finish high school. So, at eighteen he became a lead cowboy, and at twenty-two he was managing eleven pastures. Nobody else was willing to move to the isolated range on the southern edge of the reservation, so he volunteered. Today, he had to return *Yaz*, the big mixed-breed bull, back to the River Pasture just north of the Gila and east of Bylas.

Cowboy had witnessed the birth of Yaz, because the mother cow had gotten caught in some old barbed wire that had been carelessly left in a tangle on the range. She was badly cut around the legs and left hind quarter and was starting to get infected. She was a wild old range cow and went crazy when he approached to help her, inflicting more damage to herself. He roped her and tied her short to a nearby juniper and covered her head with a piece of tarp.

Then with wire cutters, he cut out and removed little sections of the wire until he had her free. Keeping her blindfolded, he led her back to the holding corral and put her in a squeeze chute where, to her great protests, he cleaned out the wounds and applied antiseptic salve. She had maggots on the infected area, so he left them there until the dead flesh was eaten, then he cleaned that wound and salved it. In a couple of weeks of isolating her in a small pen and giving her hay and occasionally oats he had her tamed, so that she would come to him when he approached.

When she dropped the calf, it was really big, and momma required help getting the job done. In the end, both the calf and momma were fine. The baby was mostly Hereford red and had prominent black highlights on the head and legs; but from the top of his curly head to the base of his tail, the entire back was white. So, Cowboy name him "*Yaz*," Apache for snow, because it looked like he had been standing in a snowstorm. He knew the minute he saw the size of Yaz that he would make a good bull, so he treated him like a pet. Yaz grew a full head taller and weighed a ton—200 pounds more than any other bull on the rez. But he would come when called and would eat oats out of Cowboy's hand.

Cowboy drove across the mesa-like flat to within thirty feet of Yaz, opened the ramp gate on the trailer, and called in Apache, "Let's go find some more girls, Yaz." The big bull walked to cowboy and gently bumped his huge head against his shoulder. Cowboy held out the hand with oats in it. Yaz ate them, then walked slowly up the ramp into the trailer. Cowboy closed the gate and started on the fifty-five mile trip to Yaz's next pasture.

Cowboy wondered why the tribe had never connected to the county road on McKinney Wash. Using that route would save him almost an hour and about ten miles of driving on a jeep trail to get to the pond across the river and north of Black Point, which would be Yaz's home until spring. Yaz liked to be near water, so Cowboy always accommodated him.

He drove to the center of the flat area between three low hills about an eighth-mile west of the pond. The sun, glowing red through the distant haze, was beginning to set. The sky was a light pink, while the earth was in a blush of orange alpenglow.

Cowboy lowered the tailgate and patted Yaz.

"Go down it," he said in Apache. "Good, good." Yaz backed out and headed over to the pond for a drink. As Cowboy watched the bull go, he caught a glimpse of movement from the east on the highest of the three knolls.

Looking more intently, he saw a man in camouflage shirt and tan pants step behind an inadequately sparse palo verde, apparently not wanting to be seen. He saw he was a big white guy, so maybe that's why he hid; didn't want to be caught hiking on the rez without a permit. Maybe he would check on the guy, just because he seemed so antsy.

He closed the tailgate and hopped in the truck and drove further east on the jeep trail to the turnaround. He was only an eighth mile from the county road here, but this was as far as his road went; just an eighth of a mile would save him so much time. He noticed a red sedan parked off the wash road with a yellow Hertz sticker on the back bumper. This time there was not another bush large enough to hide the guy, so Cowboy turned off the engine, waved and shouted over to him.

"Are you lost?"

The man walked about half the distance between them. "No, I'm not lost. I was exploring the interesting little mountain."

Cowboy thought the man had some kind of Polish accent. The man was also an extraordinarily massive fellow, maybe six-five and three hundred pounds with no apparent fat.

"I should warn you, this is the Apache Indian Reservation."

"Yes. I saw a sign on the fence, but only I'm looking around."

"It's fine with me, but if a game warden or policeman sees you, they may cite you for not having a recreational permit. It's required to hike on the reservation."

"I did not know that requirement."

"I just wanted to make sure you didn't need help. Have a good afternoon."

"And you the same."

As Cowboy drove away, he could see the man was walking east, away from the reservation. He had noticed the man had a commando knife on his belt, binoculars and a camera around his neck, and his pockets were full of other gear. He could also see the outline of a large handgun in one of the cargo pockets. He seemed prepared for war, not day hiking. As he topped out on a little ridge, he looked in his rearview mirror and saw the man heading south past the construction office by McKinney Wash. Cowboy felt a bit uneasy about that man.

Chapter 8

Deputies Haley and Sanchez left their keys in the office, put their equipment belts and weapons in their lockers, and picked up their "new" civilian cars in the parking lot.

In her mind, Pat Haley officially put away her reality, and put on Cathy Winn, chemical analyst. Her car was a six-year-old VW Jetta. Bren had assured her it was in perfect working order, so she could depend on it when needed. It was actually a pretty good ride, so she didn't mind. She went home and changed into jeans and a dark blue T-shirt.

She went to Walgreens and picked up a dark brunette hair color, then stopped at the eye doctor's and got some quick training on her new brown eyes, along with a box full of drops, cleaners, soaks, and instructions. She was surprised that the contact lenses didn't bother her at all. At home she read and followed the instructions for coloring her hair and was shocked at what a change it made in her. She dried and brushed her hair straight with bangs combed to one side.

Pat grabbed the map to SWI and headed out the door. She drove west on US 70 to Ft. Thomas where she took the dirt River Road to the McKinney Wash Road and almost immediately turned left to the newly-cut road to the SWI field office. She arrived fifteen minutes early, but seeing a car there, she went in.

Kiko rose as Cathy came in. She offered her hand and said, "I'm Cathy Winn, reporting for the analytical lab technician position."

"I'm pleased to meet you and happy you are willing to help me out. Do you have the application information?"

She handed him a Manila envelope. "Yes, plus copies of my birth certificate, driver's license, resume, physical, drug test results, and background check."

"Great! That will satisfy HR. Have you had any chemistry training?"

"I took high school chemistry and Chem 101 at college. I probably don't remember much of it."

"That's okay. That background will help you get the hang of this faster. You need to master five or six procedures and be familiar with a handful of others. I've put together this little notebook of analysis, which you can take home and study. We have the rest of this week and a couple of days next week for you to practice. Then you will go to work in our real lab near Miami. Most of what you will be doing is running liquid copper samples through this machine, an atomic absorption spectrophotometer, usually called an AA machine."

"We did get to run a few samples through an AA at the University; we also did some wet titration analysis. I don't remember much about either, though. That was at least six years ago."

"Still, it is well ahead of where most new employees start. The processes in the first section of the notebook need to be committed to memory, which will be easier once you have performed them. Today I will get you trained in lab safety. Do you know the first rule of working with acids?"

"Yes, never pour water into acid; slowly add acid to water while stirring."

"Good, you're going to do fine. I got your clothing sizes from the sheriff and have a set of our lab uniforms for you. Fresh ones are issued, and the worn ones returned for laundering each Friday. Also, you will be issued lab coats which you must wear in the lab as well as safety glasses. When you get to Miami, you will need your safety boots as described in your orientation material. Now, let's sit down and get started."

They worked until six in the evening. Pat gathered up her homework and drove home. She freshened up a bit and redid her hair and makeup and was ready to surprise her fiancé, Deputy Andy Lopez, when he arrived. He was startled at the change in her.

"Wow, you really changed your look."

"It's for work. I've got good news and bad news."

Andy looked nervous. "Lay it on me."

"I'm going to be doing homeland security training for the next two or three months out of town except for weekends. It's good news because it's good for my career, but it's bad news because we'll be apart all week."

"Does your transformation have something to do with this?"

"Yes. Part of the training is learning to safely play an undercover role. I'm getting some preliminary training and preparation right now, but starting sometime next week, I will be gone. Beyond that, I can't talk about it at all."

"Okay, I get it. I won't bother you for details. You are beautiful, but I like the real beautiful you better. When you can, I hope you go back to being you."

Pat smiled flirtatiously. "I don't want to keep this look, but it is kind of fun. I know we were planning on going out, but I'm not supposed to be out in public much; if you want, we can get take out, or we can go out of town and eat out."

Andy smiled and said, "Do you feel like barbecue? We can go to Wilcox and eat in a train car."

"Sounds good to me. You can tell me what happened during your shift today." Pat was grateful that Andy was supportive but was pretty sure he was as apprehensive as she about being separated; they were normally together for a few hours every day.

~

Manny Sanchez was likewise trying to get his head around his new assignment. He was having a real problem with the thought of Jenny spending all week for several weeks alone out at the trailer. He was also having a problem with being away from her that much; the highlight of his day was coming home to her. He knew from the fact that the sheriff was personally involved that this investigation was a big deal. It would be good for him career-wise, but he didn't feel very enthused about it.

He drove the 2010 Jeep Sahara home and changed out of his uniform. He decided he would spend the time until Jenny arrived studying the cover material. He had needed a haircut for a couple of weeks, so he had a head start on changing his hairstyle, and he was officially seven hours into growing his beard. He actually enjoyed learning about mining processes and had even gone online to get a better understanding of solvent extraction.

He realized that Jenny might be apprehensive with the strange Jeep being parked at the house instead of his department car. It had only been six months since she had to defend herself, and him, from a deadly criminal in this very place. To put her at ease, he decided to sit out front on a lawn chair to read until she arrived.

Jenny drove up to the trailer and Manny was surprised that Candy was with her. He decided he better warn her not to ask about the Jeep, so he walked to the car and greeted her with a kiss.

He whispered, "I'll explain later." Noticing a box of school stuff in the back seat, he said, "I'll get this stuff out for you."

Jenny explained, "Candy started working today as my aide, so she will be riding with me each day."

"That's a nice surprise. Good to see you, Candy. It's great that you won't have to make the trip alone."

"I could have ridden the bus in with the children, but this is much better. Jenny even offered to have the kids ride with us, but they like riding the bus."

Jenny explained, "Candy and I are going to sit at the table and prepare some lesson material; it will probably take less than an hour. She and I are going to carpool while we work in Pima. She told Mr. Dosela to come get her in about half an hour."

"I've been doing some homework, too," Manny said. "But it's on the couch and coffee table. I'll kind of straighten that up. When Cowboy comes, I'll visit with him until you ladies are finished."

He sat on the couch and put his files back together in an orderly manner out of the way on a side table. He heard the sound of tires on the gravel of the driveway, so he went out to see Cowboy.

Cowboy had already picked up the kids, and as soon as he parked at the Sanchez home, they eagerly scrambled out and started exploring.

Manny turned to Cowboy. "The ladies are still working on their lesson, so we can visit a bit. How are things going on your pioneering up there?"

"Everything is pretty good, but the wife isn't very happy about having to fetch water in a bucket. We have two perfectly good bathrooms and a hot water heater, but no water. I checked out the spring up the creek from us; it has a good flow, but the sand drinks it all up in about forty feet. I'm going to clean the spring up and put a catch sump with an overflow and pipe water from it; it's only about a hundred yards. I'll let it gravity feed from the sump to a tank about halfway down and chlorinate it there, then pipe it into the house. It'll be about a twenty-foot drop, so we'll have some water pressure."

Manny asked, "When will you have the supplies? I might be able to help."

"I had to take the bull, Yaz, over by the river, so I stopped by the supply yard; got a big tank, a little tank, and all the pipe and fittings I need, so I'll work on it tomorrow."

"I'm off tomorrow, so when the ladies get off in the morning I'll come up to help you."

Candy came out of the house, and Cowboy whistled and waved at the kids who were playing in the sand wash and they came running. The Sanchez's stood in the yard and waved as the family drove off. Manny held the door for Jenny, and they went back in the house.

"I bet you had another good day at school, didn't you?" Manny asked.

"Yes! And it will be even better now that we are better organized. So, where's your car, and what's with the civvies?"

Manny said, "I'm not supposed to tell anyone about this, but I'm going to be working out of town for several weeks, maybe months. The only thing they will let me say is that I'm going to be getting Homeland Security training, and part of it is practicing undercover techniques. I'll assume a cover identity; Marco Olvera," he said with a forced chuckle, "but you can call me Mark. I have to let my hair and beard grow and not act like a cop. When I'm not at work, I have to kind of stay out of sight of the public."

"Well, that's neat. I'm proud of you," Jenny said with a smile.

Manny knew her smile wasn't easy, and he caught a glimpse of moisture welling in her eyes. "We've only been married a few months, and now we have to be separated. I'm sorry."

"I'll get dinner going. We can plan some more afterwards," she said as she went to the kitchen, mainly to hide the tears.

~

Bren was patrolling north of Pima when his cell phone rang. He pulled off the road and answered. It was the boss.

"Bear here. I was just reading your report on the dynamite accident. You did a good job of handling that. Lucky for those two dumb kids they didn't get more seriously hurt. I checked on the status of the Gustafson boy. He has a concussion but no bleeding on the brain and is going to be fine. He's going home sometime today. I see that you recommend no further action; don't you think we should cite them to impress the seriousness of the situation on them?"

"I don't think anything we could do would impress them more than their injuries have," Bren replied. "Besides, I don't know what we would cite them for. They didn't steal the dynamite. They didn't damage anything but themselves and their personal property. They didn't deliberately endanger anyone.

"I could probably have cited Cleat for not securing the explosive, but farmers have been storing dynamite in their sheds for centuries. If we pull the boys into court, they will probably attract the attention of the ATF. The kids could be on a watch list for the rest of their lives. All of us farm kids have played with dynamite at some time or another. I seem to recall a story from about 1970 about a kid who got hurt when he threw dynamite into a crevice at Red Knoll."

Bear laughed. "You make a good point. I wasn't cited, and I lost all interest in playing with dynamite. Of course, everybody in the Valley remembers that incident, so I'll never live it down. And that is without any real record of it. Imagine being federally listed. It would have destroyed my chances for a career."

Bren said, "It might not be a bad idea to send a safety alert to all the schools in the county and suggest that they have a science teacher explain the dangers, especially of old explosives—that even touching them or their packaging can poison them."

"That's a great idea! I've got a document with illustrations and photos that I used for training mine employees on this subject. I'll edit it specifically for school children and send it out." Bear changed the subject. "So where are we on our two new undercover operatives?"

"They're both studying the materials supplied by Kiko. Deputy Haley is fully in character and has her photo ID and all her documentation. Kiko says she's a fast study on the lab work. Deputy Sanchez has a while to develop a beard and change his hair style, so I'm waiting until the last minute to do his driver's license. I think this interim period is going to be really hard on Manny; he's pretty high energy and is going to find it difficult to sit around doing nothing for two weeks. I'm going try to keep him busy at home with research and file work."

"I have an idea," Bear said. "Let's have Manny work up the revised documentation on explosives; we could have him edit the document and create a slide show and handout to go with it."

"That will be putting him to good use," Bren said. "On the subject of Manny; it's pretty tough pulling the newlyweds apart all week, but I don't know what we could do about it. I had thought we would give her a fake ID and let her move to Miami with Manny, but she just started teaching in Pima, so that's out. Since the shooting last fall, Manny has been nervous about her being alone so far from help, so this will be ten times worse for him."

"Could she live in town with her parents while Manny is away?"

"Yes, that will work for a while. But soon she'll be teaching out at Klondyke, so after that she'll be alone during the week."

The sheriff thought for a bit. "Once she can no longer stay with her parents, we'll add a third patrol beat and change the three patrol boundaries out there to overlap at Manny's place. That way someone would be by frequently. We'll provide a radio in the trailer, so she can instantly get hold of the deputies if she feels the need. And Manny has secured the place like Fort Knox and armed and trained her. She'll be safe."

"That's a great plan, Sheriff, and I agree completely . . . but I'm not sure it will do much to lessen their anxiety."

~

Al Victor went to the Bylas Apache Police substation to take care of the morning meeting and stayed to catch up on paperwork. He had an internal department mail envelope waiting on his desk. It contained the results of the fingerprints he had lifted off the stolen car out on Klondyke Road. The prints belonged to the owner, his wife, his children, one from Deputy Sanchez, two of unknown persons, and several solid prints for DeVon Goode. Al knew DeVon well.

DeVon had served time in prison for manslaughter, but he didn't have a mean bone in his body; he was an alcoholic who, while under the influence, had driven head-on into a car not more than an eighth of a mile from this office. Young Paul Rambler was returning from a night class at EAC and was killed instantly. Paul was a top of his class scholar, a shining star in the Apache future, taken by alcohol: the curse of the tribe.

DeVon had dried out the hard way, in jail, and was tortured by conscience. He received intensive alcohol addiction treatment and participated in the prison Alcoholics Anonymous group; even that was not enough to keep him from his addiction. He was still on probation and one of the conditions was no alcohol. He lived with his aged mother and worked part time at the store.

Al drove over to Nelda Goode's little clapboard cottage and knocked on the door. Mrs. Goode came to the door.

"Hello, Officer Victor. What do you need?"

"I need to talk to DeVon."

Frowning at him, Mrs. Goode asked, "What do you think he did wrong?"

"I don't know that he did anything, but I know he was a witness to something."

"He's asleep."

"Is he passed out?"

"No. He's not feeling good. He's been in bed for more than twelve hours."

"Then I need to talk to him now. If I have to, I can come back with some officers. We can take him to the station to talk to him there." Al knew that if it had been more than twelve hours, DeVon might be more aware than usual.

Mrs. Goode opened the door and let Al in, leading him to a small, dark bedroom. Al switched on the light, a single bulb at the end of a drop cord on the ceiling.

DeVon stirred, then sat up. "What time is it, Ma?"

Al said, "It's ten o'clock in the morning, DeVon. Are you feeling better?"

"Officer Victor, what are you doing here?"

"I need to know how you got to Coors Grove and back the other day."

"Gato Wesley and a guy named Patrick picked me up down by the store… said they were going to a bonfire. We got stuck in the sand and walked to the camp. When we came home, Gato said he would leave the car there, and we rode with some other guys back to Bylas."

"Did you or the others mess around with anything in the car? Did you look in the trunk?"

"No, we just rode in the car. That's all."

"You rode in the back seat and didn't drive?"

"I never drive. I will never drive again."

"You know you are never supposed to drink? You can go back to jail for drinking."

"I know. Are you going to arrest me?"

"Only if I catch you drinking or drunk."

"I don't want to drink no more, and I don't want to go to jail no more. I don't want to think about that boy no more." DeVon reached under his pillow, pulled out a cheap .22 revolver and pointed it at Al. "So, I'm going to shoot you."

"No, you aren't. You have never hurt anybody on purpose, and you aren't going to hurt me. You can't trick me into shooting you; I'm not going to touch my gun. Do you think I want to feel the way you feel because I had to shoot you? Would you want anybody to feel that way?"

"You're too smart for me. I just want this to end."

His mother scolded him and took the gun away from him, giving it to Al. "He is sick; alcohol has made his spirit sick, and anything he does makes it worse. He was seeing the lady at health services, a talker to fix his mind, but it don't help. Who can help my boy?"

Al said, "I don't know. Have you tried one of the Apache healers? Sometimes they help people get their mind straight by cleansing herbs, sweat lodge, talking, and prayers. There is an Alcoholic Anonymous here. Does he go to that? They helped him a lot when he was in prison. Maybe going back to prison would be best for him."

"No. He hates it."

Al said, "DeVon, you are sober now. Go see the psychologist again and ask her what things you can do. Ask her if native medicine might help. Go every week to the AA meeting. Don't drink. Do every good thing that can help you. Remember when you felt better before you were paroled? Do you belong to a church?"

"Yes, I felt better but still guilty. We are Christians."

"My advice is to get involved in spiritual things. Go to church, a lot. Talk with the pastor and pray with the members. You feel sick because you have done bad things. Do good things, help other people. When you are doing that, you can't think about your own problems. Read the Bible. Christ has taken the punishment and pain for you; you just have to give it to him. Do all these things we've talked about. Think more of helping your mother and others than helping yourself, and you will feel better."

"I've already told him these things," Mrs. Goode said. "But he don't do it."

Al said, "DeVon, I know it is very hard. But nobody can help you if you don't try."

As he drove back to the station, Al thought about the situation but felt powerless to help DeVon; the feeble attempt at suicide by cop depressed him. He decided the next time he found the man drinking, he was bringing him in and having his parole revoked. Maybe the remaining two years of his sentence would get him to a better place.

He saw Gato Wesley walking toward the store. Al pulled over and arrested him and took him to the office to ask him about the stolen car.

"I didn't steal it. It belongs to Norbert Cassa; he lets me use it sometimes."

"He didn't know what happened to his car. He went out to go to work and it was gone. Did you forget to ask him?'

"Maybe I was drinking a little bit and forgot."

"Did you take anything from the car? Did you open the trunk?"

"No, we were just going to the party, that's all."

"I don't think your friend would want you driving his car when you're drinking. I'm going to have you wait in the holding cell. I'll get Norbert down here, and then we'll decide whether to charge you with car theft."

When Norbert arrived, he was very unhappy with his friend. After some discussion, Norbert decided to drop the charge. But he made two things clear: if Gato ever took his car without permission again, he would press charges, and Gato was not ever to drive his car if he was drinking or planning to drink.

Norbert told the officer, "I guess I just forgot he had asked permission, this time. But if he is caught drinking and driving my car or anybody else's, send him to jail."

Gato asked, "Norbert, can I have a ride over to the store?"

"I guess so. C'mon."

Al called Bren.

"I picked up the guy that took the Cassa car Manny found and have identified the two passengers, but Cassa isn't pressing charges. He said he forgot that the guy was borrowing it; not true, but what can you do? They left fingerprints all over the doors and inside of the car, but none on the trunk; so, they had no connection to the confidential file."

"Okay, thanks. I'll let Manny know. It sounds like Cassa was telling the truth about not knowing why the file was in the mail. I guess my mystery is who left that file in the engineering field office mail basket . . . and why."

Chapter 9

Relying on the name Diana had given him, Abdulov searched the internet for "Norbert Cassa Courier Service" and found a phone number. He waited until eight p.m. and drove out to the SWI office. Parking where he had before, he carefully checked the area and confirmed that he was alone. There was a single area light near the door, the only light that was on, but it was sufficient for his needs.

He slid open the window and pulled himself inside, then picked up the phone and called Norbert Cassa.

Norbert, seeing the SWI number, quickly answered. "Cassa Courier Service. This is Norbert."

"Mr. Cassa, I'm Pete Pulaski with SWI Corporate Security. I understand that you found one of our confidential files among the regular mail; is that correct?"

"Yes, sir. I set it aside to return to the office. Other than that, I didn't touch it. It had a confidential sticker as a seal, but it had been broken." Norbert thought about what Officer Victor said to say. "I didn't look inside the file."

"So, you still have the file?"

"No, sir. I left it in the trunk of my car, and that night my car was stolen. The police found it up on Klondyke Road the next morning, but the file was gone."

Abdulov wondered what else could go wrong. "Do the police know who stole the car?"

"Yes, but it turned out that it was just a mistake. A friend of mine, Gato Wesley, took the car without telling me, so he wasn't charged with stealing it."

"I see. I appreciate the information. You wouldn't happen to have Mr. Wesley's phone number, would you?" Norbert gave him the number.

Abdulov called Gato, identified himself as SWI security and said, "Mr. Wesley, I understand you used Norbert's car and abandoned it on a country road."

"Yes. Sorry, ossifer. Norbert lets me use it, but I forget to tell him I took it. It's a honest mistake."

From the slurred speech, Abdulov thought Gato had been drinking. "That sounds reasonable to me, but for security reasons, I need a statement from you. You're not in trouble; I just need it for our records. In fact, afterwards, I will be happy to take you for a drink for helping me."

"That sounds great to me."

"Where are you? I'll pick you up in about fifteen minutes."

"I'll wait at the tables in the Bylas rest area."

"Where in Bylas is that?"

"On the highway. Blue sign says Rest Area. Big blue shades over it."

Abdulov was there on time and invited Gato into the car with a handshake and a friendly smile. "Here's a cold beer until we are through with your statement."

He drove east on US 70 past Geronimo, where he pulled onto a dirt road into a mesquite bosque. He stopped and turned to face Gato, "What did you do with the file in the trunk of the car?"

"I didn't even open the trunk. I don't know nothing about no file."

"I will give you two hundred dollars cash right now for that file."

"I wish I had it. I could sure use the money."

Abdulov got out, walked around the car, and yanked the passenger door open. He grabbed Gato by the neck and, seemingly without effort, pulled him from the car and threw him to the ground. Gato scrambled like a crab backwards, then managed to stand. Abdulov's huge open hand struck Gato on the side of the face, knocking him hard to the ground. Gato was dazed and lying flat when the giant yanked him by his left arm to a standing position.

"You better tell me the truth."

With his right hand, Gato produced a switch blade and slashed Abdulov from his right chest to his left abdomen. The big Turkman instinctively grabbed the Apache's right hand, breaking the wrist as he shoved the knife, still in Gato's hand, into his heart.

Abdulov was not seriously injured, but he was bleeding quite a bit. Among the litter on the ground was a pile of old newspapers. He packed them tightly against his wound and buttoned his damaged shirt. He got his jacket out of the trunk and zipped it. He did a quick review of the scene. Using his foot, he covered all his blood droplets with sand. *No sense making this easy for the police.*

He drove back to the SWI office, reached in the window and took the first aid kit from the table. He closed the window and drove to his motel. In his room he used alcohol and Neosporin to sterilize the wound and knuckle bandages to tape the slit back together. Finally, he applied gauze and adhesive tape. He put his bloodied clothes and the newspapers in a garbage bag, thoroughly cleaned all signs of blood from the room, and put the garbage bag in the trunk of the car.

Abdulov drove to a self-carwash and thoroughly cleaned the car inside and out, taking great care to remove hair or any other tie to Gato. Then he threw the bag of clothes in the trash bin.

Back at the hotel, he took a pain reliever, got in bed, and was thankful he had nothing to do the next day. As he considered the events of the day, he thought, "What else can go wrong? I'm sorry I asked. Papa used to say, 'Whatever you put in your pot comes to your spoon.'"

~

Manny was already at a loss with the prospect of nothing to do but paper work and study. He was glad he had offered to help Cowboy with his plumbing.

As Jenny and Candy headed to Pima for school, Manny drove to the Dosela place. He found Cowboy running a Groundhog trencher. He was nearing the mobile home and continued the trench as far as he could under the house.

He shut down the trencher and shook hands with Manny. "I appreciate your help. As you can see, I have it pretty well laid out; I'm going to bury as much of the pipe as I can, then insulate any exposed pipe. I'll go up and do the box-to-tank line and the connectors. Would you mind doing the long run from here to the tank? I laid out a saw, pipe, fittings, primer and glue for you. Once we get the hookup to the tanks, we'll get started under the house. I've already enclosed the spring with a rock filter, and it's running very clean now; so as soon as the house is piped, we'll close the spring drain and put the water to the system. If I'm lucky, we will have water by the end of the day."

The pipe work went quickly. By noon all the lines were in and connected, and they put the water to the system. It took half an hour to fill the 150-gallon tank, so the spring provided about five gallons per minute. He had piped the spring box overflow through a watering trough for cattle and animals draining into the sand wash. They went inside and made sandwiches.

Manny said, "That went a lot faster than I expected."

"The part that takes the longest was already done—preparing the spring itself. I cleaned out the spring, then boxed it in, dammed it up, put in a set of outlet pipes, filled the box with clean stones and gravel, then covered it with water proof material and buried the whole thing. That keeps the source clean."

Manny said, "I can see that would take some time. So now we just fill in the ditches and insulate the pipe. What about the tanks? Don't they need insulating?"

"The spring box and sump won't need it because the water constantly feeds through it, so keeps it above freezing. The bigger tank I'm not too sure about because it only flows when the house is drawing from it. I will make a rough box around it and fill it with dirt; that'll keep it from freezing and keep it cooler in summer. I'm going to insulate all the exposed pipe. Anyway, my little momma is gonna be mighty happy tonight. Of course, she won't be really happy until the septic tank is installed. The tribe ordered it done tomorrow, so hopefully we will be back to civilized living."

"Doesn't it make you nervous having your family so isolated? I worry about Jenny being alone, and we have neighbors within half a mile."

"From what I hear, Jenny's quite capable of taking care of herself. Candy is too. I would sure hate to have her shooting at me; she doesn't miss. We've been living on the range our whole married life, so we're used to it. But I do worry about strangers wandering about."

Manny thought for a minute, then said, "We get our share of scary characters out here."

"That's true. Like the other day I had to move ol' Yaz to the River Pasture, and out there in the middle of nowhere I come across some giant Polish guy dressed like a commando, sneaking around, peeking at me with binoculars. I drove down close to him to check on him, and he said he was just looking at that little knoll by McKinney Wash. But when I first saw him he was scoping out the SWI building. I told him he was on the Rez, and he headed back to his car, parked in a bunch of bushes south of the road."

"Really? What did he look like?"

Cowboy described him, his clothes, and the fact that he had an automatic pistol hidden in one of his cargo pockets. "He was driving a red sedan with a yellow "H" like a Hertz sticker on the back."

"How do you know he was Polish?"

"He sounded like it. Well anyway that kind of an accent; maybe Polish or some foreign lingo. Something about him didn't seem right. Just a feeling."

"An Eastern European of some kind. That is odd."

They finished up the work. Cowboy started the chlorinator and got the hot water heater working. Before they headed back to meet the women and children, the water lines had been flushed and water was working to all the sinks and tubs. They had hot water, but the water lines to the toilets were still valved off until they had a sewer system. They would still have to use the outdoor toilet. Temporarily, the gray water drains flowed by pipe to the sand wash. Cowboy planned to eventually put in a gray water system and use it for irrigation; maybe have a little yard for Candy.

As he was heading back to the house, Manny took a call from Bren who wanted to drop by to talk to him that afternoon. Manny said, "My afternoon is empty except for rehashing my cover story."

~

Each day, Deputy Haley as Cathy Winn reported to work at the SWI field office. Most days she was there by herself. She brought a brown bag lunch. The office was equipped with an individual-serving Keurig coffee maker with a good variety of coffees and cocoas and a refrigerator stocked with water and sodas.

No drilling was going on because the rigs were being relocated. All the necessary land surveying and mapping was done, and construction wouldn't actually start for a few more weeks.

She had hundreds of samples, a few dry powdered ore, but mostly liquid. She would record her results on standard lab log sheets used in the SWI lab. Her results would be compared to the results of other assayers on the same samples. Kiko wanted her to concentrate on accuracy and try to get the powder precisely weighed on the analytical scale and the digested liquid exactly measured. Then in the second week, they would concentrate on speed to up her production without impacting accuracy.

Kiko drove up at ten o'clock, saying as he entered, "Good morning, Cathy. Here is your security sticker, hard hat, and ID tag. Put the sticker in the upper corner of the driver's side of your windshield. When you get to the security gate at the Miami Operation, go through the employee lane."

"Okay, thanks! I guess this makes me official now. How do you like my giant safety boots?"

"The height of mine fashion."

Every other day Kiko stopped by, and they went over the results together. From the beginning, her results were within plus or minus two percent of the professional assays. He told her, "Your results are already at professional level. As you gain experience, you will be equal to any of the other assayers."

Cathy said, "When two technicians get different results, how do you know which is right?"

"There's always a margin of error, even with the same person running the same test multiple times. For ten percent of the samples, a control sample is sent to an independent standards lab and the results are tracked per technician. Our customers also run their own samples and will sometimes challenge ours, in which case the standards lab mediates the adjustment."

"I see." Cathy added, "So the lab tech could deliberately short the measurement by a few milligrams, and it would make the amount of copper ore seem less by a percent that only they would know."

"Exactly. And if they kept it low enough, and kept track of their shortage, they would know how much copper they could steal without us knowing about it."

"That's not the only way they could cheat," Cathy said. "We calibrate the AA instrument using standard solutions each time before we run the samples, so if I wanted to short the reading, I could calibrate it a little low."

"Yes. But the control is that the instrument automatically records the calibration as found and as adjusted when they start the sample run. If the beginning measurement is consistently lower following one tech than the others, that's the one that is likely doing it. But I've been monitoring those, and there is no such pattern."

Thinking for a moment, Cathy said. "If the tech knows that each day they can grab two sheets of copper from the electrowinning harvest, they could do that and no one would be the wiser?"

"In theory, yes, but in practice there are a number of problems. While our cathodes are smaller than most, each sheet weighs something over two hundred pounds. They are thirty-six inches wide and forty-six inches high, so not easy to hide or to handle. Also, when they are pulled from solution, the pull is placed on a hanging rack and weighed on state-certified and inspected scales, so how could they be defrauding that? Yet, the balance works. All I have for sure is that the pre-mine ore survey and core samples say we aren't recovering what we should."

"So, you don't really know for sure that a theft is even happening?"

"Actually, I'm absolutely sure it is happening; my years of education and twenty-six years of experience tell me something is wrong. I just don't have evidence to prove it. My gut tells me it's real."

"That I understand," Cathy said. "I don't have the experience in my field as you do in yours, but I know to trust a gut feeling. So, my job is to look for little inconsistencies that might lead us to whatever is taking place or any suspicious behavior on the part of the people I'm around?"

"Yes. Anything you see that doesn't seem to fit. It may actually be helpful to have new eyes that are not already accustomed to what is expected. That's also why I want you and the other investigator, Marco Olvera, to be newbies. You won't be a cause for concern."

Cathy said, "I think it would be a good idea for us to have a brainstorming session with Marco. I think we should both know fully what we are trying to solve and where to start looking."

"I will suggest it to Sergeant Allred," Peralta said. "There are a couple other things you need to know. The drillers will be working again starting this afternoon, so they will be dropping samples off each shift; they leave them in the cabinet just outside the door.

"You will have company here on Monday. Diana, a technician from our Miami operation, will come in and run some field samples from the pilot plant. It's a little crowded in here, so you may have to defer to her for about an hour. It is a chance for you to get to know her. You'll be working with her in Miami. Be sure to stay fully in your cover character while she's here; you are a technician not a trainee. Just say you're doing spot checks on the pilot plant samples."

Chapter 10

Bren drove out to Manny's place and found him sitting on a lawn chair on an actual patch of lawn in front of the trailer studying his cover material. Bren thought he should come out this way more often. The last time he was here, there was only gravel surrounding the entire trailer. Now there was a fenced front yard, lawn and flower beds, a sidewalk, what appeared to be permanent stairs, and a small covered porch.

"Wow, Manny, what a woman's influence has had on your bedraggled old property!"

"Marco to you, stranger. She *has* motivated me to spruce it up some. Come around back. We're preparing a garden for vegetables," Manny said, leading the way. "Of course, I had to shoot my mouth off and say we couldn't grow anything here because of all the wildlife. So now I have to put a four-foot trench around the garden, line it with subterranean chicken wire, backfill it with dirt and rocks, then pour a curb on top of the edge of the wire, and only then put fence around it. She found the plans for this on the internet."

Bren laughed. "Do you think you will ever get enough vegetables out of this to pay for all the effort?"

"I doubt it, but I do enjoy doing these things with her. She makes it fun."

"Yeah, that's how they get you," Bren smiled. "Now the good news! I came to give you a few work assignments to do in your spare time."

"Let's go sit in front, and we can get down to business."

Bren explained what had happened with the dynamite and about the sheriff wanting to put together a school program to teach the kids the dangers of explosives. He gave Manny the ten-page training document Bitters had made for Phelps Dodge years ago.

"Bitters wants this condensed down to a lesson plan and presentation for elementary and high school teachers and an illustrated handout for the kids. He wants this done in the next few days."

"Okay, that shouldn't be a problem. I'll put something together and have Jenny improve on it."

"I also have a pile of our cold files here; I would like you to go through them and identify any leads or needed follow-up activity. It's mostly theft and assault. As it makes sense, do any research that you would like. I don't want you to resolve any of them, just give some direction and anything we could do to breathe life into them. This assignment doesn't take precedence over your undercover preparation or your dynamite show; but use them two or three hours a day to give you a break from the studies."

"I'm glad to have it. Eight hours or more of intensive study gets rough. I have all my backstory down pat, and I think I've mastered the mining processes. I take a run up the wash every day when I need a break."

"That's good, especially the exercise. We don't want you sitting around getting soft."

"Cowboy Dosela has moved up by old Aravaipa. This morning I helped him put in his water system. That was six hours of pretty good work. You will be interested in something he told me that ties nicely to the SWI file. It happened by the SWI office over across the river." Manny described Cowboy's encounter with the big "Polish-sounding" guy.

"So, he was watching the SWI office," Bren said. "That's interesting because you guys saw some kind of a Cyrillic memo in the lost SWI file. It's too much to be a coincidence. Cowboy didn't get details on the car except it was a red sedan with a Hertz sticker?"

"That's it. It was some distance away and partially obscured by brush."

"The Hertz agency closed here, so the nearest are in Phoenix and Tucson."

"I can call the airport Hertz agency in both cities and see if the description of the guy and the car can be matched up to a rental customer."

"Do it. Have you shared this story with Al?"

"Not yet, but I will; I guess I won't be going to the Pima lunch meeting anymore?"

"No. We don't want to take a chance on the wrong person seeing you with cops. And I'll let Al know about the guy snooping around SWI; we'll keep Marco as far from cops as possible. There's one other thing I wanted to talk about before I go.

"Starting Sunday, the Sheriff has temporarily added an additional officer to handle everything between Klondyke and Pima. The three beats will overlap here. Each of the three officers will keep a close eye on your place."

"You guys knew I'd be worried about Jenny, didn't you?"

"Yes. Jenny could've been given an ID as Marco Olvera's wife and gone with you to Globe, but she started working. We'll put a radio in your house. Any request from her has top priority. The way the patrols are scheduled, someone will always be within ten minutes."

"Thanks. That makes me feel better. I'm still going to hate being away from her every weekday, though."

"I'm really sorry about that."

~

Cowboy picked Candy and the kids up from the bus turnaround and drove them home. The kids were excited to see a backhoe sitting on the south side of the house by a huge pile of dirt and trenches leading south from the big hole the dirt had come from. He told them to hold his hand, and they could go look. Candy was certainly happier than the kids at the sight. There was a large white tank in the hole with black perforated sewer pipes forming a leach field in the trenches.

"What is it daddy?" asked Benny.

"It is the septic tank. By tomorrow night we will be able to use our toilets because it will be hooked to the house."

"We won't flush the toilet with lime anymore?"

"Nope. We will use the nice toilets inside like we used to. But not until tomorrow night. Until these holes are all covered up, stay away from them. If you get too close, the side will cave in and you will be buried in the sewer."

Joe drew back closer to his dad.

Then Cowboy said, "But wait, there's more! The bad news for Momma is that she won't get to heat water on the stove anymore. The hot water heater is hooked up. We can even use the showers now."

"Oh, that makes me so, so sad. Not!" Candy said. "One more day, and we will all be back to the 21st century."

They went in the house and got the kids settled doing homework at the kitchen table. Then they sat down to talk in the living room.

"You remember I told you I saw some big white guy messing around when I moved Yaz?"

Candy nodded.

"When I told that story to Manny, I could see it meant something to him. He said something about a lot of scary people being around. I've felt uneasy about that guy nosing around since I saw Manny's reaction. Keep an eye out for anyone prowling around. If I'm not here, call me . . . and strap on your .45."

"You be careful, too."

"I'm always armed on the range."

~

Harvey Richards had made his routine visit along North Klondyke Road and had a pretty good harvest of aluminum cans. He didn't really want to go home yet because home didn't feel like home.

He had lived in the same house in Safford for over forty years; he and Jean had raised their two kids there and had continued to live there for the fifteen years following his retirement. Then one day he awoke early and slipped out of bed to allow Jean to sleep. He read for two hours, then went to check on her and discovered that she had passed away in the night.

The kids lived out of state. Bobby was a physicist in Switzerland and Angie was directing editor of a large New York publishing house. They came home for the funeral and stayed a week longer, helping to take care of clearing up Jean's things. The house was too big and too empty for him, so he sold it and put his deluxe Coachman Catalina RV trailer on a lot he rented from his friend Gil Howell. He would leave for cooler climes in the summer, camping wherever he decided to go, then return in the fall.

When he didn't feel like sitting at home, he sometimes checked other back roads and places where people tended to toss out stuff. He bagged trash and gathered recyclables and turned them in for cash—not for the money but as kind of a service. And it gave him something to do besides sit at home and drink. In the last few weeks, booze had become his main staple. His breakfast this morning was a bloody Mary; that bothered him some. He had always been a moderate drinker, but without Jean, he just had so much empty time.

On his third such stop, he spotted a man lying on the ground. He called to him, but there was no movement. He got out and checked the man. He quickly determined the man was dead and called Deputy Sanchez on his cell phone.

"Harvey, you are sure the man is dead?" Manny asked.

"Yes, no pulse and cold. There's also a knife sticking out of his chest. He's holding it like he had stabbed himself."

"Did you move the body?"

"No. I walked over to it, felt for a pulse on his neck, and returned straight back to my truck and called you."

"Do you recognize the man?"

"No, but he's an Indian."

"Okay. Try not to disturb tracks or anything else. Back up to where the officer can see you from the highway and wait for him. I'm too far away, so it will probably be Sergeant Allred."

~

Bren received a call from Manny, who relayed the information of the found body to him and described where Harvey would be waiting.

Bren immediately called Al Victor.

"Al, we have a body close to Ft. Thomas. They think it's an Indian man. I'm heading there now. Do you want to join me?"

"I'm sorry, Bren. I'm at the Federal Court in Phoenix. I have to testify this afternoon. I don't have a crime scene officer on duty tonight. I'll get hold of you as soon as I get back. I hope you get the scene fully photographed before everything gets wiped out."

"Yes. I'm not putting it on the air, so we will have very few people at the scene—at least to start with. I'll text you tonight."

Bren saw Harvey waiting as expected. He stopped and discussed what Harvey had seen and done and asked him to park his truck across the road to keep anyone else from coming in.

Bren studied the "sign" in the sand. The heavy treads on Harvey's truck were easily identified. He saw that the footprints to and from the truck corroborated Harvey's description of his actions. Bren strung crime scene tape from mesquite to mesquite, establishing a barrier a good distance from the apparent scene of the action. He moved widely around the scene, taking overlapping photos from all angles and repeated the action with video accompanied by his verbal descriptions.

Bren then captured the other set of tire tracks, which left very clear tread marks in the fine sand. He could tell there had been a struggle, so he took close-up photos of all that evidence. Finally, moving to the body, he captured close-ups from all angles.

Staying off the radio, Bren used his cell phone to call the two on-duty crime-scene-certified deputies and Doc Roberts, the county medical examiner. After about two hours, they had found everything to be found at the crime scene, and Doc had field-examined the body.

Doc said, "The victim had bruising on his face and the back of his neck. He died from a knife wound to the heart, and the hand holding the knife had a badly broken wrist. I know alcohol was involved, because I can still smell beer on the victim."

Bren told Doc, "There was no identification on the man, but he's apparently an Apache. I noticed a lot of fine blood spatter on the victim's shirt, pants, and shoes. Test many of those droplets, because I suspect some may have come from the killer; maybe the victim had managed to bloody the killer's nose." Bren and the deputies helped bag the body and get it into the ME's van.

Harvey had stayed, acting as a gate for the coming and going of official cars and watching the careful work of the investigators. Bren thanked him for his help and asked if he was okay.

Harvey said, "I was in the infantry in Vietnam, so I've seen lots of violent death, but I'm surprised that this one bothers me as much as it does. Life is so precious and so unpredictable; it can end at any moment. I need to do more with my life before my final check-out. This seems so pointless."

"Yes, so often this starts with friendly drinking and ends in tragedy."

Bren was the last to leave the scene. He received a text from Al. "The trial has been continued until tomorrow. I still haven't testified, so I have to stay. I'll let you know when they release me."

~

Mergen Abdulov realized that he had made a number of mistakes that could cost him dearly if discovered by the director in the Ministry of Minerals. His position was delicate, so he thought carefully through the various possibilities and decided his best bet was a plausible lie to the Turkmen EurMino coordinator; the fool Meret was from the Ministry of Foreign Affairs, so he could overrule a decision from Minerals. He spent considerable time making his story plausible and his actions reasonable. Then he called Fourth Deputy Director of Foreign Programs, Meret Mulikow, EurMino Coordinator, at his casita at Hacienda del Sol in Tucson.

The deputy minister answered the phone in English.

Switching to the Turkmen language, Abdulov said, "Your Excellency, this is Mergen Abdulov. I have found myself in a most difficult and embarrassing situation that could cause problems for our government. I thought before I react to the situation, I should confer with you."

"Let's hope, for both our sakes, we can find a suitable response. Start at the beginning and tell me your situation."

Abdulov spoke as matter-of-factly as he could. "As you know, we are encouraged to mingle with the citizens and befriend them. In that spirit I met an American Indian man called Gato while relaxing in a rural scenic setting and invited him to share a local drink. He apparently did not handle alcohol well and, unprovoked, attacked me with a knife.

"He slashed me badly across my torso. In the heat of battle, I over-reacted and forced the knife in his hand back into his heart, killing him. I took time to pack my wound and cover my own blood spots. I secured a first aid kit and repaired my wound as best I could. I then thoroughly cleaned my room and the car of any evidence and discarded my dirty clothes in a commercial garbage bin. Then I called you."

"Good. Your story makes it clear it was self-defense. That will be our official story. Now I want the truth. What was your disagreement with the Indian over?"

"Excellency, I had found an extremely valuable new top-secret mining technology and had secured some stolen copies of the research material. The material had fallen into Gato's possession when he stole the car it was being transported in. I was interrogating him about the material when he attacked me with the knife. The rest is accurate."

"In all future proceedings in this matter, you know nothing about secret or stolen material; no matter what, stick with your original story. You do know that you were in violation of direct orders by conducting espionage activities and could face serious consequences for doing so?"

"Pardon my saying this, Excellency, but if they learn of this, you will be implicated as giving me the orders. For both our sakes, let's hope they don't learn about it."

The threat was not lost on Mulikow. "It's important that you stick with your story as agreed. Where are you now?"

"In my hotel in a town called Safford."

"Check out of your hotel and come to my lodging. I have a spare bedroom you may use until you get medical attention and this is cleared up. How long will it take you to get here?"

"Probably less than three hours, according to the GPS route."

"Are you able to make such a trip in your condition? We don't need you to have an accident in addition to your other problems."

"I know my abilities well; I have been wounded in battle many times and continued to complete my mission. I will be there as promised."

Chapter 11

Mulikow called his American EurMino counterpart Helen Dane and explained that one of the team members had innocently gotten himself into serious trouble and would need her help to avoid embarrassing both EurMino and Turkmenistan. He repeated the "official" version of the incident. She agreed to provide intervention with local officials and reminded Mulikow that Abdulov was on a diplomatic passport and a State Department Visa, so local authorities had no jurisdiction over him. She agreed to meet with Mulikow and Abdulov later in the afternoon.

~

George Simmons was happy that he had equipped his truck with a sand spreader for traction to his drive wheels. The mine sits at 4500 feet, so in winter would have freezing temperatures and some snow. The Sunday after Halloween a massive change in the jet stream had sent winter storms far south into northern Sonora, Mexico, and over all of Arizona. SWI put their loaders and road graders on the access road from Apache Trail to the mine as soon as the snow began falling, so they kept the road open and the mine was able to continue operating, just not as efficiently as usual.

George had to turn on the sand spreader all the way from the main gate to the tank house and back, turning the feed off only for the concrete apron at the weigh station. This became a routine because even after the snow disappeared, the road in the deep canyon remained icy.

After making several of these trips in and out of the mine, George noticed that the copper he was receiving was four hundred pounds heavier than the copper weighed out on the SWI scales. That was odd, but he figured it was just that his scale was not as accurate as the mine's, which is regularly calibrated, while his scale was last calibrated by the factory twenty years ago.

After two weeks, he took a large scrap copper load to the dealer in Phoenix, and the dealer's certified scale found he had over a ton more copper than he expected. This premium copper scrap sold at two and one-half dollars per pound, so this load gave him a five-thousand-dollar bonus. When he got home, he pulled all his scale tickets and went through everything, but he couldn't figure out why he had an excess of copper.

~

Sergeant Al Victor finished his testimony in the Federal District Court in Phoenix. Al was happy to have his part in the federal prosecution over with. His car had been parked on the uncovered top floor of the parking garage, so the car was hot inside; he started it, turned on the AC, and logged into his computer. He had several messages to respond to, including one with photo attachments from Bren Allred. He responded to the other messages first, because they could quickly be dispensed with, then opened the one from Bren.

He read Bren's note describing the murder scene and what they knew to date. He opened the photo titled "Unknown Victim," and immediately recognized Gato Wesley. He called Bren's cell phone, but after four rings it transferred to voice mail.

"Bren, your victim is Gato Wesley of Bylas. He worked part time stocking and cleaning at the store, when he was sober enough to do so. He wasn't a bad guy, just an alcoholic. I'll get home in about three hours. Could we meet at the Bylas substation?"

Al drove east on US 60 and relaxed a little as he pulled away from the last traffic light past Apache Junction and Gold Canyon. From this point on, he felt at home in the familiar desert and mountains and fell into a reverie for the remaining eighty-five miles to Bylas.

This was the territory claimed by my ancestors as they moved into these rugged mountains and basins from the Great Plains. With the aid of a warming, drying climate, the Apaches drove the previous Pueblo agricultural peoples to the south and west into the river valleys.

The almost impenetrable mountains served as a fortress against the Spaniards and Mexicans who labeled the area Apacheria. With the coming of the Americans, the fate of my people was sealed. They fought the Americans fiercely for thirty-five years, but in the end, they were subdued and provided with reservations in the heart of their homeland.

While they were still able to hunt and gather as they always had, they could no longer raid their neighbors to take horses, livestock, grains, other foodstuffs, captives for trading or integrating into the tribe, and any other thing they needed. That important mainstay of the Apache economy was ended, and the men had little purpose. That missing purpose has been poisonous to the culture.

We have always been a resilient and adaptive people. We still have a long struggle to regain a meaningful identity, but we have come a long way. The Apache will be okay.

He loved this drive past the craggy cliffs of Apache Leap, where a surprise attack on an Apache raiding party in the 1860s had ended with many of them leaping off the cliff to their death. Travelling through the towering rocks and cliffs of Queen Creek and Devil's Canyons, over the Pinal Summit, and on through Miami and Globe to Cutter and the wide expanse of the reservation, he arrived at last in his little town of Bylas.

Bren was waiting for him at the substation. "You made good time, Al."

"Drove the speed limit all the way. No hang-ups. What can you tell me about the death?"

Bren handed Al a flash drive. "I videoed the scene and talked about what I was seeing. The car tracks, footprints, and other sign is clearly visible in the sand."

They watched the video, then opened the still photo file and reviewed each of them without much conversation. Finally, Al reopened the picture of the knife in Gato's hand stabbed deep in the man's chest.

Al asked, "What's the matter with his hand?"

"Doc said the wrist was broken and had torn ligaments and tendons; his hand was almost twisted off. He said that is the kind of thing you might see in an industrial accident. This was obviously not an industrial accident."

Backing through the photos, Al stopped at the one that showed tire tracks closest to the body. He pointed with the tip of his pencil. "According to the sign in the sand, the car stopped here. The driver got out and walked around to the passenger side, but the passenger never stepped out. It looks like he was thrown out on the ground and then stood up and was thrown or knocked down about five feet further. Then he stood up and, according to the blood, was stabbed and fell to the ground a third time."

Bren nodded. "I see what you mean. It doesn't look like a fight. It looks more like a beating."

"That's the point. Also, he usually carried a pocket knife, but the one in his hand looks more like the handle of a dagger to me."

"It was a faux pearl-handled switchblade, cheap like a carnival prize. The handle does look like that of a dagger."

"Odd," Al said. "He was a frequent overnighter in our jail. I've emptied his pockets many times, and he never had a switchblade. I'll have to find out more about that."

"Do you see anything else in the tracks that I missed?"

"Not exactly, but there are a couple of interesting things," Al continued. "There are beer cans scattered around, but none close to where the car was parked. But look at this cylindrical impression next to where the victim first hit the ground. I think that was made by a regular glass beer bottle, but there are none on the scene."

"So, the perpetrator must have picked it up."

Al asked, "Did you get finger prints off the beer cans?"

"Yes, but none of them were the victim's, and from the amount of dirt on them, they were likely there for a while before our incident."

"Bren, there's a lot about this that isn't right. I expected the typical pattern when a group of guys get drunk: an argument breaks out, ends up in a stabbing. They load the stabbed guy in the car and go get help. They don't abandon him, and they don't stop to pick up beer bottles . . . or clean up evidence. This was something else—maybe personal revenge. Also, Gato was an average-sized guy, but judging from the sign at the scene, the killer was a huge man."

"That may narrow it down. Do you know anyone in Bylas that size?"

Al thought for a bit before answering, "Only one. Baxter Thomas, and he's known to get kind of mean when he's drunk. But he has been on the wagon for over a year now, so I don't think it would be him."

Bren chuckled. "We know from personal experience that he's like a bull when he's drunk."

"I'll interview him for sure, but I'm tending to think the killer was not from the reservation."

"Was Gato into drugs? Maybe he had trouble with a dealer or enforcer."

"No. He was strictly an alcohol man. He didn't even do pot; of course, the ME will be able to tell us if he had recently used drugs. If so, then that would be a real possibility. I better go visit with his family.

~

EcoAnthro, LLC, owned by Mike and Jill Fulton, was a well-established Tempe preconstruction archeological survey company. They had all but given up dreams of expanding into general preconstruction surveys by adding environmental, hydrological, and geological experts. The murder of an archeologist and their involvement with the investigation brought an unexpected offer from the Fort McDowell Tribe to replace the criminally-convicted general survey contractor on their reservation.

EcoAnthro added an engineer/planner, a hydrogeologist, and an ecologist, as well as their support staff. In a few months they had to again increase their specialists to handle all the work coming to them from Arizona agencies and Indian reservations all over the West.

Mike Fulton had taken a call from a man called Kiko Peralta, asking for a meeting to discuss a possible contract for work on mine developments in eastern Arizona. Thinking he had been invited to a meeting of potential contractors to receive information he needed to make a bid, he was surprised to find that he and Graham County Deputy Bren Allred were the only invitees. Since the only two who did not know each other were Mike and Kiko, Bren did the introductions.

Kiko described the mine areas near both Miami and Pima and explained that he wanted a full preconstruction survey for mine expansion, including archeological, historical, environmental, endangered species, ground hydrology, and rain water control.

Kiko added, "I have selected your company for this solely on the recommendation of Sergeant Allred and his sheriff. We want the survey to be thorough and to include recommendations for meeting all potential legal liabilities, as you would normally do. But the project does not end there.

"There is a second purpose—that of surveillance to ferret out a theft ring in our operations. You will need to secretly include in the bid the costs for paying police undercover operatives as employees and providing genuine tasks that let them move freely in all parts of our property, thus providing a legitimate reason for them to both be there and to provide cover from suspicion."

Mike thought for a moment, then said, "Of course I want to help with your problems, but I don't want to put my employees in danger."

Bren said, "Your employees will be asked to do nothing different from what they normally do as part of their job. They are not to even know that the surveillance is taking place. They will think our operatives are just employees you hired. We prefer that only you and Jill even know this is happening and that your work be treated as business as usual."

Mike nodded, and Bren continued. "You will hire an operative, perhaps as an industrial hygienist/environmentalist. This will let him move freely anywhere he wants, for the purpose of taking air and dust samples, studying processes, and such. We will need to place weather monitors in strategic locations; they will record real data on weather, surface water, and air quality, but will also provide electronic monitoring of human activities. Depending on how the investigation develops, we may add additional similar operatives."

Mike said, "That sounds okay. So, I will hire them as I would any other employee and put them through our company and the mine safety training and orientation. They will need documentation like birth certificate, social security, driver's license."

"We'll provide you with full documentation," Bren replied, "including medical exam and background check for the cover ID of each employee. Give us a sample of the forms you use so they will look valid."

"Alright, I'll e-mail the sample documents to you as soon as I get back in the office. Do I need to submit a regular bid to you, Mr. Peralta?"

"It won't be necessary. I will send you a general scope of work and a cost-plus contract with a high cut-off limit and an additional work clause. It will be flexible enough to handle whatever we need to do. You will then need to send me an estimate of the specified work and acceptance of the additional work clause. We will both sign it as our contract. In the future, we won't do business that way. You will have to bid competitively, but this gives you a foot in the door to our future work as well."

~

After her phone call with Abdulov, EurMino Southwest Area Program Manager Helen Dane knew she would have to contact her boss in Washington, something she always found unpleasant.

The man was insufferable toward women, particularly toward Helen. He had not only made passes at her but had shipped her to the office in Tucson when she had rejected his advances. Her boss was Mo Abba, Industrial Aid Chief Coordinator, Office of US Assistance to Eurasia, a State Department seventh-level office of about fifty employees.

Helen explained the self-defense killing of a drunken Native American by a visiting mining envoy travelling under a diplomatic passport and a Department of State visa. Mo yelled into the phone, "How did you let such a thing happen? You are as incompetent as ever."

Helen expected this, his usual negative response. She knew Abba's concern was for his own political vulnerability in the State Department. She breathed in deeply, and calmly continued.

"We have six of these envoys and seventeen students, each visiting a different mine or plant scattered across the Southwest. They live there for weeks or months at a time and are free to travel at will. We've been doing this for eleven years, and this is the first such incident.

"There is no blame, since he was doing nothing he was not expected to do. The department encourages them to befriend the people they meet and socialize with them. The issue is important because we need to keep it from damaging the fledgling relationship we've established with the Turkmenistan Ministry of Mineral Resources."

Abba replied, "Yes, we have to minimize the incident. As I understand it, Abdulov was drinking socially with this drunken savage who attacked him with a knife, and it is clearly self-defense. We need to try to head off any local or state investigation and avoid publicity of any kind. Who is the FBI Agent in Charge in Tucson?"

"Tucson has no AIC. The office is based in Phoenix. His name is Edmond Lee."

"I will contact him and instruct him to take charge of the investigation, to walk lightly, and to get it cleared up quickly and quietly. I will ask him to have you present when they deal with Abdulov. If he speaks with local police agencies, make yourself available when he does so. If you haven't heard from this Agent Lee in thirty minutes, you call him."

~

Helen received a call from Agent Lee's assistant referring her to an agent in the Tucson office, Special Agent Gabriel Garcia, who would be working the case with her. It amused Helen that apparently Agent Lee was unimpressed with Abba's direction to personally handle the case. She called Agent Garcia and introduced herself.

Agent Garcia said, "I understand we have a political hot potato we need to take from local law enforcement. Please explain the situation to me."

Helen explained the program, Abdulov's importance, the self-defense killing, and his diplomatic immunity and status as a special guest of the State Department.

Garcia asked, "Where is Mr. Abdulov?"

"At his hotel here in Tucson."

"But the killing happened near Safford? Did he report it to the police?"

"It happened in a rural area near Safford, but he did not report it. Instead, he called his boss and, on his instructions, drove to Tucson."

"So, Ms. Dane, he was stabbed but he drove to Tucson? Why didn't he get medical care?"

"I didn't think to ask that. You can call me Helen."

"Okay, since we are partners on this case, call me Very Special Agent." Gabe laughed. "Call me Gabe. We have his word that he killed a man, was stabbed himself, did not report the death, did not seek medical help, and drove hours to Tucson? I want to see him right now."

"Gabe, just remember that he is a diplomatic guest of the United States and is not suspected of any wrong doing, but a friend who has fallen into a bad situation in a foreign country. Treat him with deference and utmost courtesy. He is at the Hacienda del Sol. I have an appointment set up for 2:00."

"Where are you now?"

"In my office in the Federal Building on West Congress."

"I'll pick you up in ten minutes."

Helen introduced Agent Garcia to Meret Mulikow and Mergen Abdulov and they settled into Mulikow's comfortable casita's living room. Helen explained that Special Agent Garcia had been assigned to the case because of his extensive experience in dealing with sensitive matters of state; thus assuring that the guest would not be slighted by the presence of a common FBI Agent. Garcia took that as a cue to play the part. Helen recounted the events as she had been told by Mr. Abdulov and explained that Special Agent Garcia would need more details, so invited him to go ahead.

"Thank you, Ms. Dane. First, Mr. Abdulov, I understand that you were wounded by the deceased, but that you have not sought medical assistance. I suggest we have a doctor examine you to make sure that you recover without problems and to determine the extent of the damage."

Abdulov took off his shirt and ripped off the large bandage, and considerable chest hair, to reveal the 22-inch diagonal slash down his chest and abdomen. Gabe was impressed that Abdulov didn't even wince.

The big Turkman said, "The man, Gato, surprise me with a switch-blade knife, but lucky for me he slash, not stab. I bathed it and applied balm, and tape the wound closed, then made the bandage. I had tetanus inject before departing Europe. I'm taking Panadol for pain."

Helen, seeing the question on Gabe's face, said, "Panadol is a common brand name for Tylenol in Europe. Mr. Abdulov, the deeper wound on your chest looks somewhat inflamed. We better call a doctor. I think you need stitches and an antibiotic shot."

Abdulov looked questioningly at Mulikow, who nodded agreement, and asked, "Ms. Dane, could you arrange for a doctor to come here?"

"Of course." Helen called the front desk and requested a doctor be discretely sent to the Grande Casita. The desk said they would have a doctor over right away, so Helen excused herself and went to intercept the doctor and have a word with him before he came in.

Garcia asked, "What happened to precipitate the attack on you?"

"I don't know what anger him so. He was before drinking when I first engaged him. He complained to be out of beer. I told him I want to learn about Indians, so I share my bottles with him. We drove off the reservation and pulled over to talk. When I asked what kind of work he did, he started getting angry. Next thing is he attack me. My military training made me forced his knife back into his chest.

"When I'm conscious of what I do, I'm scared and use pile of newspapers to stop my blood, then try to hide evidence. I call my leader, and he says come here. That is all. It is tragedy; nobody should be hurt."

Gabe said, "If you had gotten help, the man might have lived."

"No. He was dead already; I checked for heart throbbing. The knife cut his heart."

"How big was the deceased?"

"He was not so high as you and very, um . . ." He looked to Mulikow. "How you say *inçelik?*"

"Slender," Mulikow replied.

Gabe said, "You are a very large and strong man. It would be crazy to start a fight with you."

"Maybe crazy, but mostly drunk," Abdulov said. "It is bad. My react was too fast."

Mulikow interrupted, "Special Agent, you must understand about Abdulov. As a young man he served as a Soviet *Spetsnaz*, similar to your special forces, in several years of combat in Afghanistan. While he has been out of that service for decades, he cannot lose the deeply entrenched survival instinct. It is automatic. Also, while he does very well speaking in several foreign tongues, he is proficient but not fluent in English. He is not familiar with American legalities or customs. I instructed him to come here before doing anything else so that he could work through federal jurisdiction rather than local. That is why we contacted Ms. Dane and the FBI. We are cooperating fully with you and will continue to do so."

"I understand that, sir, and appreciate it. However, for me to be able to deal appropriately with local law enforcement, I must anticipate the questions they will have and be prepared to counter their resistance to what they will perceive as federal meddling in their affairs. I want to handle that as professionally and diplomatically as possible."

Gabe added, "In the US, federal jurisdiction is very powerful, but our local agencies can be very good at meeting the legal letter of the law, while resisting our work or leaking information we wish to suppress to the news."

"Thank you for that. As you know, neither of our governments wants press on this."

Helen met Doctor Steiner in the courtyard in front of the casita and informed him of the sensitive diplomatic nature of the situation, then brought him inside and introduced him to the group.

The doctor did a quick inspection of the wound, then checked Abdulov's heart rate, temperature, and breathing. "Are you taking any medication?"

"I take two Panadol every three hours for pain."

"You are running a slight temperature, and you have an elevated heart rate. I see signs of infection in the wound. We need to remove some of the infected flesh, stitch this wound, and get you on intravenous antibiotics. I have a surgery center nearby. We can drive there and avoid drawing attention. I will give my report to Agent Garcia, so my legal reporting responsibility is covered."

Gabe said, "Ms. Danes and I will follow you and bring Mr. Abdulov with us and return him here afterwards. Would you also like to go, Mr. Mulikow?"

"No. I will wait here. In the meantime, I will properly report the incident and ask further course of action of my superior. You are in most capable hands, Mergen."

Abdulov was surprised by the use of his first name. Mulikow did not make such friendly gestures to his underlings. He made a mental note to watch for treachery.

Chapter 12

Sergeant Bren Allred pulled up in front of his house and called dispatch, reporting off shift. Lizzy and Layton were sitting in the porch swing, and Lizzy was reading from one of the *Little Golden Books* Monica had retrieved from her parents' attic. Lizzy was in first grade, and she had really taken hold of reading. Listening to her read while looking at the picture books was one of the few things that almost-three-year-old Layton would sit still for.

Bren knelt in front of them and enjoyed a group hug. They chattered about the little engine that could pull up the hill, then Bren asked, "Where's your Momma?"

"She wasn't feeling very good when she picked me up from school, so she asked me to read to Layton so she could rest. We've read all of these books." Lizzy pointed at the six books on the porch rail.

"Okay, you guys keep reading. I'll go check on her," Bren said with an uneasy smile. Monica was about six months pregnant, and she had a history of miscarriages. She was lying on her back with her feet on pillows. He sat next to her and kissed her. She grabbed him and held him tight.

"What's wrong, Sweetheart?"

"I'm scared. I started spotting this afternoon."

"How bad is it?"

"Just a few drops, but—" Tears were welling in her eyes.

"I'll call Larry. He said if you had anything that worried you, he wanted to see you."

Dr. Larry Layton was Monica's cousin and their doctor. He understood how much Monica wanted a good-sized family and how hard she had taken her earlier miscarriages.

Bren dropped the kids off at his mother's, then continued to the doctor's office. They arrived before the doctor, and Nelda had already taken Monica's vitals and noted her response to a list of questions. Monica didn't have any pain or discomfort. Nelda said, "Don't worry honey, this probably isn't serious. The doctor just drove in."

Nelda at age 51 had been Doctor Earl Layton's nurse, and continued with Larry when he took over his dad's practice. She was surrounded by an aura of competence and credibility that was already calming Monica.

The doctor listened as Nelda described what she had found. Then he said, "Let's have a look with the ultrasound." As he explored the condition of the fetus and the placenta, he described what he was seeing as the others watched the screen.

When finished he summarized, "The condition of the pregnancy looks terrific. The placenta is smooth, symmetrical, well-attached, and very healthy. As for the spotting, it is not abnormal. I'll have Nelda get a urine sample from you, so we can check for an UTI, but I doubt if that would be a problem, since you have normal temperature and no discomfort. As your baby grows, it exerts more pressure on everything, so occasionally a capillary will leak a bit."

Larry made a note on Monica's chart and continued. "We'll let you know if the lab test produces anything. I don't think you have anything at all to be worried about. It's okay if you get a small amount of spotting, but you can probably reduce it some by being aware of bending and lifting. Maybe instead of picking Layton up from the floor have him stand on the bed or a chair to pick him up. If you need to pick up something from the floor, have the children or Bren do it. Take frequent breaks to elevate your feet, and when Layton naps, you do too."

"I'm sorry to bother you unnecessarily," Monica said. "I was really upset when Uncle Earl retired, but he found a perfect replacement."

Bren shook hands and thanked the doctor, who told them, "We want to make sure nothing goes wrong, so if the bleeding gets worse, or if the discharge changes to tissue, get hold of me right away. Otherwise, we'll see you at your scheduled appointment."

Bren drove by his mom's house and retrieved the kids, and they all went to McDonald's for dinner before heading home. Once at home they had a family meeting, where they explained to the kids what had happened, and they talked about what the kids could do to help keep it from happening again.

~

Al Victor awoke early and sat in his back yard watching the sunrise glowing bright magenta on the east end of Mt. Turnbull. He heard the sounds of Bonnie making breakfast, so went in to help. He walked behind her and slid his arm around her waist, kissing her behind her right ear. She turned in his embrace and kissed him gently on his lips. Looking at his eyes she said, "What are you worrying about? When you get up early and go outside, you are worried about something."

"I'm bothered by the murder of Gato Wesley. There are things about it that don't make sense."

"Isn't that true with every murder case? Murder doesn't make sense. I know you, and you are uneasy when you think things are not going right. Just trust yourself. You will eventually put it all together. You always do. Go get the kids up while I get breakfast on the table."

Eight-year-old Joe was a sound sleeper and always slow to awaken, so Al turned on his light, opened his curtains, and gently shook him awake. "Come on, Joe. Time for breakfast." He carefully lifted the boy from bed and sat him on the side. Then he went to Angie's room and gently brushed her hair from her face.

Her eyes sprang open. "Hi, Daddy."

"Hi, Sweetie. It's time to get up. Go to the bathroom and come to breakfast."

Joe was still sitting as Al had left him, on the edge of the bed with his eyes closed. Al stood him up and walked him to the hall bathroom, where he splashed his face with cool water. Joe was finally awake and surprised he was in the bathroom.

Al said, "Finish up here and come to breakfast."

They gathered at the table, and Al said grace. They talked about what was going on at school, and Joe said he had to do a science project for next week, and that he wanted to do it on Gila Monsters.

"Do you have any idea of how you want to do it?"

"Kind of . . ."

"Before I get home tonight write down your ideas and maybe draw a picture of how your table display will look."

They finished up breakfast and everyone carried their dishes to the sink. The kids hugged and kissed Al, as did Bonnie, and they all waved from the door as he headed to work.

Al thought, "She knows me too well. I'm bothered by the murder because I know there is more to it than we are seeing. I'm also bothered by the e-mail from Bren telling about the big stranger snooping around SWI. Too much coincidence."

~

Diana Niyazov was relieved that Abdulov did not yet have the secret SWI files she had been entrusted with. She felt terrible that she had violated that trust by attempting to give the files to him. The Americans had been nothing but kind to her, all of them. Those she worked with on EurMino, at the University, and at SWI had accepted her as an equal and had provided her with important work on an amazingly wonderful project.

She was sick from worrying about the situation. On the one hand, she was betraying all these good people in favor of a government that she hated and feared; but on the other, her family, who were also good and kind people, were at great risk if she failed to do as Abdulov commanded. Each night she lay in bed fretting, running scenarios through her mind, trying to find a way out of the quandary. She felt she would die from lack of sleep but was never able to get more than a few hours before the fears and regrets returned. She was eating little, and what she did eat often came right back up. She was weak and shaky, a nervous wreck.

Relief came strangely after several nights of such torture. That night had begun the same as other recent nights, with her lying on her back staring at the dark ceiling, her mind spinning through the jumble of thoughts. She had gone to bed early because she was exhausted, but the disturbing thoughts wouldn't let her sleep. After an hour or two she glanced at her dimly lit clock. *11:11*, it said.

Her mother believed that the number sequence 1111 was a message from an angel that you were on the right path. She laughed, because she never gave much stock to such superstition. Then she asked herself, "What was I thinking when I looked at the clock?" She was wondering if she might be able to sabotage the next duplicate work file before giving it to Abdulov.

"That's really a good idea," she thought. "Abdulov will not know if the data in the files is accurate or not and, since it is a new area of research, neither will any scientists at home. I can increase the amount of power required and decrease the copper recovery for the best techniques and change the values in the opposite direction for the worst techniques. That would cause any research undertaken as a result of the stolen files to go in the most worthless direction. I will be cooperating with him, so my family will be left in peace."

Within minutes of accepting this idea, Diana had fallen into a deep, restorative sleep.

~

Sergeant Allred stopped by his house for lunch. Before exiting the car, he checked on the ankle bracelet's location and saw Benson was in Mesa.

Monica was her normal cheerful self. He was relieved that all was well with her. They had alphabet soup and BLT sandwiches with peaches and cottage cheese for lunch—not quite as robust as Bren's usual lunch, but the kids ate it well.

Bren stopped by his office for about two hours, and as he was leaving, his cell phone rang. The call was from the sheriff's office.

"Sergeant Allred, this is Jessica at dispatch. I got a strange phone call that I thought you might want to personally handle. It is a self-reported DUI."

"A self-reported DUI?"

"Yes, she called herself in as driving under the influence and wants an officer to meet her at West Central Road and Dillard Drive. She said she had been drinking and started for town, but then realized she shouldn't be driving and reported herself. I told her to take the keys out of the ignition and put them in the trunk. She did and is waiting in her car."

"Well, that's a surprisingly responsible drunk. Did she give her name?"

"Yes, that's why I called you. It's Wilma Dillard."

"Oh, no!" Bren was stunned. He regained control and said, "Thanks for contacting me, Jessica. I'm on my way."

Bren was troubled because Aunt Wilma was the widow of his mother's half-brother. Uncle Seth died about six months ago at age sixty-five, and Wilma was about ten years younger than him. They had raised Walt, her son by an earlier marriage, and two daughters of their own, all of whom lived out of the area now. Bren knew that Wilma had been having a hard time adjusting to being alone, but he had never known her to drink. In fact, she was LDS like Bren, and Mormons who practice their religion don't drink at all.

When he arrived, Wilma's car was parked on Dillard Drive at its junction with Central. She was sitting in the front passenger's seat. It was cloudy and cold, and as usual the wind was blowing.

As he approached, she opened the car door and started to get out, saying, "I'm sorry, Bren. I will go quietly."

"No, just stay put for a minute, Aunt Wilma. It's too cold to do this out here. We'll go to your house and talk there. First let me park my car, then I'll come back and drive us back there."

Bren asked Wilma to pop the trunk. He retrieved the keys and pulled the car into her garage. Once they were relocated to the living room, Bren said, "Legally, I can't do much because you never got on the public right of way, which is a good thing."

"That's not right. I was driving drunk, and it's wrong to treat me different because we are related."

"Believe me, I wouldn't go easy on you. That's because I love you too much to let you drive drunk. Dillard Drive is signed as a street because of the 911 addressing, but it is actually your private driveway, so I cannot arrest you for being drunk on your own property."

"I didn't know that. So, I should have pulled out on Central before I parked? Then you would arrest me?"

"If you had been on a public street, I would have had to arrest you."

"Nuts. Let me have my keys, and I will do it right. But I'll be careful not to hurt anyone, just park on the side of the road."

"So, you were trying to be arrested for DUI?"

"Yes. That's why I called the police."

"Why would you want to be arrested?"

"Because I need to be forced into treatment. I don't have the will power to stop drinking on my own. The court would make me get sober."

"I see. This is too much for me to get my mind around. I've known you all my life, and I've never known you to drink; why are you drinking?"

"I'm drinking because I lost my resolve. I was an alcoholic for ten years in my first marriage; we both were. He became abusive to Walter, so we divorced. The court wouldn't let me keep Walter until I was sober, so I was ordered into treatment, and he went into foster care. When I completed the treatment, I continued with AA where your Uncle Seth volunteered as a counselor. He got the court to allow Walter to be cared for by your grandparents. After remaining sober I got Walter back and Seth started dating me. After about a year we were married, and he adopted Walt. All that happened before you were born."

"I never knew that. I always remember you as teaching Sunday School and working with the Young Women. You were even Relief Society president and worked in the temple. I had no idea you had problems with alcohol."

"I thought it was all behind me. But after Seth died and I came home to our empty dream house, I became depressed. I should have gotten help. I can't explain why, but I relapsed—tried to self-medicate, I guess. I should have known better. Anyway, being ordered into rehab worked the first time, and for all those good years, so if I'm ordered in again, it should work again."

"Do you have any alcohol left in the house?"

"No. That's why I was going to town, until I thought better of it."

"Are you feeling alright, other than the effects of the alcohol?"

"That's all that's wrong. I'm incredibly sleepy, better lie down."

"I'll see what I can do about getting some help for you. I'll come back this afternoon, but I want all the vehicle keys before I go."

~

As Dr. Steiner drove from the resort to his surgery center, he contacted a surgical nurse, told her to prep a room, and called out an anesthesiologist. Abdulov arrived and was taken in for surgical prep as the doctors scrubbed. The surgery itself took nearly an hour—most of it, as Dr. Steiner said, doing needle-point. After four hours of recovery and an all clear for infection, Abdulov was released to return to the resort.

Abdulov was settled in his room to rest under the care of an attending nurse arranged by Mulikow. The nurse administered the antibiotics, pain pills, and sleeping pills prescribed by the doctor and settled into an easy chair with a book. The doctor's plan was to keep the patient sedated for about twenty hours, then inspect the wound and change the dressing. If everything looked right, he was to be allowed up for "light duty" until the wound was healed.

Helen and Gabe relayed the doctor's instructions to Mulikow and said they would contact the local authorities about the death of the man Gato. They returned to Helen's office and made arrangements to visit with the Graham County Sheriff in the morning about "a sensitive matter within the jurisdiction of the US State Department."

Sheriff Bitters was cordial and cooperative, but he said, "What is the nature of this matter?"

Agent Garcia replied, "It involves a death, possibly one not yet reported. I can't say any more about it right now. We will discuss it in person tomorrow."

Chapter 13

Bobby Bitters was pretty sure the mystery death referred to was Gato Wesley, since it was the only recent death in the county. He pulled the file on Mr. Wesley and thoroughly studied the case. He made a duplicate of the file, which he returned to the file room, and stored the original in his desk drawer. He talked with Jessica, the combination office dispatcher, evidence clerk, and receptionist, and told her about the appointment and instructed her to show them to his office when they arrived.

The minutes of the morning command meeting and the beat shift notes for the previous day were on his desk, so he was reviewing them when the guests arrived. Bitters asked if they would like a beverage, and Agent Garcia asked for a Coke. Jessica brought a can and a glass of ice. They introduced themselves, exchanged pleasantries, and talked about the drive up from Tucson. Bitters joined them at the small conference table in his office and asked, "How can I be of service?"

Agent Garcia said, "What we need to talk about will be a lot easier understood if Ms. Dane provides the background first. So, Helen, you take the lead on the discussion."

Helen explained EurMino, its mission, and its activities in the Southwest. She talked about diplomatic status of the foreigners involved in the program and their freedom to travel and befriend Americans. She then told in fair detail about the killing of an Indian man in self-defense by one of these diplomats and said that they, of necessity, required the investigation be conducted by the FBI and not by the county.

"I think that makes sense," Bitters said. "But you should know that we have already been investigating the death of Mr. Wesley, the man called Gato. He is a member of the San Carlos Tribe and a resident of this county."

Agent Garcia said, "The fact that the death occurred on the reservation should have automatically moved it to FBI jurisdiction."

"The death did not occur on the reservation, but in rural Graham County, so it lies clearly in our jurisdiction; however, that is unimportant because State has already pre-empted the jurisdiction. In this case, because of the diplomatic immunity, that seems completely appropriate to me. So, I'm not resistant to yielding authority to the FBI. I would like to walk you through the evidence we have, and as you will see, it does not exactly support the story you were given."

Ms. Dane said, "I don't think that will be necessary."

"Let's see what they have found, Ms. Dane," Garcia said. "Since I'm the investigator, I'm interested in what they've done."

"Very well," she said hesitantly. "As long as it's understood this is our investigation."

Bitters picked up the phone. "Jess, pull the Wesley murder file. Bring the complete file including photos, videos, and physical evidence. Then prepare an evidence transfer form for our signatures, me as releasing and Special Agent Gabriel Garcia, FBI, as receiving; bring that to us when it is ready." Bitters saw Ms. Dane relax, and the tension was replaced by a faint smile. He then asked, "So I can stop saying *the suspect*, can I have his name?"

"Abdulov," Garcia said. "Mr. Abdulov."

Jessica placed an accordion file and a standard evidence box on the table, then retreated to prepare the transfer form. Bobby carefully removed the typed sheets from the file, placed a flash drive in the digital projector, and pointed out several things that were, in fact, consistent with the story.

"There was a struggle, and the evidence supports that Wesley probably attacked Abdulov with this switchblade. It's a cheap knife, not one someone like Abdulov would carry.

"However, the big inconsistency in the story is that Wesley initiated the struggle. Take a look at the way the car was parked and the fact that the first contact Wesley had with the ground was when he was violently thrown from the car and landed several feet from it. He then stood up and was attacked by Abdulov, who knocked him down again, then pulled him to his feet a second time. And *that* is when the spatter on Wesley's extremities happened. The spray and spatter on the shirt sleeves are not Wesley's blood, but the assailant's. I'm pretty sure that blood is Mr. Abdulov's."

Bitters let them think about that for a moment then summarized, "The evidence clearly shows that after the two men in the car arrived, Abdulov exited the car, forcibly removed Wesley from it, and threw him to the ground. He attacked Wesley, a much smaller and weaker man— not once but twice—before Wesley pulled the knife and slashed Abdulov in self-defense. Abdulov, breaking Wesley's wrist in the process, shoved the knife in Wesley's hand into his heart, killing him."

Ms. Dane and Garcia sat silently as Garcia studied the photo of the footprints at the crime scene. He finally nodded his head and said, "I can't disagree with your findings."

Bitters added, "So this is not as clean as you thought, and I'm glad I don't have to deal with it any further. If the government wants to cover up murder for political expediency, so be it; I'm happy to wash my hands of it. Of course, the family of an inconsequential Indian man may view it differently."

Jessica entered with the transfer form and said, "Please sign both copies. Agent Garcia will keep one, and I will file the other."

"This is great work," said Agent Garcia. "I appreciate your cooperation. What comes of all this will be decided by more important people than any of us. It's been a pleasure meeting you, Sheriff."

~

Harvey Richards awoke with a pounding headache. He looked at the clock and was astounded that it was almost noon. He couldn't shake the image of the young Indian corpse.

"So much life to live, and now it's gone. For what? A drunken party probably."

The feeling that life was short, and that he was wasting his, stayed with him. He had watched television, drinking rum and Coke, until about halfway through the news when he was so sleepy he went to bed. He had slept for more than twelve hours. It dawned on him that he had gotten stewed on rum; no wonder his head was hurting.

"Hair of the dog. I'll have a bloody Mary for breakfast."

He used the bathroom, washed up a bit, took three aspirin, and headed for the kitchen. He poured some V8 Bloody Mary mix and added a dash of Tabasco, but the vodka bottle was empty. Then he remembered he had also made a few screwdrivers last night. The only booze left in the house was a half jigger of rum, so he put that in the mix.

"I'll call it a bloody Jamaican. A weak bloody Jamaican."

He sat at the table and took a mental inventory. No rum, no vodka, no bourbon, and no beer. There was a time that he rarely had alcohol in his house. He had consumed more in the last month than in the decade prior to Jean's death. This being so alone, so disconnected, was the worst thing he had ever experienced. He wondered if that's why he'd started drinking—to make him forget that loneliness.

"If so, it hasn't helped; I felt as alone when I finally dragged in and collapsed on the bed as now when I'm sober and hurting from the booze."

He decided this was a perfect time to quit drinking. He wouldn't need to replenish his bar stock; all he had to do was to make up his mind and quit cold turkey.

"Yeah, sure. The only turkey involved is me to think I can just stop. I need help. I'm going to go get a burger in Pima for lunch; I will ask that nice lady if there is an AA group here."

He drove to the Taylor Freeze and ordered a double burger. As usual, he exchanged pleasantries with the lady he assumed was the owner, then blurted out, "Do you know if there is an Alcoholics Anonymous group around here?"

"I'm not sure, but there probably is. I know that my church hosts a recovery group using the AA twelve-step program. It's on our church announcement each week; I might have one in my purse. Let me see."

She found her purse and pulled out a program. "Yep. Here it is. You can just keep this."

Harvey thanked her, took his meal and the program to a table, and studied the announcement as he ate. The announcement had a paragraph about the program with the location and time. It specifically mentioned it was for alcohol, drugs, and other addictions and gave a contact phone number. It concluded with: All welcome. No appointment necessary. The meeting was on Thursday of each week; it took him a few minutes to figure out that the present day of the week was Wednesday. He resolved to go to tomorrow's meeting.

He didn't feel comfortable just walking into a room full of strangers, so he decided to call the contact number and talk to someone. He stopped at the market and bought a bunch of his favorite snacks to give him something to do for the next thirty hours until the meeting, then decided to spend the rest of the afternoon exploring the back roads.

At the old mines near Fresnel Wash, he picked up some interesting mineral samples. Then he set up his tripod and took some shots of the snow-capped Graham Mountains in the fading light. He enjoyed the effect of the low-angle filtered light moving quickly toward sunset, and the way it emphasized the rugged topography of the range. It was also a rather unique angle—from the south west, rather than a full mountain profile. As much as he enjoyed the moment, he decided to leave and get back on North Klondyke Road while there was still a little light.

Harvey got home at seven-thirty and made the phone call. The man said his name was Carl Hawley and that he was a clinical psychologist who volunteered as the leader for the group. They talked for about fifteen minutes, and Harvey felt more comfortable with the idea of going to tomorrow's meeting. At least he knew what to expect.

"I'm glad I've done this," he thought. "I feel better about myself already."

~

Sheriff Bitters arranged for Bren Allred and Al Victor to confer with him about the death of Gato Wesley. They sat at the conference table in Bear's office, and he described the meeting he had with the federal officers. He explained about EurMino and the diplomatic status of the man who killed Mr. Wesley.

Bren asked, "How do they justify this diplomat's killing of Gato?"

"His name is Abdulov. He claims that he was having drinks with Gato when he suddenly became violent and produced a switchblade, slashing Abdulov across the torso. They showed me a photo of the wound; it runs from near the shoulder to almost the opposite hip."

Al objected, "I don't doubt that Gato surprised his assailant with the knife, so had one chance to defend himself before his knife was turned back on him. But it is clear in the impressions in the sand that the diplomat assaulted Gato first. In fact, he was knocked to the ground twice before he was killed."

"I made that clear to Agent Garcia," Bear replied. "I actually talked him through the evidence, so at least on that point, they know that Mr. Abdulov did not portray the altercation accurately. The man may get away with at least second-degree murder because of his immunity against prosecution. There's nothing we can do about that."

"The Wesley family is powerful and well respected on the reservation," Al said. "They are tribal leaders and very influential; don't be surprised if the tribe officially protests the action of the State Department."

A slight trace of a smile played across Bear's face as he said, "State wants all news about this suppressed. No statements to the press and no further involvement of this office. So, I have to officially ask the San Carlos Tribal Police to keep this low profile, but I have no authority to interfere with anything they do."

"I understand. We will use that to our advantage," Al replied.

"There is, however, a related matter that we are going to continue to investigate," Bear said. "The matter of the stolen SWI Confidential file. In fact, we have an in-progress undercover investigation going into possible industrial espionage. I would like to include you as part of this investigation, but it would have to be kept to yourself alone for a few months before you could involve anyone else from your agency."

"I can do that as privy cooperation, but if I become an active participant, you will need to read the police chief into it."

"Understood," Bear said. "In that case, it occurs to me that since your witness, Cowboy Dosela, reported seeing a "very large Polish man" nosing around the SWI Field Office, it's very possible our murderer may also be our SWI spy."

Bren injected, "That would make some sense of the killing of Gato; perhaps Abdulov was supposed to be the recipient of the confidential file. If he somehow found out that Gato was the car thief, he may have demanded the file of Gato, and then when the poor guy didn't know what he was talking about, tried to beat it out of him."

Al said, "If Abdulov found out about the car theft, it must have come from Norbert Cassa. Only he and Gato even knew it was stolen.

Either Norbert is lying and was actually part of the theft, or he for some reason told Abdulov or someone else who did know it was stolen. I will question Norbert again."

"Please do," Bear said. "This Abdulov is looking guiltier the more we consider it. As far as the man is concerned, we know he is an Eastern European, from one of the former Soviet bloc countries, because Garcia said he had been a Soviet Special Forces member in Afghanistan. The name seems to be a Russianization of the Islamic name Abdul, so he is probably from one of the "stans" like Uzbekistan or Kazakhstan."

Bear thought a moment, then continued. "Abdulov is here to study mining and mining techniques, so he'd be very interested in any industrial secrets SWI would have. EurMino puts people inside US companies to overtly study, so it wouldn't be much of a stretch to imagine they would do some covert stuff if the opportunity presented itself."

Bren turned to Al. "Manny and Pat Haley are undercover as employees or contractors at SWI; so, if you run into them, do not acknowledge them. Wait for an introduction. The same for any other place you may encounter them. They don't even know they are investigating industrial espionage. Their assignment is a copper theft ring, but we expect to discover the workings of the technology theft as a byproduct of their investigation."

Al asked, "So they are undercover 24 hours, seven days a week until the investigation is completed?"

Bren nodded in agreement. "Essentially they are. They are home and off duty on weekends, but even then are staying out of sight."

Bear said, "As you know, the murder happened off the reservation, so it legitimately belongs to this office. We will officially say that we have no suspect in the killing of Mr. Wesley, and the FBI has taken over the investigation. That will take the political heat off you concerning his murder and allow you to keep it on the back burner until the appropriate time. Tell Chief Walker this official line today, and tomorrow we will release it to the press."

"Sounds like a plan. I'll let you know what I find out from Norbert."

Chapter 14

Marco Olvera made his debut appearance at the SWI Field Office at the invitation of Kiko Peralta. Kiko and Cathy Winn were already seated at the center work table. Manny had to look pretty hard to figure out that Cathy was Deputy Hailey.

Kiko introduced himself and Cathy to Marco and went to a cabinet to retrieve a respirator. He handed it to Marco and said, "You will need to trim your beard so that it fits inside the respirator, but keep as much of the sideburns as you can and still get a good seal."

"Thanks. I'm glad to have this. I read that I would be required to be clean shaven on the contact area. Having a respirator will let me get it right."

"The filters on this mask are for dust; you will need that in some areas of your work outside the tankhouse. However, you will need a second one that is equipped to filter out the aerosol vapors. Make sure the one they give you has the right filters; a favorite prank is to hand you a dust filter, then laugh when you get a breath of the acid. As an industrial hygienist, you would know to check that. Being super safety-conscious for yourself and employees will give you credibility. Don't hesitate to butt in and correct safety and hygiene problems when you see them."

Marco said, "I have that down. My response is, 'Working safe lets you get home in once piece; proper industrial hygiene lets you enjoy health, and your retirement for many years.' I'll tell them I may be annoying, but it's better than the alternative."

"Good. We take this very seriously at SWI, so your approach will fit our culture. The purpose of this meeting is to clear up any questions before we dive into the investigation and to brainstorm as a group some things we may watch for. Cathy and I have discussed this some, so I will let her recap our thoughts."

Cathy described the metallurgical balance process and the points where it could be gamed. "However it is that they are inserting the error into the balance, in the end the most difficult part for the thieves is the physical removal of the cathodes from the property."

Manny asked, "How often are cells harvested?"

Kiko replied, "We have an eight-day cathode pull. We are a smaller but very efficient tankhouse. Our cathodes are about 30% smaller than those in most companies. We have two sets of forty-eight cells, with twenty-four cathodes in each cell. We are pulling sixteen cells per day. So, 384 cathodes per day and we are losing two cathodes per day—that's slightly under one percent. Still that would be something over four-hundred pounds per day. Comes out to maybe one half-million dollars per year, and when the copper price is up, much more than that."

"When a tank is pulled, do you dip them or spray them off?"

"Both. The refinery cathodes are dipped in a bath, then loaded on the machine that rinses them with a hot water spray, blows them dry, straightens and spaces the cathode, and stacks and bundles them for loading by a forklift. The forklift deposits them on the scale, the weight stamp is attached, and it's loaded for shipping. The starter sheets go through a different machine where they are stripped from the cathode blank, deburred, crimped, bundled, banded, and racked to go into the refinery cells."

"They are shipped on flatbed semis, right?"

Kiko nodded.

Marco asked, "You have trucks coming and going often?"

"Yes, pretty much around the clock."

"Is there other truck traffic?"

"Yes. We receive daily supply shipments of all kinds. We have our own work trucks for a wide variety of jobs. We have a couple dozen contractors with their equipment. So, there are many ways they could be hauled from the property, if that's what you are wondering. If it is done frequently, it could be a pickup truck."

"So once the cathode is separated from its group and outside the tankhouse, it could be fairly easily removed from the property?"

"Yes, that's the rub. Nobody touches an individual cathode anywhere in the tankhouse, and when they leave the tankhouse, they are in weighed bundles; our customers would certainly let us know if they were short by a pound. Somebody is doing something very clever."

"Could it be they are stealing pregnant solution from the SX plant and hauling it in tankers before it ever gets to the tankhouse? You get regular deliveries of sulfuric acid, so maybe they could be hauling solution rather than leaving empty."

"That would be highly unlikely because a tanker loading at one of our solution tanks would be pretty obvious. Also, the tankers are weighed into the property and out of the property, so if one was loaded, we would know it."

Marco asked, "Could the person doing the weighing be complicit?"

"Of course, the weighmaster on the gate could be one of the culprits. But again, the weighing process is automated, so not much opportunity there."

Cathy asked, "What if the driver of the theft truck is allowed to simply drive past the scale without weighing?"

"It would be obvious, and it would be on video. I don't think they could get away with that, but I like the way you both are thinking. They are apparently doing something we don't think they could do."

They each thought a bit without saying anything, then Kiko said, "These are the kinds of things you will be watching for, Marco. Cathy will be watching for irregularities in the starting entries to the metallurgical balance. But both of you keep an eye out for anything irregular."

Kiko asked if they had any more thoughts. When none were offered, he finished up, "You will both go through two days of new miner training and orientation. Take that very seriously. It is a matter of your personal safety. Cathy needs to not be too familiar with the safety aspect, and Marco can flash a little expertise."

~

Bren Allred called Noah Flake to discuss Wilma Dillard's request to be ordered into rehab. Judge Flake was the long-time Superior Court Judge of Graham County, who had recently gone into semi-retirement but was appointed a Judge Pro Tem. He still handled several cases each month, plus served as a consultant to the newly elected judge. Additionally, he was Monica Allred's cousin, and he was a member of the Thatcher Stake Presidency of the LDS church, an upper hierarchical pastoral position.

Bren felt he was the ideal counselor to translate Aunt Wilma's legal and spiritual situation. Judge Flake asked Bren to come to his home office later in the afternoon.

Bren then drove to the Boy Begay Rehab Center and went to the office of Amanda Kennedy. Mrs. Kennedy was pleased to see Bren and greeted him with a hug. They spent a few minutes catching up.

"I wonder if I might be able to refer my aunt for alcohol rehab," Bren asked. "She is not a tribal member and she is not pregnant, which is the focus of the Foundation, but she wants the kind of help you offer. I know you have nice individual suites for residents, plus common socializing and recreational areas. I think it would be ideal for her."

"Brother Allred, you should automatically assume that I would assist you with any good thing you ask of me. I owe your father so much for his kindness; and then the help you gave me in setting up the foundation was immense. We would welcome her for free."

"Thank you. She is comfortably well-off and will be happy to pay. How long does recovery usually take, and how soon could she be admitted?"

"The time required varies some, the longest would normally be one month. Most people are past all the detoxification and the urgent drive for alcohol in about one week. If they are really determined to stay clean and have support, they can often go home in eight or ten days. Is she currently still drinking?"

"She called me wanting help two hours ago. She was drunk and very sleepy. She has no alcohol available to her, and she said she would sleep for a long time."

"You need to get her in as soon as you can. In eight to ten hours, she will begin to suffer withdrawal. She needs to be admitted before that starts. It's good she is asking for help, but the withdrawal gets so bad, most people quickly change their mind. If she is self-admitted, I can't keep her if she decides to leave."

"Actually, she wants me to get a court order placing her in rehab; I'm talking to Judge Flake about it this afternoon."

"That's wonderful. He is a wise and kind man."

Bren said he would bring her over as soon as he had the court order and drove to the Judge's home office.

Bren explained the situation in detail to Judge Flake.

"So, she never actually drove on public roads?" Judge Flake asked.

"She did not." Bren chuckled as he said, "She wanted me to look the other way so that she could pull out of her driveway and park on the side of the street and I could arrest her for DUI. She wants help."

"As a law officer, in your opinion, is she a danger to herself or the public?"

"Yes."

"Good. That takes care of a legal justification. Now, I don't know Wilma very well, but I am actually shocked that she was drinking. How did that happen?"

"I didn't know it before, but when she was in her early twenties, she and her first husband where alcoholics. She joined AA, and Uncle Seth was a volunteer with them. They eventually fell in love and married. She never had a problem again until a few months after his death, when she relapsed. She wants to detox and get back in the program."

"That's good. She has the right attitude. Do you have a place in mind for me to send her?"

"Yes, Amada Kennedy is preparing a place for her at the Boy Begay Rehab Center."

The judge signed a blank document and placed it in a manila envelope. He called the Court Clerk's office and explained that he needed a rush order, gave them the particulars, and said he would send a signed blank with Deputy Allred for the order to be printed on. He handed it to Bren and said, "Go right away so you can get her in today."

After Bren left, President Flake called Wilma's Bishop and told him that she needed to have ministering sisters assigned to her who could spend a lot of time with her. "She needs a sister who is non-judgmental and has the time to check daily and spend social time with her as needed."

~

Norbert Cassa was at the Bylas Police Station within ten minutes of Sergeant Victor's call. They sat in the guest chairs in Al's office. Al offered him a water, which he declined.

"Norbert, I need you to tell me everybody that you have talked to about your car being stolen, besides me and Gato of course."

Norbert thought for a minute, then said, "My wife and the security man from SWI who called me about the confidential file. I don't think there was anybody else."

"What security man?"

"I don't know. He said his name was Pete something and that he was SWI security just following up on the missing file. I told him I found it in the mail, and when I saw the confidential sticker, I locked it in the trunk of my car to take it back the next day. I said the car was taken by a friend who forgot to tell me, so I reported it stolen. I remembered that you said not to know anything about what happened to the file, so that's all I told him. He asked me who my friend was, so I told him Gato and gave him the phone number."

"How do you know the call was really from SWI Security?"

"Because it was on the caller ID. It said SWI."

"Is it still on your phone's call history?"

Thumbing through his calls, he handed the phone to Al. "There it is."

Al wrote down the phone number, date, and time. "It was after regular business hours. It shows the call was made at 8:10 p.m."

"Yeah, it was after dark."

"Norbert, think about the caller. What was his voice like?"

"He was courteous, had a very deep voice, and he had some kinda foreign accent."

"What kind of accent?"

"Well it sure wasn't Indian . . . maybe German or somethin'."

"Okay. Thanks, Norbert. That's all I needed."

As soon as Norbert left, Al dialed the number taken from Norbert's phone.

A familiar female voice said, "SWI Field Office."

Caught by surprise, Al asked, "Is this Pat?" He immediately realized his mistake.

"No, this is Cathy Winn. Who were you trying to reach?"

"I'm sorry. I must have dialed the wrong number," he said and hung up. "That could blow her cover," he thought.

Al called Bren Allred and told him about the Cassa interview and that he confirmed the call was from the SWI Field Office. He asked Bren to share it with the Sheriff. He then said, "It sounds like that Abdulov guy was Cowboy's Polish guy and he stalked and killed Gato looking for the confidential SWI file."

"That ties everything together."

"One really bad thing . . ." Al said. "Telling Norbert not to tell that the police had the file probably cost Gato his life. If Abdulov had found out we had it, he would have dropped the whole thing and not gone after poor old Gato."

Bren answered, "We had no way to know that. It's the normal thing to not let details of an investigation out."

"True. But it doesn't change how I feel. Sometimes winning hurts more than losing."

As soon as Al hung up, his phone rang. It was the SWI field office. He answered, "Bylas Police."

"Hi, Al, this is Cathy Winn. I'm alone right now if you need to talk about something."

"Thanks for calling back. Your voice caught me by surprise. I was just confirming that the number on a cell phone was actually SWI. I apologize for my slip up."

"No problem. It's just me and you and the fly on the window."

~

Bren picked up the court order, called Mrs. Kennedy and told her he would be delivering Wilma Dillard in an hour, and drove to Wilma's house. She was awake and eating a chocolate bar when he arrived. He showed her the court order and asked if he could help her get her things together. She would need enough for two weeks.

"Oh, I packed before I pulled my little driving trick. I just need to put a few things in my makeup kit." In ten minutes, they had secured the house, loaded her things in Bren's car, and were on their way.

At the rehab center Mrs. Kennedy accompanied Wilma to the office where the personnel admitted her and copied her insurance information. She was alert and seemingly fully functional, though she said she still felt tipsy. A nurse checked her vitals and drew a blood sample. She asked how long Wilma had been in this bout of drinking.

"I've been drunk for three weeks. I'm an alcoholic who had been sober for over thirty years before that. I went through rehab then, so I know what I will be facing to dry out; not looking forward to that."

"How long were you drunk before your first rehab?"

"Two years."

"Then this withdrawal should be significantly easier than your earlier experience because the longer you are intoxicated, the worse the withdrawal; but it will still be unpleasant. When you went through before, there wasn't much they did for withdrawal. They more or less let it run its course. We now treat with hydration, pharmaceuticals, and vitamins and nutrients that lessen the symptoms and help heal the damage caused by the alcohol."

"Well, that's good news."

"For the first few days, you will be in a hospital room with IV's and monitors. Once you are past the severe withdrawal, you will be allowed to disconnect from the wires and tubes and go to your living quarters. When we both agree you are ready to go home, you will be released with outpatient follow up."

Chapter 15

Manny Sanchez's cover cell phone rang. He grabbed it and answered. "This is Marc"

"Is this Marco Olvera?"

"Yes, it is."

"Mr. Olvera, this is Connie at EcoAnthro in Tempe. I have been processing your employment paper work and everything appears to be in order, so Mr. Fulton asked me to set up an appointment for tomorrow morning to begin your employee orientation. Could you be at the Tempe office tomorrow morning at 9:30?"

"Yes. Could you e-mail me directions and anything else I need?"

"I actually just sent all the material out, so check your inbox. If you don't have it, call me back right away. Otherwise, I will talk to you in person tomorrow."

"I'm looking forward to it. Thank you."

Manny noticed it was noon; Jenny would be on her lunch break. He called her cell phone. She stepped out of the lunchroom to take the call. He told her about his call from "Homeland Security" and said he had to leave at six in the morning.

"So now it begins. I'm going to miss you so much."

"I will be back home tomorrow night. I don't know if I start on Monday or not. If so, I'll be gone until Friday next week. Are you still going to stay with your folks until you start at Klondyke?"

"Yes. I'll have to let Mom know it might start on Monday. I'll also have to let Candy know that she'll have to ride the bus once I'm staying with my folks."

"Good thinking. I'll have dinner ready when you get home tonight."

Manny tried to sound upbeat, but he felt anything but.

For her part, Jenny went into the restroom, wiped her eyes, and blew her nose. She composed herself and touched up her make-up before returning to the lunchroom.

~

Diana Niyazov duplicated the spreadsheet containing the in situ electrolysis research data and saved it with a slightly different name. She then altered the data to show the poorest results for the most successful processes, with not good, but somewhat better, results for the poorer processes. Her hope was that it would discourage any attempt to replicate the study in Turkmenistan. But she was pleased that if they did, they would only have disappointing results.

This was a frightening but somewhat liberating act for Diana. As a top student, her country had invested in her education and her participation in EurMino, and she knew that if her deception was discovered, the punishment for this would be severe—not only to herself, but also to her family. She would be considered a traitor.

It was liberating because never in her life had she dreamed of confronting the strong-arm tactics and oppression of her government. While she loved her homeland, she hated the government and what they did to citizens. They hopefully would never find out about her little rebellion, but she was glad she had done it. Now she would simply wait for Abdulov's instructions, then deliver the worthless information to him as he ordered.

~

The caller ID on Bren's phone indicated Judge Flake.

The Judge said, "I'd like you to assist me tonight in administering to your Aunt Wilma. This is going to be a hard time for her. I think she needs the support, and invoking the blessings of the Lord will help her."

"What time would you like to do it?"

"I was thinking seven, if that will work."

"Yes. I appreciate you doing this for her."

"I'll pick you up at twenty 'til seven."

Judge Flake was acting in his position as first counselor in the Thatcher Stake Presidency, which consists of the Stake President and First and Second Counselor, all addressed as President. A Stake President in The Church of Jesus Christ of Latter-day Saints is a local pastoral leader over a group of six to twelve neighboring congregations called wards.

When President Flake arrived, Bren was waiting in the porch swing with Monica, watching the kids play.

They arrived at the Boy Begay facility and were ushered back to Wilma's room. She seemed to be doing very well and smiled. "It's so nice of you to come."

Brent gave her a hug. "We thought you might like to be administered to."

"Yes, I would."

"Good," President Flake said. "We will do it in a bit. How are you holding up?"

"So far, no delirium or shakes, so it's better than I expected. They are very nice here. Plus, I have this great view," she said, indicating Mt. Graham glowing red in the last light of the sun. "Am I in an Indian hospital? The other patients and about half the staff are all Indians."

President Flake answered, "It's not on the reservation, but its primary mission is housing pregnant alcoholic mothers from the reservation. It just happens to be the finest treatment facility in this part of the state. I'm on the board and am legal counsel to the foundation."

"I agree with it being an excellent place. I hope you don't think I'm complaining. Everyone has been wonderful."

"I didn't take your question that way," Flake said. "I thought you might be wondering why you were with a bunch of expecting patients. Do you feel like talking about what caused you to relapse after so many years?"

"It's no mystery. I haven't handled Seth's death well. I thought in a few months it would begin to ease, but a hundred times a day something pops up that I want to tell him. I awake in the night, unconsciously feeling for him next to me. We used to share a snack at night. I still want something, but the sharing was what it was all about, so there's no pleasure in the snack. He was such a part of me that everything is just . . . empty."

"Every relationship is unique," Flake said. "I can't know exactly what you are feeling, but when my first wife died, I had very similar experiences. In addition, I found out that she did so many things for me, that I didn't know about, or that I can't do; it was like half my world fell into an abyss. I talked with my bishop and my mom and got some good advice and support, but as soon as we parted, the loss kept coming back.

"I finally went to a professional counselor. He gave me lots of good advice, but the thing that helped most was that he said to keep busy. I put everything into my work, my church calling, and Rotary and participated in every civic activity that came along. I even volunteered nights at the library. It helped, if only because I was too busy to think and so exhausted when I got home that I actually slept."

"I can see that would help, but I don't feel like I have any dedication or desire to put into it. I was shopping one day and thought being drunk would be better than this. Of course, it isn't. The grief was still there, so running away to alcohol did nothing but make me physically hurt and spiritually ashamed. That's why I decided to force myself to get help."

"That's interesting." Flake continued. "One of the things my counselor told me stuck with me, and in a couple of years it proved to be true. He said, 'Trying to outrun grief is like trying to outrun your shadow; even time doesn't make it go away. We eventually become acquainted with it, and we find we can tolerate its companionship. You will know when you reach that balance when the memories make you smile rather than cry."

Wanda grabbed the tablet and pencil and wrote down the quote, then asked President Flake to repeat it. "That's what I want to get to. That will be my goal as I work on my sobriety."

As they finished up the visit, Bren placed a drop of consecrated olive oil on the crown of Wilma's head, then placed his hands on her head in prayer stating that he anointed her with oil consecrated for healing in the name of Jesus. Then both men placed their hands on her head and President Flake prayed, sealing the anointing she had received, and blessed her with strength of body and spirit to overcome her addiction and to bear her grief. He promised her that as she followed her program and relied on the Lord for strength and guidance, she would regain her joy in Christ and her love of life.

After the men left, Wilma asked Roberta, an energetic Apache RN, if she could have a poster board to write the quote on.

Roberta read the quote. "I like that. Let me take this to Lita. She is our art volunteer, and she will make you a beautiful poster. What is your favorite flower?"

"I like lilacs and pink carnations about equally."

"What's your favorite color?"

"I like anything blue; maybe a shade of teal or turquoise."

~

Sheriff Bitters had spent much of his quite time thinking about the murder of Gato Wesley. Of course, it bothered him as much as it did Al and Bren that Gato's murderer would likely never have to answer for the crime, and in fact would continue to be treated as a VIP guest of the American taxpayers. As much as it galled Bitters, he was realistic enough to accept the inevitable and push it from his mind.

As he did so, it created a mental vacuum that was filled by a related thought: Kiko Peralta had stressed the value of the technology that had been targeted by corporate espionage. Competing companies were thought to be behind the attempt to steal highly confidential metallurgical files from SWI.

What if the file is actually what Abdulov was trying to beat out of Gato? The Turkman is a mining technologist of some kind, so perhaps the secrets are the target of foreign espionage. But would new mineral extraction technology warrant that government losing the financial and developmental support being offered them by the United States?

The Sheriff decided the only one who could answer that question was probably Kiko, the only person who knew the whole picture of the project. He took out the burner cell phone and called Kiko.

"Hello."

"This is Don Evans. Do you have enough privacy to talk for a minute?"

"Yes. I'm just driving into Pima. I'll pull to the side."

"I would like to talk with you about the business we've been discussing."

"If you are free, meet me at Ft. Thomas. I can show you the property."

They met at a pull-out on Ft. Thomas River Road, and Bobby joined Kiko in his SUV. As they drove across the bridge, Bobby scanned the interior of the truck for bugs, then explained his concerns about spying by an agent from Turkmenistan. Then he asked Kiko if he thought that the Turkmen government would consider stealing the extraction technology at the risk of losing American funding and goodwill.

"Honestly, Bobby, I don't see how they could know about the real value of the project. Certainly, if they understand the value of the extraction process, they would be interested in it. But there are two big *ifs* in that possibility. First, they would have to know about the project, which is known by very few people; and second, they would have to believe that the process could be made commercially viable; so, they would have to also know about the new power technology as well."

"But how else can we explain the coincidence of the guy who was driving the car with the confidential file in it being killed by a Turkmen mining man with diplomatic immunity?" Bobby asked. "I'm telling you, the guy was trying to beat information out of the poor drunk, who knew nothing about the questions he was being asked. There's too much smoke in this situation not to have some fire there."

"You make a good point. We did have one of the guys associated with that mining cooperation group from the former Soviet states meet with our operations people and get a tour of the operation in Miami. I was supposed to meet with him but had other commitments. Not a single one of the middle management people he met with know anything at all about the project. Even the mine manager thinks it is just an ordinary mine start-up."

As they started up McKinney Wash Kiko shifted into four-wheel drive and veered off on a rough dozer road cut up the side of the eastern ridge to the relatively flat top. He stopped where they could overlook the project area, pointing out the portable field office, the exploratory drill holes, and where the shaft would be driven down to the ore body. "This long flat we are sitting on will be a giant earth battery, which will drive the primary power for our process. So, you understand what a valuable intellectual property this scheme is, I'm going to give you a somewhat detailed overview. Again, this is for your ears only. Don't share it with anyone."

"Good. I think I need to fully understand what we are dealing with."

"Well, Bobby, you are familiar with the use of electrical currents to determine the presence of ores in native ground?"

"Yes. It basically measures resistivity or, conversely, conductivity of in situ geological bodies to identify specific compounds or ores."

"Exactly. Nowadays we often introduce the current between arrays of poles to map the measurements, but in the earliest days of the science, they used what they called natural telluric currents to detect these electrical characteristics."

The Sheriff nodded. "Those would be the same natural currents that were used to power the old telegraph system by tapping an earth battery; basically, a copper rod and an iron rod driven into the ground."

Kiko continued, "Those telluric currents are the basis for what will soon become the breakthrough technology of the century. We are building what we are calling the Nicholson-Lamont Generator, after William Nicholson and J. V. Lamont. Nicholson discovered electrolysis and Lamont identified telluric currents. For mining, this patent will be worth billions of dollars. Not only that, but it will also be a major breakthrough in power generation."

"Let me think about that for a minute." Bitters paused, then asked, "So exactly how will generating earth currents help mining?"

"You've got it backwards. The NL generator uses the small telluric currents as its power. We use a series of earth batteries to create a current to the NL Generator, which boosts the power. We place electrodes on each side of the ore body via shafts and tunnels underground, driving a large controllable current through the ore body. The current carries the metal atoms through the untouched moist earth to a cathodic wall where it concentrates. Periodically, we remove the high-grade concentrates and ship them to the smelter."

Grinning, Kiko continued. "Think about that, Bobby. No traditional mining takes place; only access shafts and transportation tunnels are driven. Other than development, there is no waste to dispose of. In most instances, the natural moisture provides sufficient current media, so we don't even have to add water. No chemicals or acids are required. So, there is very little surface disturbance, no waste, no pollution, and the only utility costs are for lighting, ventilation, hoisting, and if needed, dewatering."

"Okay, I'm impressed," Bitters said. "There are potential problem byproducts, though—hydrogen at the cathode and oxygen at the anode. That could be very dangerous underground."

"Yes. In our tests we used hoods and fan-vented the hydrogen from the test drift; but in our production model, we will actually capture, compress, and either sell hydrogen as a byproduct or use it for fuel in our vehicles. The oxygen was not a problem in the test; its only side effect was that it improved the air quality in the anode drift. However, we are looking at bottling the oxygen as a byproduct, as well.

"And, as the late-night TV commercials say, there's more . . ." Kiko said. "Since the current will move all metal and semi-metals from the ore body, unlike leaching, we will get all the precious metals. Not only will that increase our valuable byproducts, but it will leave the ground free of almost all heavy metals, and it will create a more porous and purifying aquifer. Then finally, since we can produce this power for free, we believe we will be able to apply the same technique to produce utility-quality power."

Bobby shook his head. "This is not just a mining bonanza, but a big technology leap. Metal prices will drop due to low production cost and increased supply, but profits will increase due to a much lower cost of production and a huge increase in product metal types. Almost every product manufactured depends on metals, so the costs for everything from canned foods to aircraft carriers will drop. If utility-quality power can be produced, it will revolutionize both grid power and individual home power. This will be worth trillions of dollars. It changes everything. World economies and governments will change."

"I think you have finally grasped what I'm telling you," Kiko said. "This knowledge is wonderful and extremely dangerous to possess. There are only seven of us who have any knowledge of the N-L project; we've kept the development highly compartmentalized, and each of the seven developers knows only the details of their portion. I'm the only one who knows the combined details of the high-power earth battery, the NL Generator, and the in-situ extraction process."

They sat in silence for a while, each deep in his own thoughts. Finally, Bobby said, "Seeing your field office reminds me of one more link to your Turkman." He explained about Al reporting that a "Polish guy" had been seen nosing around the office the day before the confidential file appeared. "That was also about the same time as our suspect murdered the guy he probably thought had stolen the file he was after."

Kiko exclaimed, "Oh, no! Something just fell into place for me. We have a field technician who is a participant in this EurMino thing, and she is from one of those 'Stan' countries. She works primarily in the research lab, testing the in situ electrolysis theories. She would have access to those analytical files and works one day a week in this field office. Diana could be the link in the spy theory you postulate."

"So, you do have a person outside your privy group that knows about the project!"

"Not really. But she has been working on tests that measure the effectiveness of applying current directly across ore-bearing rocks, what works and what doesn't; but she also knows that even the best results are not financially viable. So, based on her small amount of connection to the overall project, it would be crazy to risk the investment potential of American aid on her findings."

Kiko thought about it, shaking his head at the rashness of the theft. "But you are right. This has to be all connected to the Turkman and the murder. What should we do about it?"

"Nothing at all. We let it play out. But I'm going to warn my operatives to watch their backs. This is more risky than we thought."

Chapter 16

Judge Flake paid a visit to Wilma Dillard at the Begay Treatment Center and was pleased that Wilma seemed to be doing well. When he arrived at the center, he stopped by the Director's office and learned from Mrs. Kennedy that Wilma had actually had a fairly easy time with "drying out" compared to most patients and was in good spirits.

Wilma mentioned that the new treatment methods were a lot better than what she had gone through many years ago, so she was thankful for that and happy to be feeling so much better, in spite of feeling embarrassed and ashamed. She mentioned that Bren and Monica visited her each day. She had friends come to see her often, and the people at the center are "just wonderful."

As the Judge was saying his goodbyes, Wilma told him, "By the way, I loved the thought on grief that you gave me. In fact, Lita, the arts and crafts person, is making me a decorative poster of the quote for me to keep on my wall."

"Well, I'm glad to hear that, I felt it was some of the best advice I ever got as well."

As he left the patient area, he asked where he could find Lita. She was introduced to him and agreed to credit the quote to its originator, his old counselor.

~

Al Victor had arranged to work with EcoAnthro as a field technician in order to gain access to the property and as an excuse to enter anytime that he needed. He would not be assigned full-time with EcoAnthro, as Marco Olvera (Manny Sanchez) would be, but he'd be able to contact the two undercover officers without raising suspicion.

Part of Al's cover would be to help place and maintain monitoring devices on the roads accessing the SWI Miami site. The environmental study included installation of a number of air and water monitoring stations and motion cameras on game routes. The criminal investigation of SWI copper cathode losses would take advantage of these monitors to look for unauthorized vehicle traffic.

Al did not use a cover identity but was taking a part-time job with EcoAnthro as himself, because there was a fair likelihood that someone from the reservation would recognize him. His best cover story was no cover story.

Al met Mike Fulton, owner-operator of EcoAnthro, at the breakfast room in the Best Western in Globe. At first Mike didn't recognize Al, who had let his hair grow for a couple of months and had a scraggly mustache. He was dressed in a western shirt, a big black Stetson hat, Levis, a roping-trophy belt buckle, and western-style safety boots.

Mike laughed and greeted Al with a handshake. "I didn't know who the big Indian cowboy was!"

"Just blending in. How are you, Mike?"

"Doing well. We are really happy to have you back working with us again. Did you bring your personal safety equipment?"

"Yes, it's in my truck, and I have my MSHA training certificate and the mine orientation card."

"Good. Here's your contractor ID and SWI sticker to get you past their main gate and provide freedom of movement in the property. I have us set up in a small conference room. Let's have breakfast in there while I explain what you will be doing today."

As they ate, Mike used a topo map and projected slides to show where they would be placing weather and environmental stations, water monitors, and game trail cameras. He identified the mining claims SWI had acquired, the current active mining and plant areas, and SWI's plans for expansion. He oriented Al on the monitoring equipment and game cameras and the method for installation of the gear. They'd been at this about an hour when Manny Sanchez, in the role of Marco Olvera, joined them.

"Al, you remember Marco Olvera who was in your MSHA training class in Phoenix. Marco is our liaison in SWI, so he'll be coordinating or facilitating our work both here in Miami and in Safford. The vineyard across the street has given us permission to use their lot to train you on preparing the ground and setting up our stations. Elton Godwin will show you how."

Elton was one of the EcoAnthro field techs, who had mild mental limitation and learning disabilities, but he was a good worker and a very fast visual learner. He first demonstrated the scraper/bucket and auger attachments on a four-wheel ATV, then let the others try it.

He explained, "We use this ATV instead of a dozer to not hurt the ground, so it will look good when we take out the stations. We mark the place for four poles on the corner of a square and one for a single pole in the middle to hold the station equipment. We auger the anchors down until the flange is on the ground, which is 18-inches deep. The poles are ten-feet long. Once the four corner poles are in place, we attach four panels to the side. The one with the gate goes where it opens best."

Elton used the auger to set two of the anchors four feet apart, slipped a pole on each, and bolted them solidly to the anchor. With the help of his trainees, he moved a welded chain-link panel into place and bolted it onto the two poles.

Mike explained that once the fence was assembled it could only be disassembled from inside, so with the locked gate it was pretty good protection for the monitor, which included weather and air monitoring instruments and a remote-controlled video camera.

"We do this because some components, like the solar panel and video cameras, are very attractive to thieves. We use cell phone telemetry to monitor the instruments from anywhere. If someone starts messing with a station, we get notified right away. You guys will have the app on your phones. We will also install single-trail cameras along the game trails. These are also very attractive to thieves, but we depend on discrete placement and camouflage to keep them from being stolen."

Elton confidently led the way, pulling the ATV trailer with a loaded two-ton flatbed Ford. The two contractors followed, driving for the first time up Tinhorn Gulch through the old Copper Cities Sleeping Beauty Mine area into the eastern side of Myberg Basin where SWI had built its initial plant area. Both the employee gate and the contractor gate were unmanned, card-operated sliding gates, monitored on video by the weigh station operator/security guard at truck scales installed across the road from the main office.

~

In her first week working at SWI Miami, Cathy Winn (Deputy Pat Haley) had met only four of her fellow assay technicians. She already knew and liked Diana Niyazov, whom she worked the most with since

Diana was one of two permanent weekday day-shift workers in the lab. Diana had oriented Cathy on the lab and would provide any needed task training.

The lab was a long rectangular building. The employee entrance was on the south end, and the locker rooms and bathrooms were on each side of the door; a wide aisle went north up each side of the building with connecting aisles several places between the two. In the center were the rooms with analytical scales, AA machines, a lunch room, the platinum lab, various storage rooms, and plasma and X-ray spectrometers.

Along the outside walls were the individual lab work areas. Cathy's area was the second-to-northmost station on the east side, opposite Diana's on the west side. The fire assay lab, Lee Gallo's office, the secretary's office, receptionist area, and visitor's entrance filled the north end of the building. The environmental and research labs were separate buildings next to the main lab.

Their boss, Leonardo "Lee" Gallo, was the Chief Chemist—a genuinely nice man of about fifty who always seemed to be slightly nervous and perhaps a touch embarrassed. Lee held degrees in chemistry and metallurgy and a doctorate in chemistry from Penn in his home state. He had worked in lab management for the last ten years.

The police tendencies in Cathy made her curious about Lee's nervousness; maybe he was jumpy because he had a secret. In spite of her curiosity, Cathy liked the boss.

Lee Gallo approached Cathy Winn's lab station. "Cathy, we'll get an oversized number of samples from Pima early tomorrow morning, and I would like to get them assayed and reported by noon. Would you be willing to start at five in the morning to get them out on time?"

"Sure, no problem."

"The lab will be open because Jack Locke is on a six-to-six night shift, so you'll overlap him for an hour."

When Cathy arrived a few minutes before five, she was surprised at the number of sample envelopes she had. The samples were specified by titration. "Wow," she thought. That will take extra time."

She quickly counted them and realized she would be short two racks of beakers for digesting the samples into solution. She headed for the supply room, but it was locked. Through the platinum room window, she saw Jack weighing his cleaned electrolytic sample cathodes. She tapped on the door.

Jack opened the door. "Hi, Cathy, come on in. Lee told me you'd be working early today."

"Yes, but I just counted, and I'm short two racks of beakers for that large sample batch. Can you unlock the supply room for me?"

"Strangely enough, I can't. I have a key to everything but Lee's office and the supply room. Kind of strange isn't it? I can come and go all I want in the platinum room, but not the glassware and paper closet."

Cathy chuckled. "There does seem to be some irony there."

"You can use as much of my glassware as you need. Just leave them cleaned and racked for me. Help me log my cathodes, and I will help you weigh out your samples. That way you'll get started much sooner."

"It's a deal."

Cathy was never assigned to work in the platinum room, though she had been trained on analysis by electrolysis and in the procedures for tracking the platinum ware used in that process, as well as other processes using platinum crucibles and bowls. Each platinum item was stamped with an ID number and was precisely weighed on an analytical balance and recorded. Each time an item was used and cleaned, it was weighed to track any loss of material. She'd learned that there should be no measurable loss in the electrolytic process, but there would be a slight milligram loss on some of the fire and chemical analysis.

Jack said, "I'll read the number and the weight, and you record it on the log. If any measure is low, stop me and we will recheck it."

The log sheet listed various sizes of crucibles, then bowls, and finally the thirty cathodes. Today he had only used fourteen cathodes. She entered the values as read, and all were as they should be. She noticed that the last row for ten large bowls had a handwritten note: *None received to date.* She looked at the first paper in the file, the supplier packing list, which showed the large bowls were back ordered.

They left to weigh out Cathy's samples, and Jack secured the platinum room. Jack's lab station was adjacent to and north of Cathy's.

He picked up two racks of his beakers, carried them to the scale room, and added them to Cathy's ten racks.

Cathy asked Jack, "Why would they specify titration rather than AA?"

"Honestly, there is no valid reason. Some mining engineers and mineralogists have always used titrated samples and trust the method. It's simply their preference. If Lee wasn't so accommodating, we would always do things in the fastest and most accurate way—AA."

As they began weighing out the samples, Cathy felt like a distance runner being lapped by the leader. Jack was much faster on the balance. He weighed out eight racks to Cathy's four.

"There you go," he said.

"I can't believe how fast you are, Jack. Thanks for your help."

"I'm glad to help. By the way, Lee said I could leave the lab's main door open when I left; but if you would feel better, I can lock it. Lee can open it when he gets here."

"No need. It's less than an hour."

"I'm outa here, then. Have a good one." Jack slung his backpack over one shoulder and headed out.

As she was filtering the solids out of the samples, Cathy ran low on filter paper at her lab station, so she tried Jack's paper drawer. She found an open box of filters, but it was nearly empty. She pulled the drawer all the way out and found another box near the back, stuck among miscellaneous forms and junk. As she moved the box, she saw what looked to be platinum bowls covered by papers. She lifted one out and could see it was indeed platinum, and it was the large size. There were six others, and none were stamped with an ID.

She thought, "These should be numbered and secured in the platinum room; but I'm sure the inventory for large bowls read 'Not yet received'. Jack, or somebody else who used this station, has possibly removed these and is in the process of stealing them. During training, Lee said the medium-sized bowls were over five-thousand dollars each. These would be much more."

Cathy took a metal scribe from the tool cabinet and put a small scratch on the bottom of each bowl and photographed them with her phone. She took out the number of filters she needed and put everything back in the drawer exactly the way she found it.

She got back to work and thought, "I'll not mention the platinum to Lee or anyone else in the lab, because at least three of them have access to the platinum room. With the value involved, any of them could be the person who hid the platinum; even hiding it in Jack's work station would be smart, because it would cast any suspicion on him rather than the perpetrator."

Cathy had the samples well on the way when Lee came in. "Man!" he said. "You've really made good progress! How did you do this so quickly?"

"Jack finished up early, so he helped me measure out the samples. He did it much faster than I do, so it made a real difference."

Cathy was resolved for the time being to keep quiet about the platinum mystery and just observe the stash of bowls.

Chapter 17

Cathy found the work she was doing very interesting, though she imagined it could get boring once she had mastered everything and the days became a routine of running hundreds of the same analyses every day.

She was worried about staying in shape, so she began to run up the ridge behind the lab for fifteen minutes every day on her lunch break. It was a pretty strenuous workout, and she enjoyed seeing the wildlife, cattle, and the varied rugged country around her. It was cold enough that she didn't break a sweat, and she walked the last half mile back. The walk cooled her down so that she could have her light lunch in the last half of the noon break.

Today, as she ran up her regular route, a crew of men on four-wheel ATV's were putting up a fence. She slowed to a walk as she approached them. A big native guy looked at her, then did a double-take. He put down the wrench he was using and walked toward her.

"Hi. Did you know this is private mining property?"

She recognized the voice and did her own double-take. Overcoming her surprise, she said, "Yes. I'm an employee. I run up here every day, but this is the first time I've seen anyone else on this hill."

Al stuck out his hand. "I'm Al Victor, a part time employee with the contractor doing the site survey for SWI. This is Elton Godwin, our field foreman, and Marco Olvera, an environmental and industrial hygiene specialist."

"Cathy Winn, assay technician in the analytical lab," she said as she shook hands with the other two.

Al continued, "I just help out once in a while to earn a little extra money. They'll be putting several of these monitoring stations on the property and I'll help with some of them. Marco will be evaluating all the work areas from an industrial hygiene point of view, so you will probably see him around a lot."

"Well, now I won't have to wonder what all this is about. I better head back so I can have my sandwich before lunch is over. I guess I'll be seeing you guys around."

As she trotted back down the trail, Cathy wondered why Al was in the open instead of undercover. She was glad that her first encounter with them was more or less in private, so no one would see her surprise. She also wondered if Elton Godwin was an operative or if he was really a contractor as Al said. That name sounded familiar for some reason.

~

There were seven people, along with the group leader, in the addiction meeting that Harvey Richards attended. Karl went through the rules of the group and welcomed Harvey. As part of the anonymity, everyone used their first names only.

During sharing time some of the group chose to remain silent and others explained their challenges or accomplishments. There was no discussion or responding. It was the individuals' time to express their own thoughts. Some of those having difficulty staying on the program had really bad home situations, and even legal troubles.

One lady was addicted to pain relievers, and her terrible home life made it hard to give up the relief from reality the opioids gave her. Another attendee was stealing from his mother to support his drinking. It made Harvey realize that people were struggling with harder things than he, yet weren't giving up.

When it was Harvey's turn to share, he mentioned that one of them had said that it was important to be honest about your addiction, especially to yourself.

He said, "Honestly, I don't think I'm an alcoholic, but I know I have developed a serious problem with drinking. My wife died a year ago, and my days are so empty that in the last month I've fallen into a routine. I explore the back roads all day and then get drunk at night. The last time I drank was Monday night.

"The next day I found the body of a young Indian man—a life wasted. It occurred to me that I was wasting my life. I know that if I don't do something different, I will become an alcoholic. I'm hoping to get more life in my life. I'm hoping this group can help me."

After the meeting closed, Karl approached Harvey. "I tend to think that you have come to the right conclusions on your own. There is a difference between alcohol addiction, and a serious drinking problem. I think you have the latter. Can we help you? Yes. As you may have picked up from the sharing of others, we don't solve your problems; but we support you in solving them."

"I feel good about tonight's meeting," Harvey said. "To be honest, I was a little worried it would be preachy and pushing church, but it is very practical on understanding and dealing with the problem. I'm anxious to read the handbook you gave me."

Karl asked, "You identified your reason for drinking as the loneliness of missing your wife. I think that is also true. You may want to look into grief counseling or participate in a grief support group . . . or both. Here's a brochure on grief, a list of certified counselors, and contact information for a grief group."

"Thanks. If nothing else, I'll at least read the brochure."

"Something you are doing that you may want to change is avoiding others—or at least not seeking association with them. Try to talk with people every day: visit friends, call your children, get involved in hobby clubs; and if you have a church, get involved in that. Do you have a hobby?"

"I'm a retired professional photographer, and I still frequently do landscape photography. I do enjoy it. Since retiring I've had some photos in *National Geographic* and *Wanderlust*, the UK magazine. I occasionally sell to *Arizona Highways*, *Sunset*, and other such journals. But it is a solitary activity. Maybe I'll try to find a local group to associate with."

Karl said, "Well, it sounds like you still have a real passion for your art. That's a good thing, and you may be able to use it to fill some of your unproductive time. If it can involve friends, that would be good, too. Consider teaching photography at the college. And keep coming to the group each week. We can't help you if you don't."

~

In his first week on the job, Marco Olvera helped set up five monitoring stations, installed hidden game cameras on twelve trails and jeep roads, attended a meeting with plant operations managers to discuss their concerns and goals related to environmental and hygiene within the various departments, and made a preliminary inspection of each area.

Marco began reviewing each of the venders and contractors that made deliveries or picked up items from the various departments of SWI.

He was also asked by Mike Fulton to get all the mining history on the claims SWI was trying to consolidate; fortunately, the chief geologist provided him with a copy of the ownership history and description of mining activities that had taken place on each of the claims.

Evenings were lonely. After work Marco would often have dinner out. Frequently, he stopped at Guayo's, the first restaurant he reached after getting on the state highway. It was convenient and had great Mexican food. The area had at least eight really good Mexican restaurants, as well as a good number of other ethnic and American restaurants; but he didn't enjoy eating by himself, either out or in his apartment. By the end of the week, he was mostly cooking small easy-to-prepare meals at home, eating as a matter of necessity. The highlight of his day was talking online with Jenny.

The conversation was hard for him, because she couldn't know where he was or what he was doing. He talked about things on the news, the book he was reading, or a TV show he watched. And he told her too often how much he missed her.

"I'm glad you do, because being apart is even worse than I had feared. These five days AND NIGHTS are so long, and the weekends so short."

"I know what you mean about the nights. I usually eat by myself, and I don't like to do that at a café. I end up eating what I can microwave at home. There is a nice library here, so a couple of nights a week I visit the library. That's about it. Thankfully the days are very busy, and this work is interesting. I usually spend ten hours at work, so the days aren't as bad."

"Oh, my poor sweet man. I do have it better because mom and dad are good company. Mom does all the cooking and tries to do everything else for me, and I do preparation for class and grade papers at night. Of course, I'm not looking forward to being all by myself in a couple of weeks."

"Yes. I will be a lot more worried about you then. I can hardly wait for this assignment to get wrapped up."

"I'm so looking forward to the normalcy of a weekend when we will prepare and eat meals together. Anything we do will be better, because we will be together."

This, his first Friday as Marco, finished at two o'clock . . . as soon as Elton, the hydrologist, and the crew of archeologists decided to call it a day. He and Jenny had decided to spend the weekend at their place in Klondyke, so he texted her to let her know he would be home two hours earlier than they had expected. Once out of town he pushed the speed limit as much as he could without being stopped. As he drove, he mentally organized and analyzed what he had learned about possible copper theft.

There was a flow of both employee and commercial traffic in and out of the property during normal business hours; additionally, SWI employees passed in and out of the property as part of their jobs many times a day and even during the night shifts. The vast majority of all this traffic consisted of equipment that could move copper: semi-rigs, commercial freight, light delivery vans, and small trucks of every type. Most of the employees drove either pick-up trucks or SUV's that would be capable of hauling a few hundred pounds of copper.

While there was no actual physical guard inspecting vehicular traffic, the video cameras at the gate, at the major intersections inside the property, and at freight or loading areas allowed the guard on duty to see who was in the vehicle, keep track of truck movement, and observe the light vehicles enough to see if one was loaded that shouldn't be—all from his office.

All the freight and hauling vehicles were weighed coming in and leaving, and a copy of each bill of lading was received by the weighmaster. Liquid tankers would all leave empty, because they hauled things like fuel, bulk oil, sulfuric acid, or organic media for the solvent extraction plant. They were paid in part on the difference between the full and empty weight.

Marco thought that was a lot of traffic, but he knew only a small percentage of the truck traffic got anywhere near the finished copper cathodes, the end product sold by the property. These were eighteen-wheel semis pulling empty flat beds. Marco knew the cathodes were packaged on pallets held together by steel bands wrapped around each package and that they were weighed and stamped by certified scales in the tankhouse. The loaded trucks were weighed leaving the property, and SWI's two customers had their own certified scales at their yards to weigh them on delivery. The weights had to agree, because payments were based on those weights.

As far as the monitoring devices he'd helped place on the dirt roads and jeep trails, none of them had recorded a single instance of suspicious travel. *The copper isn't going off the property via primitive roads.*

The one thing Manny had zeroed in on was the scrap removal process. All copper scrap generated in the tankhouse ended up in a portable waste bin. This included irregular electrolytic growths of copper that were removed from the cathodes, damaged cathodes, and reject sheets or hanger bands that came through the starter sheet and stripping machines. Those generated by the machines automatically dropped into the scrap bin. The scrap created in other ways was manually tossed in a chute to the bin.

The salver contractor picked up the bin every other day, or as otherwise needed, with a standard heavy-duty portable waste bin hauler and left an empty bin in its place. But similar to everything else, the truck weighed in empty and weighed out full, and the salver paid SWI a reduced copper scrap price based on the difference between the tare and loaded weights.

But it just didn't seem to have any way to cheat the system. Even if a conspirator was tossing good copper into the bin, it would still be accounted for in the metallurgical balance as scrap. So, he thought, "I have produced no evidence of wrongdoing."

By the time Manny had thought all that through, trying to find exceptions or loopholes but ending up at the same conclusion that there was no way for copper to be physically removed without being spotted, he was fifteen miles up Klondyke Road and only a few minutes from Jenny, a shared meal, and home.

Chapter 18

As soon as he finished his Monday roll call, Bren checked Billy Benson's GPS position and saw that the man was heading east out of Apache Junction. He then called Manny in Miami, who answered, as he should, "This is Marco."

"There is a delivery man I would like you to check out. His name is Guillermo Benson. He works for Just-N-Time Industrial, and they make deliveries a couple of times a week to SWI. It occurs to me that since he is weighing in loaded and weighing out unloaded, he could stow a few cathodes somewhere on the truck and no one would know the difference. In addition to their processes, I'd also like your personal impressions of Benson."

"Yes, SWI has hundreds of vender salespeople and delivery people that frequently visit the property. I've started interviewing the largest first, but I will arrange to interview Mr. Benson the next time he shows up."

"That will be great. This is really involving a separate investigation, so keep the discussion of Benson strictly between you and I, not the team. Of course, include your review of the Just-N-Time processes in your report to SWI along with the other vendors."

Two days later, Bren heard from Marco. "In regard to Just-N-Time, it turns out that they have two types of delivery. Heavy loads come up on flatbed semis and are typically delivered to a laydown yard, rather than a warehouse, and occasionally directly to a shop or a construction project."

"Benson goes by Billy rather than Guillermo. He drives a medium-duty stake side truck and delivers only to the receiving dock, so he never approaches any of the plant or mine operations. The receiving dock is a busy place on day shift, serving also as a distribution point to other parts of the operation. The foreman and three clerks work there as does an internal delivery driver, and it is well covered with video surveillance. So, there's very little likelihood that even with an accomplice he could remove copper from the property."

"I agree. It sounds like nothing to be concerned about. What did you find out about Billy as a person?"

"He's a very gregarious, personable guy; the receiving people like him. He often brings donuts or breakfast burritos to them, and sometimes he brings lunch, which he eats with them. He's also very open about himself. He volunteered that he is on parole from prison, having served almost twenty years. He says he deserved what he got and is just glad he's been given a chance to get on with his life. He gives all the signs of telling the truth. I have to say I'm favorably impressed with him."

"Good job, Marco. Thanks for letting me know."

Billy is building a credible reputation and a large audience of supporters, Bren thought. *He's making himself look like the good guy, being picked on by a bad cop. So now I'm sure he plans to put me in a badly-compromised position and cause me to violate the law.*

~

Cathy and Diana stopped at Guayo's on the Trail for dinner. They often experimented and picked different items from the menu, but having eaten there many times, they each had a favorite. Diana ordered the twelve-ounce *carne asada* (a butterflied ribeye covered with cheese and green chili) served with rice, beans, and a tortilla. Cathy chose the #6 combination: a taco, enchilada, and regular burro. "Regular burro" was a unique name to Globe-Miami. It referred to a mixed bean, cheese, and red chili meat burro.

They sipped their drinks and feasted on the chips and salsa as they visited. Cathy said, "Jack Locke helped me out with the extra samples I had this morning, so it saved a lot of time. He seems like a very nice man."

"He is," Diana said. "He has been very helpful to me, and before his wife became so sick, they had me come to dinner two times at their home. It made me feel as if I am with my own parents. The last time was for Christmas dinner. They had a gift for me even though I am not a Christian. Then shortly after that, she became very ill and it turned out that she had cancer. She has had surgeries and various treatments and is in hospital in Phoenix now. He often goes to spend the day there with her, then drives up to work for his night shift. I feel so sorry for them."

Cathy gasped. "I would never have guessed. He seemed untroubled, and he was so helpful."

"The Lockes love hunting and fishing and had a nice camping caravan, a big boat, and a powerful truck to pull them. To pay his wife's medical, he has sold all their nice things, even his guns and fishing kits. All they have left is their house and one car. He doesn't say anything about it, but I know he is troubled about the cost."

The food came to the table, and their attention turned to eating. It was up to its usual high standard, and the women were famished from a hard day's work. It was a fine way to finish the day, but Cathy was troubled by Jack Locke's strong motive for theft.

~

Bren and Monica Allred asked Bren's mom to watch the kids, then drove to the Begay Center to visit Aunt Wilma. She was in good spirits, dressed in regular clothes and watching Jeopardy when they entered her room. She turned off the TV and greeted each with a hug, telling Monica, "You look so good! You must be doing a lot better."

"I am. Dr. Layton says that the baby is strong and healthy and that we are now at the point that an early delivery would be perfectly safe. I feel like a weight was lifted off."

"Oh, how wonderful!"

Bren interrupted. "But we want to know how you are."

"I'm doing well enough that I will be going home tomorrow. I'll return once a week to talk with a counselor, and they want me to start attending the local AA meetings each week. I'll do that, although I feel like I'm not likely to slip again. Arlene Griffin will pick me up tomorrow morning and take me home."

"That's great. Arlene's been a good friend for a long time."

"Yes, and she's just been assigned to be my ministering sister. Since we are both widows, she thinks we should figure out things to do together. It will help both of us."

Monica noticed an inspirational poster with a floral border and commented on how pretty it was. Wilma explained that it was a gift made for her by the arts and crafts director at the center.

"It was something Judge Flake told me about grief. I thought it was so good, I wrote it down. Lita found out and made the poster. I was thrilled with it. Then I noticed they had put an attribution on it in small print."

Monica and Brent moved closer to read the quote:

Trying to outrun grief is like trying to outrun your shadow; even time doesn't make it go away. We eventually become acquainted with it, and we find we can tolerate its companionship. You will know when you reach that balance when the memories make you smile rather than cry. –Seth Dillard

Monica gasped and teared up.

Wilma smiled through her tears. "Judge Flake's grief counselor was my dear husband, and now his words have come back to comfort me."

~

Cathy sat on her patio for a few minutes. She could see the lights of the Freeport-McMoRan smelter looking to her like a giant ship on a dark sea. Once in a while she would hear the whoosh of the air into the converters or the PA system giving some important information to someone, indistinguishable at the distance. None of it was loud, but it was reassuring in its own way. Production was churning along, unconcerned with tragedies, triumphs, or personalities.

It's feeding homes, utilities, and millions of other businesses' and products' need for the red metal. At the same time, it's supporting thousands of people in their daily livelihood. She shivered a bit and realized she was getting chilled, so she moved into the warmth of her apartment.

She rested at her table and pondered the discovery of the "missing" large platinum bowls. She was troubled. Jack Locke's shrinking resources in the face of his wife's medical expenses certainly gave him plenty of motive to steal such a valuable cache. She wondered how the shipment of platinum was invoiced by the supplier as undelivered, yet the bowls were hidden in a paper drawer in the lab.

"At least most of them are there," she thought. "Three are missing, meaning whoever put them in the drawer has probably already taken those from the building. For whatever reason, the person is taking them out in small numbers—maybe even removing them one at a time. But if they are safe taking one out, they would likely be as safe removing them all at once."

Cathy noticed the clock radio sitting on the counter. It occurred to her that she could use that to help solve the mystery of the vanishing platinum. She got it at a Law Enforcement and Security show in Phoenix because it included a motion-activated hidden video camera that recorded to her cloud account. She bought it to monitor any break-in to her apartment. It was positioned on the counter to tape anyone coming in.

"I could plug it into the outlet next to my exhaust hood, and it would record anyone using Jack's paper drawer."

She immediately got up, unplugged the radio, and put it in a cloth bag by the door to take to work with her in the morning.

She called Marco Olvera's cell phone and explained that she had noticed a possible protocol lapse in handling of platinum lab ware. She could use his help in checking out how such high-dollar specialty items were ordered and received.

"Wait, you said *platinum lab ware*. You mean like the special electronic sensors in atomic absorption?"

"No, crucibles and lab bowls made of platinum or high platinum content alloys. These are worth thousands of dollars each, and you could easily carry them out in your hand. The lab has good controls and security in place in the lab itself, but I want to know about the processes and controls on ordering and receiving high-dollar items."

"Sure. I've reviewed their purchasing and receiving processes, and they have a good separation of duties and auditing oversight. The originator of any higher dollar item is usually the end user or operator. Depending on the value and based on an escalating power of approval, it is approved in the originating department by a supervisor, department manager, general manager, president, or the board of directors."

Marco added, "Once it's approved for purchase, it goes to one of several types of purchasing agents, such as a procurement manager or commodity manager who checks for compliance to company guidelines and to competitiveness of the pricing. Then it ultimately assigns to a buyer who sources and places the order."

Cathy said, "Okay, so it's unlikely a person would be able to order something that wasn't needed or was extravagant. But what if it's improperly shipped . . . or the wrong thing is shipped . . . or the guy who receives it decides to keep some for himself?"

Marco replied, "The receiving is done by the receiving department, where a clerk handles specialty items differently than run-of-the-mill receipts. For a routine example, if they get a bunch of hammers, the clerk actually inspects each item, compares it to the invoice and the purchase order, and sends them to the warehouse for stocking."

On the other hand, on a special direct order, the clerk calls the "owner" listed on the invoice who goes to the receiving dock and observes the unpacking and inspection, and if it is a small enough item, the owner takes possession. If it is too large, it ships by the internal distribution department on the next available truck and is delivered to the owner. The owner then inspects and stores it in their own facility. Copies of the receipt go to everybody who touched the original order, so they know the transaction is complete, and the bill is paid by accounts payable. They audit inventory in both the warehouses and plant storage on a semi-annual basis."

"I agree they have good processes," Cathy said. "But suppose something really odd happens. Say the shipper actually completed the entire order, but for some reason they mistakenly listed one line item as back ordered. The clerk and the owner compare the items in the box, and four items are properly there, and they already know the fifth item is not there because the invoice says *Item back ordered*.

"So, the large crate is delivered to the owner's storeroom. At some point an employee finds the missing items, and knows they officially don't exist. The guy is holding something in his hand the size of an egg carton worth eighty thousand dollars, and nobody knows it even exists. So, he takes it."

"That could happen." Marco mused, "It seems highly unlikely that the shipper could make such a mistake, but if they did, the loss would be to them because they will eventually ship the back ordered items.

"All the thief would have to do is remove the 'non-existent' items from the property unnoticed, which could be easy, considering the small size. There would be nothing at SWI that would find that kind of dishonesty, and SWI would suffer no loss."

"That would sure be a strong temptation," Cathy said.

Chapter 19

Deputy Pat Haley was finding it a little harder to be herself after weeks of being Cathy Winn. She decided this part-time ID change was harder to pull off than being fully immersed in her character. For a person who had never been particularly concerned about her looks, she would be happy to be herself again.

She had put on a different character once before, changing from her tough girl to a sexy detective to appeal to a suspect's ego. She pulled that off successfully, but it was only acting the part for one or two hours at a time while questioning the hospitalized suspect.

She did not like this assignment. The theft investigation seemed to be going nowhere. That was frustrating enough, but now she had discovered a good man who might be about to commit grand larceny to care for his wife. She wished she had never discovered the wayward platinum. The money would go to help a good couple, and it would be small potatoes to a giant insurance company. She wished she could have amnesia, but that was just not in her.

As she got out of Globe, she pulled over and called her fiancé, Deputy Andy Lopez.

"Hey, I'm on my way home. I'm pretty tired and dirty . . . and also hungry. Could you pick up something to eat after I've had a chance to shower and change?"

"Of course, I can do that. I was pretty sure you wouldn't want to drive out of town tonight, so I was planning to grill a couple of tenderloin filets on the balcony, along with corn and potatoes. I'll make my special red-wine salad and dessert. Which would you rather have?"

"I like your plan best!"

The dinner was the start of a nice weekend of the two of them enjoying relaxation and down time. Sunday night, since Andy had the night shift, they parted company at 7:00. Andy went home and slept until eleven, then arose to get ready for his midnight shift.

Pat went to bed at eight and immediately fell asleep until the four o'clock alarm launched her on her way back to the mine. As she drove west across the San Carlos Reservation, she once again mentally put on

Cathy Winn. In her mirror she saw the new day pushing against the darkness until the clouds began to grow pink, then a blazing magenta. As she reached the lab the gray light of the basin was beginning to flee west from the march of the sun.

In the lab she checked her work area, making sure her reagent bottles were full, set out racks of beakers, and filled her acid burettes in preparation for digesting powdered samples. The Chief Chemist, Lee Gallo, spoke to her.

"I've been wanting to get you acquainted with our research lab. The core samples from Pima are delayed this morning, so I'm going to have you go with Diana who will introduce you to the work we are doing there. Join her in my office. I need to explain some things to you and have you sign a form before you begin."

In the office, he asked her, "Have you heard of our research lab?"

"Yes, Mr. Gallo. Diana works there sometimes."

"Uh . . . nobody calls me Mr. Gallo. I go by Lee. We work on a first name basis here."

Lee explained, "The large barn across the parking lot is our research lab. We are working on trying to improve our mining and refining processes, so some of the work is proprietary. It's important that it not be discussed with anyone."

He handed her a form and a pen. "If you reveal this information, you will not only be fired from the company, but theft charges could be filed against you. If you are not interested in being part of this, tell me now and you can return to your normal work with no problem."

The form was three paragraphs long but basically said what Lee had told her, in legalese. She signed the agreement and accompanied Diana to the lab.

Diana walked her to each of the experiments currently in progress and explained its purpose and what their role as technicians was in each. Cathy thoroughly understood the copper leaching, solvent extraction, and electrolysis process from studying the material she had been given by Mr. Peralta, so she quickly understood what was happening in the leach towers and test pads. But she was quite surprised by what Diana referred to as *in situ electrolysis*.

Cathy said, "I didn't even know that was possible."

"Neither did I, until I worked here." Diana explained the in situ electrolysis process to her and added, "We change out the cathodes about once a week, then analyze and quantify the deposited copper. The engineer uses that with his electrical measurements to calculate accumulation rates of metal and cost of production; the accumulation rate is very low, and the cost is very high. They hope to find ways to make it more efficient."

She then demonstrated the process of changing out the cathodes, removing the deposits from them, and operating the arc optical emission spectrometer, which gives a measurement of all metals in the sample.

Cathy found it interesting that iron, copper, zinc, molybdenum, lead, arsenic, silver, gold, and platinum, ordered by percent of the sample, were present in the rock. Diana pointed out that the elements after molybdenum were only a trace.

Diana read off the measurement for each element from each of the in situ experiments, and Cathy entered them into the spreadsheet. Diana said, "This is nice. I usually have to interpret the scan, make a handwritten list of the values, and then take that over and type it in. It's much more efficient to be able to just read them out loud and have you enter them."

She then told her that as work load allowed, she would task train Cathy in all the research processes. "That way they will be more willing to let me take time off once in a while!"

Cathy found it all very interesting, and it appealed to her love for learning. But as she reviewed the processes in her mind, she didn't see how any part of what they were researching could be used for copper theft. For one thing. the quantity of ore and copper involved was minute and certainly couldn't add up to the magnitude of the suspected theft.

Even the record of the tests and assays they meticulously recorded were in a non-production data base, so they had no effect whatever on the production copper balance. They returned to the lab before eleven o'clock.

At noon Cathy took her daily run on the game trail along the ridgetop. The environmental station was now fully assembled and, she assumed, functional, which meant that the survey company and her fellow law officers would record her presence past the station every day.

It was set up at an intersection of the trail with a jeep road. She thought that made sense for both environmental and investigative reasons. Any vehicles on the dirt road would surely create dust, and the intensity and duration of the dust would be recorded. For the investigation, any person or vehicle on either the trail or the two-rut road would be photographed.

She had been improving her distance in the fifteen-minute uphill run each day, and today she reached the saddle at the base of Webster Mountain. Sleeping Beauty Mountain had no resemblance to the fairytale maiden when viewed from the northwest.

From here she could see most of the scattered mine property. The hills and valleys of the basin were covered with juniper, cedar, and piñon, with cottonwood and willow on the wash banks. She could see that old roads and trails were all over Myberg, Granite, and Ruin Basins and Gerald Wash. It seemed to Cathy that it would be nearly impossible to keep unwanted traffic out of the mine property if someone really wanted to trespass.

~

Billy Benson made it a habit to ask the Morenci mine receiving people if they had any pallets or warranty items for him to carry back, because it often extended his trip to an overnight stay. The overnight not only gave him opportunity to spy on Allred, but also took him out of the semi-confinement of the halfway house. Even his computer research was easier in the hotel, because he had little privacy at the house.

He thought he had found a phone number for Deputy Allred on the fourth time he opened up the Graham County Sheriff's page. Going over each screen carefully, he found a link called Staff. it listed the department officers, including fifteen sergeants. Sergeant Allred was listed with a phone number.

Unfortunately, it was the same number for every member of the staff, so that was another dead end. He figured he had spent close to 100 hours trying everything he could think of on the internet. He would give up looking for an electronic footprint.

One of his friends at prison had told him about a hacker who could get into any system for a price. A copy of Allred's driver's license would give all the information Billy would need. That would most likely cost more than Billy could afford, and it would be too risky. If the guy got caught, so would Billy.

I don't need to be found associating with other criminals; that would land me right back in the pen, and not as a trustee.

He decided instead to get a police scanner. Then when he identified Allred's transmissions, he could go where he was, trail him from afar, and plant the magnetic GPS tracker on his squad car. From that he would find Allred's home and other personal things about him.

The scanner he bought was a handheld device with a car charger and an earbud connection. That way he could keep it in his backpack and listen wherever he went, even at the park by the sheriff's office. Which is where he now was, watching as the three office ladies came out of the office for their noon time walk. This was the third time he had been able to hang around town, waiting to make a pickup at the mine. He used the time working on his Allred trap.

He was surprised that a fourth walker was with them—a giant of a man in a department uniform with a bunch of stars on the collar. It must be the sheriff in person. Billy could hear his friendly chatter with the ladies and figured this must be something he did every so often.

They followed their usual route west on the south side of the park, north at the end of the park, back east to tenth street, and then past his sitting place on their way back to the office, thirty feet from him. But the sheriff paused to look at the rented ATV. The ladies stopped to wait for him.

Billy took the ear bud out and called, "Is there a problem, Sheriff?"

"Is this your Rhino?"

"Yes, kinda. I'm renting it."

"I was just checking that it had a street license. Pretty nice little buggy!"

"Yeah, I like it enough that if I can ever afford it, I'll buy one."

"Well, I better get back to work. Have a good one."

"Thanks. The same to you and your lovely ladies!"

He put his earbud back in and resumed his reading as the little group entered the building. He waited until it was time to head to Morenci for his pick up. As he was driving back to turn in the Rhino, he heard, "Dispatch to 502."

"This is Sergeant Allred. Go ahead."

"The sheriff would like you to call him about a schedule glitch when you have a chance this afternoon."

"Thanks, Jess. Probably about half an hour."

Aha! 502 is probably his badge number. Now I have a way to know when he's on the air.

~

Judge Flake had been asked to sit on a case in Gila County as a visiting judge due to the illness of two judges. He had heard that Wilma Dillard was being released from the Begay Center that afternoon, so as he drove to Globe, he stopped by to visit Wilma before she checked out. She was in the arts and crafts room facing the view of the Gila Mountains through the glass wall. She was adding water color to a line drawing she had done of the mountains.

He walked up beside her and said, "I didn't know you are an artist."

"President Flake! How nice to see you. What are you doing here?"

"I'm on my way out of town and thought I would stop by for a minute. I understand you will be going home today?"

"Yes, after lunch. They like to have a celebratory lunch in honor of patients leaving. They let me pick what I would like, so we're having the Apache tamale pie. It is so delicious!"

"I've never heard of it. How's it different from regular tamale pie?"

"It is beef red chili on a bed of Fritos with a thin layer of masa, Indian colored corn, piñons, Mexican white and cheddar cheese, strips of green chili, yellow pepper, and diced tomatoes topped with mild sauce and a scattering of cheese. You should stay for lunch."

"I wish I could, but I have to be in Globe before one. So how are you feeling?"

"Pretty good. I have had several hours at a time when I don't feel like crying, so that's better. And I have no desire to drink. I really like the quote you gave me from Seth. Since going to grief counseling helped you, I wonder if it might help me."

"No two people deal with grief the same way. Some who stoically push through it do just fine, while others who use that approach get worse. For you time is not lessening the pain, so maybe discussing it will help you. A good way to 'test the water' is to visit the Gila Valley Stakes' grief group that meets at the Central Building on Thursday nights."

"I may do that. I'm committed to attend the addiction group and weekly counseling here at the Center. I guess one more group would help fill the time."

He added, "They deal with coping. As usual with groups, it's anonymous and open to anyone, so drop in if you want; or if you would rather just talk with a counselor, make an appointment."

~

Sheriff Bitters called Agent Scott, told him about Bren's concerns, and then said, "I had occasion to speak with Benson briefly in a chance meeting. He was very friendly and open, seemed like a pretty nice guy. Do you think Bren's overreacting to the situation?"

"I most assuredly do not. There's no question the guy has charm; he's witty and friendly and easily wins people over. Before years and prison uglied him down, women would fall all over him. But he is also without empathy, though he can fake it, and has no conscience whatsoever. He's a master kiss-up, manipulator, and the most convincing liar I've ever met.

"My opinion is he is a classic psychopath. His time in prison hasn't changed him, unless it made him even better at kissing up. The guy is capable of unlimited cruelty. He's using his charm to sway public opinion in his favor, so when he gets Bren in a compromised situation, and it comes to believing him or Bren, it will be hard for people to not trust him."

The Sheriff said, "In the short minute or two I spoke with him, he didn't display any sign of nervousness or hesitation or have any lie indicators. He didn't blink excessively, smiles were whole face, no tells of any kind. Of course, it was a casual situation, so not much of a test."

Agent Scott said firmly, "As I said, he's the best liar I've seen. He has great self-control. For example, when he said 'no hard feelings' to me, he allowed his eyes to smile with the rest of his face, and it was very convincing; but when he spoke to me of Bren, he had the same smile, but his eyes were hard and mocking. He did that on purpose as part of his plan against Bren, knowing I would warn him, thus increasing Bren's anxiety."

"I appreciate your honest appraisal. I'll continue to take the situation very seriously. I trust Bren's integrity, and he's probably the wisest judge of human nature I've met."

~

Cathy Winn arrived at work earlier than usual, plugged in her radio, and used her smart phone to adjust the field of view on the hidden camera such that it provided a clear side view of Jack's paper drawer where the cache of platinum dishes was hidden. She set the camera to send a text to the cell phone anytime the camera was activated between five p.m. and seven a.m.

That's when there will be enough privacy for the thief to remove more of the bowls.

She installed the spy radio on Tuesday and monitored the video from her apartment that night. Having Stouffer's lasagna and some snow peas, she watched as Jack started digesting a batch of samples in 500 ml beakers. He left the screen but reappeared in the distant background through the window of the platinum room where he appeared to be preparing the electrolysis samples. The lack of motion in the vicinity of the camera caused the camera to shut down after two minutes.

A similar thing happened two more times as Jack came back to his station and re-liquefied the digested samples, took them in, and started the electrolysis. The next time the camera came on, he took a big stainless-steel Thermos from his backpack and poured a cup of soup into the cap, sat on the stool, and ate it.

Surveillance was boring, and this surveillance was proving to be as boring as most. Finally, at ten o'clock Cathy decided to go to bed and get up an hour earlier in the morning to review the other intervals of his visits to his work station.

There were eight more instances of the camera recording periods of two to thirty minutes at a time when Jack did more routine stuff, including finishing off his soup at about two a.m. The only time he opened the drawer, he removed a form, filled it out, and delivered it to the receptionist's office. It was most likely a supply requisition.

The highlight of the night was at 11:40 when the security guard walked through, waved at Jack, and exited the building. Nothing unexpected happened and finally, Jack turned out the lights, and the infrared kicked in for two minutes of nothing as he walked past the camera on his way to the exit.

Cathy was pleasantly disappointed that there was no apparent interest in the platinum, perhaps because Jack knew nothing about it.

"I truly hope so," she thought. "I would hate to catch him in a felony; he has more heartache than any person deserves to have."

Chapter 20

Billy Benson was heading west to Safford on US 70 approaching Solomon when his scanner picked up a conversation between dispatch and Sergeant Allred. The court clerk had some papers requiring his signature right away, and Allred responded that he would be there within ten minutes.

Billy drove to the health services parking lot and sat with his engine running where he was hidden among cars but had a clear view of the courthouse police parking spaces.

He saw a sheriff's SUV pull into the police slot at the corner of South and West Court Streets. Sergeant Allred, looking as fit as ever, walked across the lot into the back door of the courthouse. Billy snapped a photo of Bren with his SUV in the background.

The street parking space next to Allred's SUV was empty, so Billy parked there. He walked to the front of the police vehicle and attached the magnetic GPS tracker inside the front push bars. He then drove back to US 70 and continued his return trip to Apache Junction.

He stopped in Pima at the Taylor Freeze drive-through and got a burger, fries, and a large crème-de-menthe milkshake. He pulled across the street to an almost-empty parking lot where he checked the GPS positioner on Bren's car. It was working fine; the SUV was still parked at the courthouse.

He folded the paper back on his hamburger, got the fries and ketchup set up on the truck seat, and ate as he eased out of Pima to the open highway.

"I'll be home, such as it is, in less than three hours," he thought. "I feel like celebrating, but it's hard to do by myself."

~

Meret Mulikow did not inform the Ministry of Mines about Abdulov's foolishness. Instead, he went to his office near the campus of the University of Arizona, removed a satellite phone from his safe, and called his contact in the Political Crimes Division of the Bureau of Internal Security. They spoke in Turkmen.

Aziz Orazow answered, "My friend, Meret. How can I be of service?"

"I need you to determine if anyone in the Ministry of Minerals authorized Abdulov to steal industrial secrets from our host companies here in the United States. Don't make inquiries of anyone, but check all communications with him. Not only is he running an operation to steal their research, but he has killed an American citizen in the process."

Orazow replied, "As I mentioned when I heard he was assigned on your project, he may have never stopped working for our friends in the Great North. Since that time, I have found encrypted communications between Abdulov and a former KGB Station Chief now working in Kazakhstan. We haven't broken the encryption yet, but I suspect Abdulov takes his orders from Moscow."

Mulikow thought about that for a bit before replying. "That is most interesting. If we find he is a traitor, you may need to arrange a special return trip that doesn't cause him concern. Continue checking for any legitimate orders or discussion on intelligence operations during our EurMino activities. Also look into Abdulov's finances. Find out if he has income from sources outside his salary."

"I will check all his communications and analyze his income, investments, and spending habits."

"Yes, as quickly as possible. Send me a short text about the weather and local news, and I will come to the office and call you on the sat phone as soon as I am able. I don't want Abdulov to start thinking he is at risk. He is a very dangerous man."

~

Bren finished up his business at the courthouse, visited with a couple of his friends on the way out, then drove to his office in Central. He was careful to park the car in the warehouse. He took care of his daily log and the shift reports, made a couple of phone calls, and then decided to check on Billy Benson's location.

Benson was on the outskirts of Globe traveling west. That was a relief. Bren would not have to worry about him tonight. Earlier, the last time Bren checked, Billy was on 191 nearing the US 70 junction, so he reviewed the position history for the hour and twenty-minute gap between the two checks.

It didn't take long for Bren to realize that Billy had sat in the parking lot and watched him going into the courthouse. He then moved over and parked next to Bren's SUV for only about a minute, then left heading west.

Bren pondered for a while, ending up with more questions than answers.

Benson seems to have known where I was going at that specific time. The only way to know that is if he is monitoring the SO radio communications. That would be no big deal for him; radio scanners are inexpensive. He was doing pure surveillance, because the psych ops move would be to let me know he had found me. But he kept out of sight. Then why bother to stop at my car? Maybe he wanted the car number and the plate, but what good would that do him?

~

Lee Gallo stopped by Cathy's work station. "We are going to be getting the core samples from the site of the future main shaft at McKinney Wash next Monday evening, so I'm going to need you to repeat the early morning on Tuesday."

"That won't be a problem."

"I appreciate your attitude," Lee said as he headed for his office.

Cathy was happy to have another opportunity to talk with Jack Locke, and she wondered how she could make the best advantage of it. She had not yet shared her suspicion with her fellow officers because she was hoping to find at least one other viable suspect.

She had been monitoring the cache of platinum in Jack's drawer for nearly a week. She hadn't seen any activity in relation to the cache or any suspicious behavior on his part.

She didn't know if the best strategy was to just keep surveilling or do something to spur some action.

I could broach the subject of platinum security as just a curiosity question, or maybe move some of the dishes to a different hiding place and see what he does when he finds it missing. As long as I'm passively observing, I can keep it to myself; but if I'm going to take action, I will have to at least clear it with Sergeant Allred.

Her decision was to continue surveillance through Tuesday. Nothing changed during the remaining time. No one, including Jack, checked on the hidden lab dishes. Jack kept his normal work routine with no variance.

On Tuesday Cathy was up by four a.m. and quickly checked the video record of Jack's Monday shift, which would last until six a.m. He had his normal two o'clock cup of soup, rinsed out the cup, and screwed it back on the Thermos. After that he spent most of the shift filling his reagents, cleaning and organizing his work station, and other mundane chores.

At four o'clock there was a change in his routine. He stood just to the right of the paper drawer and did something with his backpack. He then opened the drawer and fiddled around in it. Both these actions were partially blocked from the camera by his body. He then put the Thermos in the pack and zipped it.

Cathy could not be sure what he had actually done, but he was very likely putting some of the lab bowls in his pack. She decided to head to work and check the drawer as soon as possible. If she found it empty, she would call Bren, and Jack could be apprehended before he got away with the stolen platinum.

At the lab, she was greeted by Jack, who seemed to be in a good mood. He said he had an unusually small number of samples this shift, so he'd mixed and filled all his reagents and done all the odd chores there were. He again offered to help her weigh out her samples.

They sat side by side at the analytical scales, carefully weighing the powdered samples into beakers.

Cathy asked, "Why did you choose to become an assayer?"

"I really didn't make that choice, just sort of fell into it. My major was ecology, and my degree is environmental engineering. I actually worked for the National Fish and Wildlife Service as a researcher. I became disillusioned with environmentalism when I discovered that in government practice it was more an ideology or religion than science.

"There was a mine near where I lived in Challis, Idaho, that needed a chemist. I applied and got the job. The assay chemist was retiring. He decided I would make a good assayer, so he trained me. The rest is history."

"Diana mentioned that you are a skilled outdoorsman. I guess your original career was because of that."

"I grew up on our family ranch spanning the Arizona-New Mexico border, so nature has always been part of my life. I thought working with Fish and Wildlife was a dream job, and in some ways, it was. I'm just not cut out for government bureaucracy. I still enjoy hunting and fishing when I can. My brothers operate the ranch, so I go up and help with roundups. I like this job because it pays well and has good benefits, low pressure, regular hours, and weekends off."

"Your hours seem kind of severe to me. Six to six every night would be rough."

"That's the schedule I chose. I could be on five day shifts with weekends off, which I was for years. Lee let me do three twelve-hour shifts, basically thirty-six hours for my full salary so that I could have most of my days off. My wife has had cancer for several months, and this schedule lets me spend more time with her. I'm working when she normally sleeps. So, I nap for three hours, drive to her hospital in Mesa, drive home at three, take another nap, and go to work. Then Thursday through Monday I stay with her until I leave for my six o'clock shift."

"That is nice of Lee. But that sounds like a strenuous schedule."

"Funny the things you can adjust to when needed. But I get good sleep the four days I'm at the hospital. I think that I'm helping Emma by being with her so much, and if the worst should happen, I want to spend every minute I can with her. It's worth it."

During the conversation, Cathy had been trying to keep pace with Jack's rate of measuring out the samples, but he was like a machine. She would occasionally get too much on the scale and would have to remove the excess, which slowed her down. Jack's careful hand seemed to almost magically tap the spatula, dropping the exact weight onto the scale the first time.

"Jack, what's your secret for weighing so quickly and accurately?"

He chuckled. "It has something to do with having performed the task millions of times. You are probably doing better than I was at your level of experience."

They finished up the last of the samples, and he helped carry the racks of beakers out to her lab station. Jack took his leave, slipping his backpack on one shoulder, and headed out the door. Cathy waited until she was alone and rushed to check the platinum in the drawer.

To her consternation, there were ten bowls in the drawer—the seven she had marked and three additional. That accounted for all the line items the list showed as not yet delivered.

I expected them to be gone. What does this mean? Why would he move the remaining three bowls from the platinum room to this drawer? Is he planning to take them all at once from here? It makes no sense. It does, however, prove that Jack is the one responsible for the bowls being in his drawer.

~

In his room in Apache Junction, Billy decided to try a different way of looking for the deputy on social media. He knew that Deputy Allred did not have a social media page at all, though he had looked at half a dozen Brendan Allred accounts, plus spelling variations. None were his guy.

He decided to try FaceBook to find family members in the Gila Valley and go through their photos. Maybe his parents, siblings, or other relatives had him in group pictures taken at family events. Positively knowing any of his close relatives would be valuable.

He grudgingly admired what a good job Allred had done on protecting his privacy. He had been doing everything he could think of to get his personal and family information for weeks now, and the only thing he had was his police radio ID, familiarity with his police cruiser, and a recent snapshot of him in the parking lot. Of course, the GPS bug he had on the cruiser would shortly lead him to more information. But finding a family portrait identified with names would be a bonanza that he could easily weaponize against Allred.

After hours of concentrated searching, he found what he was looking for. Allred's photo with his family was in an album called Mother's Day 2017 on his mother's page. She had captioned it "Bren and his sweet family: Monica, Lizzie, and Layton." Billy created an Allred family file of the families of Bren's sister, Ann, and two brothers.

I have enough personal information to scare the guy to death now. Now to figure out where he lives, his family's daily routine, and how to communicate with him.

~

Sheriff Bobby Bitters asked Sergeant Bren Allred to arrange a phone conference with the two officers on the SWI case and Sergeant Al Victor of the San Carlos Police to update the status of the theft investigation.

"Have them call into your office in Central and let each of them report on their activities and observations to date. I will sit in on the meeting, but I don't want anyone but you to know I'm there. I won't say anything, but if I want a question asked, I'll pass it to you in a note. What time do they finish work?"

"Normally at four o'clock."

"Alright, have them call from their apartments at five."

The Sheriff arrived at Bren's office at quarter to five. Everyone called in early, so the meeting started a few minutes before the scheduled time. Bren called on Sergeant Victor to speak first.

"I've been able to visit all of the mine property. It touches on several basins including parts of Myberg, Granite, Ruin, Syphon, and Gerald Basins. It's quite rugged—lots of ridges and valleys—and many old mines, mining camps, ranch pens, water structures, and cattle fences. There are trace roads and trails all over the place.

"However, there really appears to be only three reasonable access points for vehicles. On the south side, the mine main gate is at Prince Charming spring, and the road comes off the Apache Trail up Tin Horn Wash, through the closed Sleeping Beauty Mine, into Lost Gulch, and turns north just before the spring. The main gate can also be accessed from Pinto Valley Road, through the Diamante Ranch. But coming either way, the mine itself can only be accessed through the main gate.

"The main gate has an employee entry and a delivery-contractor entry. Both are access card gates with continual video monitoring by a guard. There is also a speaker box, so a visitor with no access card can have the guard admit them. At the guard office, they log in and out and are escorted to their destination in the mine.

"The other two access points—one from the east via Gerald Wash and one from the north up Devore Wash—have conventional lock and key gates that are always locked. So really the only public entry point is the main gate.

"We've installed cameras at all gates that capture the driver and passenger and the rear license plate, so we will have a time-stamped record of who enters and exits. They seem to have very good security. At this point, I can't see how cathodes could be removed undetected. That's my report."

Bren looked at the Sheriff and silently mouthed, "Any questions?"

Bitters, who had been penciling notes on a spiral notebook, shook his head.

"Manny, why don't you tell us what you have."

"I've come to the same conclusions on security and access as Al. I've also observed the processes for handling cathodes in the tankhouse and for shipping them out. The stuff is weighed at every hand-off from one step in the process to another, so any shortage would be noticed. One area that I think could be a source of theft is the handling of scrap copper.

Manny explained the copper scrap process, finishing with, "A contractor comes in every two or three days, replaces the bin, and hauls the scrap out. He has similar bins at the repair shops where any scrap metal is tossed, and he picks that up as needed. The shop's clerk calls him when it is getting full."

Bitters had pushed a note across the desk to Bren, and Bren asked the question on it. "If our thief was somehow tossing a couple of cathodes a day into the scrap bin, would they be taken with the rest of the scrap? Sounds like a fine way to get them off the property."

Manny replied, "That is true. However, it really wouldn't create a loss in the metallurgical balance, because the empty bin tare is noted as it comes in the gate, and the loaded bin is weighed as it leaves. Scrap is accounted for in the formula. This is the most likely place for copper theft I could find, but it seems to be a dead end."

Manny paused briefly, then continued. "However, we did set up a dust monitoring station near the scrap bin, so we are now capturing all activity that happens there on video. I plan to view each trip it makes for a couple of weeks. The video is activated by motion, so even a pedestrian would be captured. In the end, like Al, I can't find anything wrong with the process."

Bren asked, "Pat, what have you found in the lab?"

Pat decided that possible platinum theft was not relevant to the core investigation and wanted to give Jack every benefit of doubt, so she chose not to mention that development.

"The lab is actually four labs overseen by the Chief Chemist, Lee Gallo. Three of the labs are located at the general mine complex by the main office. They are different buildings, but they're within fifty yards of each other. The assay lab is staffed and operated around the clock, though only a single technician works nights, and two on dayshift during weekends. Generally, four or five people are working in the lab during the week days.

"The environmental lab is basically a water quality lab and a dust analysis facility. Nothing they do impacts the copper balance. There is a lab tech and a guy who cleans and maintains respirators and air and water monitoring equipment.

"The research lab is physically the largest building. It is a Butler barn that houses an office and a small lab area, but mostly with silos and pads for leach testing, a tiny little tankhouse section, and the in situ rock leach pads. I am in training in these processes and will work a few hours a week in the lab. These are mostly long duration processes unattended except for performing occasional operational tasks and scheduled analysis.

"The fourth lab is really just a table, an AA machine and a cabinet with lab supplies, located in the engineering field office near Pima. Diana travels there on Mondays for a few hours' work. This is where I did my lab training. Only the assay lab has any bearing on the copper balance, so the others are irrelevant to copper theft.

"Everybody I've met has been very professional. I've reviewed report entries of all the techs and spot checked their results against my own, and nothing looks the least bit suspicious. I was introduced into the research lab this week and found some interesting things." Pat paused and chuckled, "By the way, I had to sign a non-disclosure agreement to work in there, so if I tell you about them, you may have to arrest me."

Bren laughed. "I'm pretty sure your permission from Kiko has you covered."

Cathy continued, "Anyway, they actually produce a few miniature copper cathodes in the pilot plant they have in that lab, but it's not in operation except for specific short tests. I'm not sure what they do with those, but they mostly seem to be piling them in a corner of the lab. Since nothing in the research lab is on the met balance, that copper is unaccounted for. But it would average less than a few pounds per month."

Her tone became a bit more excited as she said, "Then, a really interesting thing they are testing is recovering copper directly from huge intact ore rocks using only electricity applied across the rock itself. Diana runs most of the tests. I will be helping with that now. But there is no copper production really involved. The amount of copper being recovered amounts to a few grams per day."

Bren received a note from the Sheriff and asked, "Tell me about Diana."

"She is very good. She's actually an engineer working on a scientific exchange through the U of A. She's from somewhere in the Middle East. Like I said before, she travels to the Pima field office once a week to do a few tests for the drillers. Her work is excellent, and we have become good friends. We fairly often do things together in the evening."

"So, you talk on your cell phones to arrange dinner and such?" Bren asked.

"Yes."

"Send me her number."

"I will. May I ask why you want it?"

"It's sensitive, so I won't explain details, but we have a person of interest in another case who is also in that same exchange program. I'm interested in how much communication he has with her and the others in the program. Continue the relationship with her exactly as you have but let us know of anything unusual."

Chapter 21

Bren told Monica that he was going to have to go to work for an hour or so after the kids were down. After supper he helped Monica clean up the kitchen, then got the kids in bed. He walked over to his office in the old store building, where he called the sheriff's cell phone. He explained what the GPS had revealed about Billy Benson's movements and that he couldn't understand why Benson went to that trouble without getting some kind of psychological jab against Bren.

"I bet he's monitoring our radio calls, so he knew where to wait for you."

"That's what I think, too."

"I'll give dispatch orders to only contact you by cell phone, and you use the radio only for routine calls that reveal nothing about your location."

"I wish he would tip his hand on what he is up to."

Bitters said, "Well, we can be sure what he did had a purpose, and since he made no effort to make you aware of it, it had to be preparatory to something in the future. You say he parked next to your cruiser. Can you tell how long he was there?"

"Not exactly," Bren replied. "The route he takes is shown as a continuous blue line. A stop is noted as a yellow dot if it is less than five minutes, and as a red dot if more. This one's a yellow dot. I figured he might have noted the car number or license plate. He was there for a very short time, because he couldn't know when I would be coming out or if somebody might see him messing around with the car."

The sheriff said, "So probably not enough time to clip a brake line or plant a bomb."

"Jeez. I didn't even consider him doing something to the car. He might also have put a GPS Tracker on it. That would let him know where I am and could lead him straight to my home. And sticking one on the car could be done in a matter of seconds."

Bitters said, "He would either have to use an adhesive or put it on the frame or other iron part. Most of those cars are plastic now. If he is tracking you, he already knows exactly where you parked. I guess that's your driveway?"

"No. Thank goodness I've been parking it in the old warehouse at the office I use. That's a short block from my house, though."

"Get a good light and hunt for a GPS tracker. If you find it, open the garage door, pull it off, and move it as fast as you can to the shoulder of the highway, as close as possible to where you're parked, and leave it there. I think the best accuracy on those is about 12 feet. With any luck, he will think it was jolted lose and fell to the ground and will not think you discovered it. And for sure, at least for a while, he will not be able to track you. Call me back and let me know whether you have found one or not."

There was no light in the old warehouse Bren used as a garage, so he took his flashlight and did a walk around, looking for anything unusual or any disturbed dust or mud. He walked to the right side of the car and thought, "Benson got out of his car on this side of it. Where would he put a magnet quickly? The push bumper. He wouldn't even have to enter the parking lot. He could walk to the front and reach through the pipe fence and stick it to the metal of the bumper. Fast, easy, and difficult to spot."

On close examination, he found the little black plastic rectangle. He paced out the distance from the garage door to the front of the car, opened the garage door, and went outside. He marked that distance and noted the corresponding spot on the road to place the device. He took out a screwdriver to pry the magnet loose, then trotted the twenty feet to the spot on the road and dropped it. Then he called the sheriff.

"I found it on the push bumper and have placed it at the edge of the road."

"One more thing to do right away," the Sheriff said. "Pull out on the highway and, coming from the east, brake hard and leave a skid mark to a point near the GPS tracker. In case Benson checks, it will provide an explanation as to why the tracker ended up there."

"That's a good idea. I'll do it right away."

"And don't take your cruiser back to your house. Shut down that little office. Make it look abandoned, and until this cat and mouse game ends, don't use it. Bring your cruiser back to this office tonight and leave it in our garage. Drive one of our "civilian" cars home; but if possible, even park *it* out of sight—maybe inside your back gate. We will have you swap out squad cars frequently."

Bren left the skid marks on the road and swapped out his car for a blue Ford Fusion. As he drove home, he was relieved that they had countered Benson's move in about the best way possible. Now he was worried about Monica.

She's bound to know something is wrong when I'm no longer bringing a police car home or going to my office. She knows I've got some officers under cover. Maybe I can get away with telling her it's all to protect them when we meet. She's not easy to fool, but her being upset could be bad for the pregnancy.

~

Marco Olvera, as part of his plan of action for improving industrial hygiene and ergonomics at SWI, arranged to observe the contractor processes and interview the contractors working on the property. His first meeting with George Simmons had been an interview conducted in a small meeting room at the tankhouse.

Marco was impressed with George's obvious friendliness and good standing with all the people he encountered as they walked through the building for their interview. Everybody they met greeted George and shook his hand. The wiry and energetic George seemed to have an inside joke with each person and knew many of their family members by name.

They talked through the contract that George had with SWI, and how he conducted his business. George explained the routine he used for picking up the scrap and how he sorted it at his scrap yard near Mackey's Camp in Miami. As he had enough to fill a load, he hauled it to Phoenix to sell to a metal dealer. He mentioned that as part of his payment for helping start the operation, he had received stock, so he was an SWI owner.

Unlike some of the other contractors who generally seemed slightly uncomfortable, perhaps wondering what the interview was all about, George was effusive and very forthcoming with information.

He knew a lot, not only about mining and the processes around it, but also about the history of the area and the old historic mines. He spent quite a bit of time talking about the Money Metal Mine and mentioned that decades ago County Attorney A. R. Edwards was one of the early owners starting in territorial days. George's dad worked for him, putting in some of the shafts and tunnels.

"Old A. R. died in the late 1940s, before I could remember him, but dad respected him and said he was smart enough to listen to advice and ended up making some real money from the old mine.

"Some time ago, I think in the late fifties, Louis Ellsworth bought the mine and hired dad and me to reopen and explore it. I was about fifteen. We found a few veins of silver and took out enough to cover all of Louie's costs, including paying us. There was a lot of low-grade copper, but not something a little operator could do anything with. Louie hoped to interest one of the two big mines in it, either Miami Copper or Inspiration, but they never bit. So, I'm really happy to see SWI mining here. It proves dad was right. It's too bad Louie didn't live to profit from it."

Marco said, "You sure know about this place. I wish I had talked to you before I submitted my report on the mining history of the property. I got good information from Hugh Holcomb of the geology department, but yours is more detailed. I really enjoy knowing the history of the places I'm in. I'll have to make a point of spending more time visiting with you."

George took that as an invitation to tell another story. "Any time. As you might have guessed, I enjoy talking about these things. I actually provided the report to Hugh.

"There's a lot of history here. Did you know that Phin Clanton and Pete Spence were the first owners of the Diamante Ranch? They ran angora goats over the whole area from Sleeping Beauty to the top of Webster Mountain."

"The gunfighters from Tombstone? They lived here?"

"Yep. A widow lady by the name of Laura Jane Jackson and her son Will Bohme homesteaded near the Clanton-Spence place, and those two old desperados watched out for them like good neighbors. They took young Will under their wings, taught him the ropes. They were both really good to him. Eventually Phin asked Laura Jane to marry him and she accepted. Poor old Pete was also sweet on her, so he did the honorable thing; pulled out to Mexico where he operated a ranch.

"After about five years of marriage, Phin got caught by a blizzard on Webster Mountain, which lead to pneumonia. He died and is buried in Globe. Laura Jane and Will called their ranch, now combined with Clanton's, the Bohme Ranch. Will named one of his boys after Phin."

George leaned on the table and continued, "Pete reappeared and eventually married the widow Clanton and worked with Will building up the ranch. After a few years, old Pete also died of pneumonia and was also buried in Globe.

"Four generations of Bohmes owned and operated the ranch until they finally sold out to Cyprus Minerals Corporation, who renamed the ranch Diamante. It has continued to be run by Phelps Dodge, and now Freeport, who use the cattle to help with revegetating the old mine. A Bohme daughter still operates a ranch not far from the old home ranch."

Marco said, "Wow. Thanks for the information. I guess we better both get back to work."

Marco mulled over the conversation with George. *As the scrap hauler, he has to be the most likely suspect, but sure seems open. No hint at all that he's lying or hiding something. He's also more invested personally in the company, than he is as a stock-holder. He really wants the mine to succeed to prove him and his dad right in their judgment of the property. Yet he remains my only viable suspect.*

Chapter 22

Billy Benson sat at the computer in his halfway house room and looked at the GPS on Allred's car. At first, he was elated that Allred's car had stopped for over an hour at the corner of Highway 70 and Central Road. He thought it was Allred's house. Then the position seemed to have leaped south a few yards and didn't move for three days.

He went to Google maps and switched to street view. There was no house there, just what looked like a long-empty business with an aging realty sign on the front. Even worse, the tracker seemed to be on a spot near a curb drain on the highway. A car would not be there without having run off the road. He decided he would check on his next trip.

Benson still had an hour before his parole officer's "good night" call, so he walked out in the back yard—about the only place he could be sure he had a level of privacy. He had picked up a cheap burner phone, which he used to call the number Ray, a fellow prisoner, had given him and he committed to memory. The dealer went by Doc. Billy explained who he was and what he wanted and gave Ray as his reference.

"Yeah, Ray said you'd be calling me. You want two injectable Special-K needles. What weight animal do you want to knock out?"

"About 120 pounds and 190 pounds."

"I'll put an S on the small dose and an L on the large dose. Don't get 'em mixed up or you might kill the small animal. In the morning leave 300 bucks in the rock pile Ray told you about, and I'll replace the cash with your medicine. You can pick it up when you want. But don't leave it too long. If you lose it, there's no refund."

Billy decided to get ready for bed. He was scheduled to make Saturday deliveries tomorrow. His cell phone rang. It was Chapo Garcia.

"Billy, we need you to start at seven in the morning because you have a run to Morenci and Silver City.

"Silver is the priority. They need it before noon, so go straight there using highway 70 all the way to Lordsburg, and at Silver go through to the mine. They will escort you to a project site to make your delivery. Then get back to Morenci before six p.m. That means you will have to push hard, but don't break the law. Take a snack and thermos with you because you won't be able to take a break until you get to the hotel in Safford."

Benson said, "A couple of things, Boss. For one thing, I'm not supposed to leave the state."

"I checked with your parole officer, and he cleared it with the judge. You have to call him when you approach the state line, when you reach your delivery point, when you return to Arizona, and of course when you are in Safford. Then he will call your hotel room after 9:30 to be sure you're in. What else do you have?"

"I've never been to New Mexico. Anything I need to know?"

"Just follow the GPS route to the address on the order. New Mexico has a little stricter enforcement of speed laws, so watch it carefully. One last thing. Until the current projects at both Morenci and Silver are finished, we will be making more frequent trips, and even more so for Morenci. We will likely make daily trips for the next six weeks as they do major maintenance on the plant. Are you willing to work a lot of overtime?"

"I will be happy to work seven days a week. For the next several months, I have nothing better to do."

"I have to offer the overtime to the other drivers until either they refuse it or until the overtime is evenly distributed to those who want it. But I'll have the schedule ready for each week not later than the preceding Wednesday."

"However, it works out will be fine with me."

Benson was out of the shipping lot and on US 60 heading through Gold Canyon by a quarter to seven. As instructed by Doc, Billy slowed after he passed the Renaissance Festival grounds and pulled off just before mile post 206. Near the power pole he found the pile of rocks and put the money under the largest rock. Then he pulled back on the US 60 and continued east.

He thought, *I'll have time to at least drive slowly through Central and maybe stop long enough to take a look at why my GPS tracker isn't moving.*

He made good time and was a half-hour ahead of schedule when he reached Central Road. He pulled into the small parking lot in front of the abandoned building. He walked to the spot his tracker seemed to be and noticed that a car skidded to the curb two feet from where he found his device. Chuckling, he picked it up, hurried to his truck, and continued his trip to Silver City.

Somebody probably pulled out in front of Allred, causing him to slam on his brakes and skid hard into the curb, which knocked the tracker loose. No big deal. I'll just have to find a time to reattach it.

~

Arriving after work at her apartment, Cathy Winn again reviewed the video focused on Jack Locke's work station. She thought about the day. Jack had surprised her by putting more bowls in the paper drawer. She went through the Monday night shift, reviewing each of the episodes captured as the camera sensed motion.

She confirmed that nothing unusual had happened until after the security guard made his pass through the lab. Then when Jack had his last cup of soup, he did something with his backpack and the drawer. That had to be when he added the three platinum bowls to the cache.

She realized that since Jack had placed the pack on the counter of his station when he first arrived, it had lain untouched except for the two lunch breaks and had never been in the platinum room.

"Since he didn't have the pack in the platinum room," she thought, "he must have brought the three bowls when he came to work! This makes less sense the more I know."

She switched to the live feed in time to see Jack start his Tuesday night shift. He placed his backpack on the counter and looked through his new samples. She could see several liquid samples in plastic bottles, a handful of dry sample envelopes, and four red-labeled high-grade ore samples that would require a fire assay. Once he organized his work, he took the liquid bottles into the platinum room and started them on electrolysis, then headed to the fire assay bay to start the furnace.

Cathy decided that this was going to be a routine night until at least the night guard made his round. She decided to get a quick microwave meal and get in bed early. She would check Jack's later actions in the morning.

Cathy was awakened from sound sleep when her alarm buzzed at five a.m. She used her phone to check the camera. It was currently off, so she manually turned it on. She could see Jack in the platinum room and his backpack where it had apparently been all night. She pulled up the video records for the night and played the eleven-thirty instance, which it turned out was caused by the guard who stopped and visited with Jack for a moment in the platinum room.

The 2:07 film was Jack removing his Thermos from the pack and having his soup. He then walked out of view in the direction of the main lab door, returned in the opposite direction to the office door, then came back toward the work station but instead went into the platinum room. Once in the room, he walked past the electrolysis area toward the storage closet, then returned to the work station with a cardboard carton that looked about a foot long and five inches square.

Jack placed the carton on the counter, opened the paper drawer, extracted the ten platinum bowls, and placed them in the carton. He closed the drawer and carried the carton loaded with the bowls back into the room from which it came. He came back to his work station, rinsed out his Thermos, and put it in the backpack. Then, as if nothing had happened, he resumed his normal work.

Cathy quickly spot-checked each of the remaining video segments until 5:15 a.m. Jack went to the wall phone and made a call that lasted about two minutes. He then walked toward the main lab door and remained off camera until the lack of motion caused it to shut down. The next segment at 5:35 showed Jack and Lee walking hurriedly into the platinum room. There, as viewed through the window, Jack brought the carton out to the table and had Lee inspect its contents.

There was some obviously confused discussion, and Jack produced what Cathy took to be the original yellow-colored bill of lading for the big platinum shipment. They put the carton back in storage, secured the platinum room, and took the paper into Lee's office. The video timed out.

Cathy realized she had to get moving or she would be late for start of shift. She made it on time and saw that Jack's backpack was still on the counter. She started working on her samples, when Jack came walking in from the office.

"Hey, Jack. What are you doing here so late?"

"It's the darnedest thing. You know that back ordered shipment of large bowls we are waiting to get?"

"Yeah."

"Well, I found it in the bottom of the original shipping box. The lab supply company had been going crazy trying to figure out what happened to them, because they just seemingly disappeared. What apparently happened is the shipping department somehow got them into the crate for shipment without ever recording that they were shipped. The supplier is so happy they are going to send a ten percent finder's fee of $8,300 to the company."

"That's great, Jack. You're kind of a hero."

"Definitely not. I'm just glad it's taken care of."

"Jack, I know better. I found the bowls when I ran out of filter paper. There were seven. Then a week later there were ten, and now the mystery of the missing bowls has been resolved and the supplier is saved from an embarrassing loss. You have terrific financial need, and this was free money that you could really use, yet you gave it back with no outside pressure. To me that's pretty honorable, even heroic."

"I'm ashamed of that and didn't want anyone to know."

"I'm not telling anyone." Cathy added, "Jack, there's no crime in being tempted. In the end you did the right thing, and I'm proud to know you."

As she got back into her work Cathy saw irony in her situation. *I am getting nowhere in my part of the investigation, which is frustrating. Now I did a great job in solving the platinum case, but no one will ever know it.* She chuckled. "That's even more frustrating."

Chapter 23

Because of deputies' scheduling complications, two of the areas in the county were short a sergeant for the weekend, so Bren was up early on what would normally be a day off. He was an on-call supervisor covering the short districts. With any luck, other than handling the morning roll calls, he would be able to spend the day with Monica and the kids. He handled the morning roll call and called into the command call, handled by the undersheriff. Everything was routine and hopefully would stay that way.

After the call, he once again checked the GPS for the location of Billy Benson. To Bren's surprise, Benson was just leaving Globe on US 70 heading toward Safford. He thought, "Billy is no doubt wondering why his tracker isn't moving. There's a chance he will stop and check it out. If I park at the old Church Avenue chapel, I'll be able to watch from inside the car and video him if he stops. It's far enough away that he won't be able to see me, but the zoom will capture everything."

Monica and the kids were sleeping in, so Bren drove the blue Fusion into the southeast corner of the parking lot. He adjusted his video and watched Benson's progress as he left the reservation, passed through Pima, and approached Central where he slowed to a crawl.

As Benson drove past, Bren saw he was staring intently at the empty building. Bren began filming. Benson's left turn signal came on and the truck pulled into the front parking lot. The truck was blocked from Bren's view by the old store building.

Benson quickly walked directly to where Bren had left the tracker by the curb and looked around on the ground. He apparently saw it, then paused and looked at the skid marks on the road. He seemed to be chuckling as he picked up the tracker. Benson hurried back to his truck and pulled back on the highway heading east.

Back at home, Bren copied the video file and sent it in a message to the sheriff. "This happened about ten minutes ago. Looks like Billy swallowed our story."

A few minutes later the sheriff replied, "Hook, line, and sinker. So, we are one up on him now."

~

Meret Mulikow received a Turkmenistan weather report from Aziz Orazow. As planned, Mulikow left Abdulov resting in his room and drove to his office where he used the satellite phone to call Orazow.

After greetings and some preliminary discussion, Orazow said, "We have deciphered the messages we discussed earlier. Abdulov has been on the Russian payroll from the beginning."

Orazow continued, "Of more interest to you, Meret, he is currently negotiating to sell some American mining research to the Russians. If this becomes known to the Americans, it could jeopardize our mining partnership with them—a potential loss of billions of dollars for us. We will bring this idiotic situation to an end as quickly as possible."

"I will be happy to have this over with. However, I dare not confront Abdulov. If he senses any threat, he could kill me in an instant. How am I expected to handle this?"

"You are not to handle it," Orazow said. "We're working on a way to quietly and quickly extract Abdulov from the US and replace him with someone with an actual mining background. You will eventually be instructed on what to do, but mostly maintain the status quo in regard to him. How are the Americans handling the situation with the murder?"

"They have moved the case from the local law enforcement to the FBI. Miss Dane, my US counterpart, seems to have accepted Abdulov's story at face value. She has made it clear to the FBI that Abdulov has diplomatic immunity and that the situation needs to be kept out of public attention."

"Does she know anything about the espionage?"

Mulikow strongly asserted, "Miss Dane knows nothing about it. In fact, only Abdulov, you, and I have any knowledge of the attempted espionage. The stolen files were to be passed to Abdulov, but he missed the hand off so never actually received them."

"Then there is one other person who knows—the insider who removed the file to begin with."

"I hadn't thought about that. I'm sure it had to come from one of the two students in that sector. They are both very serious about this professional opportunity and would not jeopardize it for anything, so whichever one it was had to have been bullied by Abdulov."

"We need to confirm their level of involvement. Subtly get from Abdulov which one it was, then send their file and cellphone number to me and we will check for any security breaches or unexpected funds. Depending on that outcome, we will decide how to handle the guilty student."

~

Billy Benson arrived in Safford from Morenci about three-thirty, so he switched to his rented Rhino and headed to a thrift store where he bought a diaper bag, toddler car seat, a baby helmet, pajamas, and a few items of clothing for an almost three-year old. Securing his purchases in the back of his ATV, he stopped at Walgreen's and picked up some training diapers, wipes, baby power, and some diaper rash cream.

He rented a storage locker, basically a small walk-in closet with a secure door, at a public storage facility. He opened the packages and removed some of the contents to make them look used and packed them in the diaper bag. He then stored his newly-acquired goods in the storage locker and headed back to his room.

From his spying via internet, Billy had found that Allred's sister Ann had posted that she would be watching Layton during school hours so that Monica and the grandmothers could rest up for the birth of the new baby, due in the next few days. From this same FaceBook page, he had learned that little Layton Allred was nearly potty-trained but still wore Pull-Ups. He discovered the boy's favorite toys, foods, and snacks and that he loved motorcycles.

He had an appointment to interview a babysitter, a woman in her late fifties named Nanna Beth, who tended children at her home near Artesia. The place looked good. It had a fenced yard with a good lawn, lots of shade, and nice-looking playground toys. The house was nice and childproofed.

Nanna Beth said, "I keep up to three children on a weekly basis and will accept two more for short periods. Weekends, long days, or overnights are more expensive."

Billy said, "As I explained on the phone, I will only occasionally need to drop my son off; but because of work, I don't get much notice when I will need him sat." They agreed to terms, and Billy returned to his hotel room.

Billy took a used Maricopa County Sheriff's Office uniform shirt he'd found in a thrift store from an overnight satchel and patiently snipped the county patches from the shoulder. He replaced them with Graham County patches he had purchased on the internet. Combined with the Graham sheriff ball cap, matching khaki cargo pants, black police duty belt and Glock, and the engraved plastic name tag he also ordered online, he was now ready to convincingly impersonate a deputy. He neatly packed the items in the satchel.

Shortly after the nightly call from his probation officer, Billy was in his comfortable bed and fast asleep.

The next morning on his way to the Morenci warehouse, Billy pulled off the highway into the storage facility and deposited the satchel in his locker. He was quickly back on the road.

Billy was at Morenci only fifteen minutes and was out the gate heading for Apache Junction. He made good time all the way to the Salt River Valley. He stopped briefly at the rock pile near the Renaissance grounds and picked up his tranquilizer needles. As he got back on the highway heading west on US 60, he got a call from Chapo Garcia.

"I need you to start early tomorrow, because I have two time-sensitive deliveries. I'll have your truck loaded by 5:00 a.m. with repair parts that Morenci will need by 9:30. They also need an electronic item by about 2:30 p.m. that we don't have yet. We will get it long after you've left, so I will put it on the Greyhound bus to arrive there at 11:25 tomorrow morning. After the 9:30 delivery, get back to Safford, wait for the part at Greyhound and get it to Morenci as soon as possible. I've sent you a text with this schedule."

That schedule worked well for Billy's plan. On his morning run to Morenci, he dropped the two tranquilizer pens off at his storage locker.

Now everything is in place. I just need a time when Allred is fully occupied away from Safford to spring the trap.

Chapter 24

Harvey Richards was now at his third weekly meeting of the addiction recovery group. The first meeting was awkward for him, even though he had read the booklet on the program prior to attending. He was more comfortable in the second meeting, so he talked about his drinking problem.

He had at first worried that they would push the church on him, but the group members really didn't talk about religion in that way. The program focused on recovery, overcoming addictions by following the steps to recovery, and having the support and understanding of people with similar problems. The spiritual aspect was limited to the existence of a loving, helpful God.

This third meeting began as the others, and a new person was welcomed to the group. Wilma was an upper-middle-aged, nice-looking woman who looked like she could not possibly have any kind of addiction—more like the perfect young grandma.

Each meeting emphasized one of the twelve steps. The emphasis this time was on restitution and reconciliation. For several of the people in the group, this was a tough one since they had spouses and children, siblings, and parents who had been hurt or neglected because of their addiction.

For Harvey it was not a big step in the process. He spoke first during sharing time. "I drank to fill the emptiness left by my wife's death. In a way, I have hurt only myself. I have met all my civic and social obligations. But, in another way, I feel I have besmirched my wife's memory, and I have been weak in seeking God's help and trusting in Him.

"I visited her grave and told her what I've been doing. I apologized for letting her down, but I don't know if I'm the only one that heard that. I've admitted my weakness to God and asked for forgiveness and help, and I feel I'm receiving that. I wish there were more I could do, but I don't know what that would be."

The new lady introduced herself. "I'm Wilma, and I'm a recovering alcoholic. Many years ago, I and my then-husband ruined our marriage and our lives with addiction. I found help through an AA program, became sober, and stayed that way for over thirty years. When my beloved second husband died, I relapsed. I went into rehab and have now been sober for one month. I'm so glad to be back among supportive people."

Harvey was surprised that this poised and gracious and obviously strong woman ever had such problems. He thought it showed that you can't judge the challenges a person faces by outward appearance.

Jess, a guy about Harvey's age, said, "Sometimes the hardest thing is forgiving ourselves. I have hurt a lot of people. Over the last year, virtually all of them have accepted my apology and forgiven me. I have confirmation by the Spirit that Heavenly Father has forgiven me. Yet, I'm still disgusted with myself for what I've done. Just this week it hit me that I need to put the guilt behind me and fully welcome my forgiven state. You can't ever really repent of something if you don't let it go."

After the closing, those who wished ate cookies and mingled and visited a while. A couple of attendees offered Harvey encouragement.

Wilma said, "I completely identify with the emptiness, loneliness, and grief being so overwhelmingly present. I thought it would naturally get better with time, but it hasn't with me. I've been advised to visit a grief support group, and I'm going to give it a try."

"Please let me know how it goes; maybe it would help me."

~

Vasily Petrov, Mergen Abdulov's handler for the Russian Federation Foreign Security Service (SVR), had provided a darknet secure communication link to allow Abdulov to safely communicate with him from the United States. It had been difficult for Abdulov to do so during his recuperation, since Mulikow spent most of his time in his casita drinking and watching European Football League games. Today something came up that required Mulikow to actually go to his office, providing Abdulov a chance to contact Colonel Petrov.

Abdulov reported what had happened and the fact that he was recuperating under care of a visiting nurse in Mulikow's hotel suite. He added that the file on the mine research had become lost in the internal corporate mail system, but that his contact had prepared a second copy, which would be delivered to him directly as soon as he was well enough to travel, which should be in two or three days. Petrov was online, so the texting continued as a back and forth communication.

Vasily: So, your wound was serious?

Mergen: No. It was a surface slice from right shoulder to left hip. It was easily sewn back, but it became infected. The infection has been difficult and made me sick. It is clearing up nicely now, and I feel much better. The file is worth a great deal. I would like to negotiate for a higher reward.

Vasily: There can be no negotiation. I will deposit 3,000 manats in your account upon receipt, as usual. The technical people will determine the value, and you will be given a ten percent bonus. If it is as valuable as you think, you should get a very good bonus. We have never shorted you and never shall.

Mergen: Very well. When I get the folder, I will let you know. Can you provide me with a drop location in Arizona? It's a good-sized parcel.

Vasily: A parcel? No. No paper. Get it digitally on a thumb drive, then send it electronically to me on this site. Don't use regular internet or phone.

Mergen: As you say, Vasily.

Vasily: Good. I await the delivery.

Abdulov disconnected and shut down his computer. As he heard Mulikow opening the door, he sat on the edge of his bed as if he were just getting up. Mulikow looked in and said, "I hope I didn't disturb you."

"No, I'm just getting up to use the toilet. Maybe I'll walk around outside a bit. I need to start doing a little more."

"Just don't do anything to cause the wound to open again."

~

Al Victor was driving to his office when he saw DeVon Goode come out of the Mt. Turnbull Apache store with a soft drink and a sandwich and head to the patio area. Al pulled up beside DeVon and lowered the window.

"Hey, DeVon. I need to talk with you."

"I don't feel like company now. Go away."

"I can either sit by you and we can talk while you eat, or I can put you in the car and take you to the office. Either way, you are going to talk to me. It's up to you."

"Ok, come on over and spoil my lunch break."

Al waited until DeVon opened his sandwich and took a bite. He asked, "On the night that Gato was murdered, did you see him?"

"Yes. He had been in the store to buy a candy bar. He left just a few minutes before the end of my shift. I walked down to the rest area and crossed the highway to the gate to Rainbow City. Gato was talking to some white guy in a car, and I saw him get in the car. They drove off east on 70."

"Were they by the road or in the rest area?"

"Gato sat on a table. The guy drove into the rest area, and Gato went to talk to him."

Al thought for a minute while DeVon ate a few more bites, then asked, "Could you see what the driver looked like?"

"Nah, he was in the car. He looked like a big white guy."

"What kind of car was it?"

"I'm not sure. Only it was a red full-sized car is all I know."

"I appreciate the information. See, that wasn't so bad was it?"

"I guess not."

"I'm glad to see you're sober. Did you go see the lady at Health Services?"

"Yeah. She talked me into going back to a meeting. It was good. It might help."

"Good. Just keep on doing the right thing. Thanks for your help."

Al left DeVon to finish his lunch in peace.

~

Manny called Jenny every evening, and they talked about Jenny's day and what they would do on the weekend. Not much was said about Manny's activities because he couldn't mention where he was or what he was doing. Instead he told her about his health, things on the news, and the distance learning course he was currently taking.

Jenny had some big news. "Mr. Willard told us the board approved the move to Klondyke School. They'll move our stuff over next week during Spring break!"

"Wow, that's happening kind of fast. I wish I could be there to help you move."

"How I wish you could be here. But moving is no big deal. School personnel are doing everything. Lymie, the bus driver you met, has been working about an hour each evening cleaning, doing minor repairs on the school building, stocking the supply shelves, and even working on the grounds. They also have some contractors putting in a satellite dish and communication wires. This Friday we'll pack all our teaching files, supplies, and personal property in moving boxes, and they'll move them for us. Toward the end of break week, we can go in for a couple of hours and get things exactly where we want them."

"That sounds pretty good." Manny chuckled. "But I guess you will have to get used to using chalk on blackboards."

"That's kind of a bonus," she replied. "They are providing chalk and erasers, so we can use the old slate boards. We also have four portable white boards with a good supply of markers and two big digital boards. We have PCs for Candy and me and learning stations for each of the kids. They installed the satellite connection to the Pima School WAN and all the same digital equipment as the main school. We will even get the same morning announcements that the school does. They want us to text them something about Klondyke school each day, so our kids are regularly on the announcements."

"Wow. It's a good thing the sheriff increased deputies out there. That school is a prime burglary target."

"Oh, that's another thing. They have installed an alarm system for both entry and fire with a silent alarm to the sheriff's office and our phones, as well as a loud audible outside alarm. It has a panic button in case we see something the system doesn't see. There are two street lights at the school, one in front and one back, and several motion-activated lights."

"That's a lot of added expense! How did they afford it?"

"Mr. Willard got grants for low-income rural schools for the electronics and some kind of state aid for one-room schools to help with initial reopening."

"That's great. It sounds like you aren't as worried about teaching in a one-room as you were."

"I'm not worried at all. Since I've been teaching for several weeks, I have a lot more confidence. I know all the kids we'll be teaching, and we've got everything a modern classroom needs. I'm excited about the challenge of teaching multiple grades.

"The only downside is the grounds are all dirt, and we have no playground equipment for the little kids. Our PTA is willing to do the work on the playgrounds, and the school is trying to get swings, slides, and a jungle gym-thingy. The parents have already put in a de-rocked baseball diamond and are rehabbing the old basketball court . . . and they're promising some spots of lawn."

"You already have a PTA?"

"Yes. They self-organized as soon as they heard we were reopening the school."

"When are you planning to move back home?"

"My last night at Mom and Dad's will be this Thursday, and break week will be my first full week back home. I'm looking forward to it. I know you are worried, but I will be just fine. In addition to the added sheriff patrols and the radio, our neighbors are really looking out for us. We just have to get used to living life as it happens. You will be anxious about me being alone out there, but how do you think I feel about you being alone in some strange place doing who-knows-what dangerous thing?"

~

Cathy Winn and Diana Niyazov often had dinner together, since both women avoided romantic relationships. Pat avoided them because she was in a committed relationship (unknown to Diana), and Diana said it was because her assignment was short-term, and any romance would become problematic, personally, culturally and politically. This evening they had Cornish pasties at the Copper Bistro.

Diana had become quite taken with the steak, potato, onion, and black pepper pie, brought to American mining communities by Cornish miners who immigrated in large numbers between 1890 and 1920.

Diana said, "It reminds me of one of my favorite Turkmen dishes, *ichlekli*—a ground beef and potato pie. The ichlekli is a bit spicier, but the steak and black pepper in the pasty is wonderful."

Cathy asked, "How does living here compare to living in your country?"

"Most everything is better here. People have more of everything. Women here are treated the same as men. Most of my people are unemployed. Having mines developed would bring hundreds of good jobs, so I'm very excited about EurMino.

"While under the Soviet Union women in Turkmenistan held positions of authority. That is not completely undone, but women are rarely in positions of power. I was born five years after the Soviet Union ended, and my country became independent. Of course, I don't remember those days. I was a small child, but my parents told me of the changes." Diana paused as her glass was refilled.

"Father is a cotton broker and mother an elementary school teacher, so we are wealthier than most. The despotic President Niyazov, the same as my name, suppressed women's rights, instituted government bullying of everyone, and spent huge sums of money on monuments and ornate buildings. Ashgabat is now called 'city of marble'.

"Father was treated well by city officials because of our name, though we are not related to the former president. Then President Berdimuhamedov rose to power. He is not much better, so all hope in the country for change is gone. Father is no longer favored, though his skill and knowledge of the cotton market is valued. Still, he doesn't feel as secure."

Diana paused, seeming almost startled by what she had said. "This is very dangerous talk. Already I've been threatened to obey or my family will be put in prison. My country, like Arizona, is sunny, but it feels dark all the time. Here it is easy to breathe; there I feel as if I always hold my breath."

Cathy said, "That's frightening. How can you be threatened here?"

"Because my family can be taken by the government at any time."

"Who threatened you?" Cathy asked.

"Mergen Abdulov told me to give him something from SWI or my family will be imprisoned and everything they own will be taken from them."

"What are you going to do?"

"I gave it to him, but he lost it; so now he wants me to do it again. I hate this. Everyone is so kind to me and helps me, and I must betray them."

"What is it that he wants?"

"The file we signed non-disclosure on. But I have a way to fool Abdulov and his masters. I have made a copy of the record with bad results on all tests. No one will know, and when a scientist looks at the data, he will say it proves the idea won't work and that the Americans are wasting their time. So, the true secret will be safe."

"Did Abdulov have you do anything to SWI's metallurgical copper data?"

"No. All my work, even the research, has been professional and accurate. The only thing I sabotage is what I will give to him. So, you must keep it secret, and it will all work out. My family will be safe, and SWI research will remain confidential."

"Yes, I think you've found a good solution. We should not talk about it again, so no one can overhear."

~

Gabe Garcia received a text from Helen Dane saying that Meret Mulikow wanted to meet with them at Helen's office at 2:00. He texted back that he was very busy, but curious, so he would be there. He wondered what the killer with diplomatic immunity had done now.

Using handwritten notes on a lined pad, Mulikow got straight to the point. "We all know that Abdulov did not tell the truth about the killing of the Indian, but there is nothing you or I can do about it because of his immunity. I don't like him. He is, as you say, I think, a rolling cannon."

Gabe said, "That's a loose cannon. So, you don't have control of him?"

"I'm his superior officer, but he does what he wishes. To be honest, I'm afraid of him. I notified the ministry of his problems with the law, and they are recalling him and replacing him on EurMino. I know that you would like to see justice done, but it is rare in cases of diplomacy. I want to assure you that Abdulov was not acting on instructions from any part of our government and had, in fact, completely disregarded our agreement with the United States."

Mulikow removed three documents from his attaché case and handed them to Miss Dane. "I have been authorized on behalf of the Republic of Turkmenistan to provide a formal letter of apology to the United States of America, including the desire to pay for all costs caused by Abdulov's unsanctioned actions. We also apologize to the San Carlos Apache Tribe and to the Gato Wesley family and send our sincere condolences for the loss of their loved one.

"Of course, we know that by rules of diplomacy we can't be sued by the victim's family; nonetheless, we would like to make recompense to them and to the Apache Tribe, for whom we hold no ill will. Therefore, we ask that you, Miss Dane, discuss with the tribe and the family what agreeable payment can be made to both. We will pay the amount you recommend, knowing it doesn't replace a person or a citizen but is the only gesture of apology open to us."

He placed his notes back in the case. "Now completely off the record and for only your information: Abdulov does not know he is under a deep investigation by our National Security Ministry for espionage against our country, and I can assure you that his crime will not go unpunished. Our penalties are much harsher than your own, and I'm sure justice will be done. Of course, for my safety, I don't want Abdulov to get any hint of this. I expect him to be traveling within the week."

Helen replied, "On behalf of the United States, we accept the apology and look forward to continued cooperation and progress through EurMino. I will provide you with a formal letter to confirm it and make recommendations on compensation to victims."

They all shook hands, and Mulikow left.

Gabe said, "Well, that was a surprise. Is it just me, or did you know it was in the works?"

"Not really. I knew that they would move quickly to mend things because of the huge amount of US money and assistance they will receive in creating a lucrative mining industry in their country. I certainly did not expect a formal apology, let alone damages; but I was pretty sure they would find some other place to station Abdulov."

Gabe said, "Since, according to you, I have "vast experience" in diplomatic matters, I should probably understand this better. But why would their government agree to pay out millions to keep this relatively minor diplomatic mess under wraps?"

"Two things: they fully understand how much this arrangement will benefit their economy, and they equally realize that it will greatly enrich the members of the president's cabal. After all, the third most corrupt government in the world is not going to let that kind of treasure slip through their fingers. But, back to business. Do you remember the name of that San Carlos Tribal Police Sergeant we met?"

"Sergeant Al Victor."

"Thanks. That will save me a lot of hunting. I'll ask him the name of the tribal lawyer I need to talk to and arrange for him to take me to meet Mr. Wesley's family."

Chapter 25

Sergeant Bren Allred participated in his daily telephone conference roll-call with the deputies assigned to the western portion of Graham County, then participated in the sheriff's morning executive call. Bren reported they had a theft of some tools at a house south of Pima, two minor accidents, one drunk and disorderly, two stranded motorists, and four traffic stops; but otherwise, "all is quiet on the western front." He mentioned that Deputy Andy Lopez would be acting sergeant this morning, while Bren took care of some personal business. More than a few eyebrows were raised with that news, since Lopez had always rejected fill-in opportunities.

The personal business was a routine examination for Monica with Dr. Layton. She had carefully followed the doctor's advice and avoided stooping, picking things up, lifting, and standing for long periods. Her mom and Bren's mom would alternate days helping Monica with the kids and doing needed things around the house. Occasionally a sister, sister-in-law, or a Relief Society lady would cover when the moms couldn't.

Bren bathed the kids and got them into their pajamas at night, and lifted Layton into his crib. He would load the dishwasher and put the clean dishes up, take out the trash, and sometimes do a load of washing, though the moms usually took care of that.

Before they had left the house, Bren's mom told them, "Go have a nice lunch together. You need a little pleasant time with each other. I'll feed Layton and take him for a walk. When you get back Bren can go back to work, and the three of us will nap until time for Lizzie to come home from school."

The doctor was pleased. He said everything looked great and the baby was growing normally. "Keep doing what you've been doing. You only have about a month to go now, so even if the baby comes early, there is no reason for concern. We are well past the critical stage now. Of course, I prefer you go full term, but if not, there's nothing to worry about. If you start spotting heavily, having contractions, or your water breaks, call me on my cell phone."

As they came out of the doctor's office, Bren asked, "What would you like for lunch? This is a celebration lunch, so the sky's the limit!"

"Let's go to Le Chez Sonic. I want a loaded double bacon cheeseburger, chili fries, and a chocolate Coke."

"Really? Maybe some Italian . . . or Chinese . . . in a nicely decorated dining room?"

"Nope. Listen up, Bucko. You said I could have anything I want, and that's what I want. We can eat in the quiet, nicely-appointed family truckster."

Chuckling, Bren headed for Sonic Drive-in. "Your wish is my command."

She smiled sweetly. "And don't you forget it."

~

Al Victor spent a day mulling over his conversation with DeVon Goode. He had a feeling that he had found an ugly truth, and it made him angry. He radioed in that he would be out of radio range for an hour or so and drove on an unmarked trace road up the slopes of the Gila Mountains to a deep little box canyon off the west Salt Creek.

His grandfather once brought him here and told him that hidden in that wall were the graves of three great Apache shaman. When grandfather was worried, he came here and scattered pollen and sang a simple Apache prayer, which he had Al memorize, then sat quietly and let the spirits speak to his mind. He said, "You will not hear them; but if you wait, you will find the answer you need—not the answer you want, but the right answer. It may be what you want, or it may be different, but you will know the truth."

So here he was scattering pollen from the small medicine pouch grandfather gave to him, which he always carried—not because he thought it was magic, but because it belonged his grandfather, the kindest and wisest man he knew, and the old man's wish that Al honor this tradition. Al had never been more troubled in his life. He sang the five little words, repeating the verse twice, then sat in the same very limited shade of the palo verde the two of them had shared almost thirty years ago.

He pondered the situation. He knew all along that the man Abdulov's story of the killing of Gato Wesley was filled with lies, but now he knew that poor old Gato had been set up from the start. He knew that the guy Cowboy Dosela had seen was Abdulov, and that he was interested in SWI. Plus, he knew the Turkman was interested in the file that turned up in the trunk of Norbert Cassa's car. Abdulov decided that since Gato had "stolen" the car, that he also had taken the SWI file. Gato had no idea what the big thug was talking about, so couldn't give him an answer. Abdulov decided to beat the truth out of Gato. Unfortunately, Gato had that silly switchblade and cut the brute with it and was then summarily killed by the knife in his own hand.

The killer was never going to see the inside of a courtroom. The worst that could happen was the State Department could expel him from the country, and he would go back to his work, home, and life in his own country as if nothing ever happened. No justice for Gato, no resolution for his family, and no satisfaction from finding the killer.

For the first time in his life, Al found himself thinking about administering rightful justice by his own hand. He knew hundreds of isolated places he could lure the big Turkman to execute him for his crime and drop his body into a deep crevice where nothing but mountain lions or buzzards ever go.

Like my ancestors did to traitors and those filled with evil.

The thought jolted him. He was not a vigilante. He was a Christian, a Deacon in the Holy Church, and a law officer; he has spent his life believing in justice, mercy, and the rightness of law and order. He looked up at the deep blue cloudless sky. "O, God. Forgive my anger and give me strength to trust in your judgment, not mine. I live in Christ's mercy yet can't give my burden to Him. Give me strength."

As he drove across the ford in the Gila River, he felt he had in fact gotten his thoughts straightened out. Instead of a plan for a perfect murder, he needed to not worry about things he could do nothing about and concentrate on things that were in his power. He would talk to Father Obion just to make sure he was back on the path, and he would share the small additional information he got from DeVon with the team.

Chapter 26

George Simmons truly enjoyed his visits with the young industrial hygienist, Marco Olvera. The guy was eager to learn, and he wasn't picky on the subject. He seemed interested in everything, but particularly in history. George had been around mining all his life and had known a dozen or so industrial hygienists or safety directors. Marco had something different about him.

George was also an excellent judge of character, and while he would be willing to trust his life with this kid, something in the intensity of those dark eyes set off a warning in George's subconscious. Marco carried a sense of mission that had nothing to do with the questions he was asking. It gave him an uneasy feeling that Marco was looking for a specific problem in the copper balance. That was odd, because so was George.

George felt bad about the disparity in the weight of copper he hauled from SWI. They had given him breaks and opportunities he would never have imagined. He was not a dishonest man. This just fell in his lap, and he needed an infusion of cash. Since then, his finances were in order, his bank account was growing, and his silver mine was in great shape. In fact, the new equipment at the mine was so much more efficient, he could now pay miners and still make a profit.

Then there was Kiko Peralta. He treated George with such respect and had been so generous that George was ashamed he might be taking advantage of the situation. But he had no idea how. He decided to discuss it with the metallurgical accountant.

On his next scrap run at the mine, he parked at Administration and went to Dave Willis's office.

"Hey Dave, do you have a minute?"

"Sure, George. How can I help you?"

Laying a file folder on Dave's desk, George said, "For some reason I can't figure out, I'm making out like a bandit on the scrap sales. I take a load down to Tempe every so often. Most of the time I have about a ton more copper than I'm supposed to have. I brought the last three months of weigh-tickets, in and out of the gate. My own scale, which isn't certified, shows more copper than the certified scales, and the weigh-tickets in and out of the certified dealer scale is higher. Both of the external scales are showing I have more copper almost every trip than the SWI scales."

"So, you aren't complaining about being shorted on copper; you're complaining about getting more copper than you bargained for?"

"Yes. I'm getting five or six thousand dollars more per load than your copper weight says I have. I'm not complaining about the bonus, but I don't want it to go on for a year and have you demand a hundred and fifty thousand dollars all at once. That would cramp my budget a tad."

Dave looked at the weigh bills. I see exactly what you are talking about, but I don't have any idea how this could be happening. You aren't picking up scrap anywhere besides SWI?"

"Nope. You're my only customer. I value the business enough that I don't want to create any conflicts. Can you check this out for me and see if you can find an explanation?"

"Yes. I'll check the balance from top to bottom and get back with you."

~

Kiko Peralta wanted an update on the status of the copper theft investigation, so the sheriff arranged a conference call. Kiko would be sitting in anonymously at the sheriff's office.

Al was listed first on the agenda, so he recounted his interview with DeVon Greene and the fact that the only explanation for Gato's murder was the Turkman wanting the SWI file. "Since he had traced Gato down with a fake call from the SWI office to Norbert Cassa, then set up a meeting with Gato, and then DeVon seeing the guy pick Gato up it is clear that he intended to get the file from Gato. Of course, poor old Gato didn't know what he was talking about, so this Abdulov guy tries to beat it out of him, leading to his murder. Then the part that we can't link is the coincidence of missing copper from SWI; it seems odd that there is no connection. Add the frustration that we can't even question the murderer, and this is the most frustrating case I've had."

Manny Sanchez reported that he had completed interviewing and reviewing the processes of all the contractors but was at a dead end. "I feel that the most likely way to get copper off the property would be in the scrap bins, but the weighing process provides really good control of that. I'm mystified, and all we can do is keep looking for something wrong in the operation."

Pat Haley said, "Well, I have some kind of bad news and kind of good news. The bad news is my friend Diana Niyazov is the source inside SWI who removed the file from Miami and attempted to provide it to Abdulov."

Bren said, "I was more or less assuming that, since she was the only one tied to Abdulov. But you have proof?"

"Better than that, she confessed to it. We have actually become close friends, and it was bothering her so much that she confided in me. She said that Abdulov coerced her by threatening to arrest her family if she did not cooperate. When she found out that Abdulov lost the file, she was relieved, but he made it clear she would have to provide another copy to him.

"But this time, she had time to think about it. She made a duplicate file and falsified all the data in it to show that the process does not work and is extremely expensive. That way, she does not have to worry about her family because she delivered as ordered, and the secrets in the file remain secret; in fact, any scientist analyzing it would write the process off immediately."

Bren asked, "And you trust her enough to believe all that to be true?"

"Absolutely. Her work is the most important thing to her. She is very professional and meticulously conscientious. She abhors Abdulov and the corruption in her country that produces men like him. My thought is that we should let her pass off the fake file. I think it would deflect all interest from the confidential work at SWI."

"Do you think she has sabotaged the copper balance? Could she and Abdulov have anything to do with rigging the weights and removing copper?"

"No. There is nothing wrong with the data or the processes in the lab."

"Well, the missing file resolution ends our meeting on something positive anyway," Bren said. "Thank you all for your work; for now, just keep your cover as normal and see if we can open any new leads on the missing copper."

Bren discontinued the conference call, and immediately received a call from the sheriff.

Sheriff Bitters said, "That is great news from Pat on the file. Mr. Peralta was in my office listening to the report. He has a couple of questions for you."

"Sergeant Allred, this is Kiko. How do you rate your officer I know as Cathy Winn?"

"She is excellent. She has good judgment and an eye for essential detail, or I would not have assigned her on this job."

"Should there be any doubt that Diana told the complete truth to Cathy?"

"I don't think so. If Diana knew "Cathy" was a police officer, then we would have to wonder if she was building a plausible excuse. But she was speaking to her friend and confidant. Also, I've done some research on Turkmenistan and the type of coercion Abdulov used with Diana is a way of life there; it is very authoritarian."

Kiko responded, "I would like to take the file to Diana and confront her with it to see her response. If she responds honestly, I may agree to let her pass off the bad data. I agree with her that it would kill any further interest in our process."

"There's a problem with that." Bren said, "We don't want to blow Cathy's cover for the copper theft investigation. Maybe surprise Cathy and Diana together, explain that the file was found in a stolen car near Safford, and then ask them the question of how the file got out of the lab. Cathy would say she had nothing to do with it. And Diana could either deny it or tell the truth. Either way, Diana would not think Cathy went to you with it, so her cover would remain intact."

Kiko looked at Sheriff Bitters, who nodded in agreement. Kiko thought about it a moment and said, "I agree. That's how I'll handle it."

~

Al Victor started his morning at the Bylas police substation for the shift change, which usually included him and two officers, sometimes three when an extra person was assigned from Peridot. One of the few formal procedures he performed was an inspection of the officers to make sure they projected a professional image of the department and were prepared for potential danger.

Al glanced through the off-going reports, clarifying a couple of things and discussing what had happened in the last 24 hours. His officers had assigned beats, so the only assignments he usually made were work passed from the other shifts or warrants or court orders to be delivered. Today none of that was needed, so the men all headed out.

He would work up to two hours a day in his office and a part time file clerk-receptionist-quasi dispatcher worked three days a week. So, on Monday, Wednesday, and Friday day shift, Clara Danny answered the phone and the radio while she worked. On Tuesdays, Thursdays, Weekends, and all evening and night shifts, the phone would ring twice and switch to the main dispatcher at San Carlos. Being a Tuesday morning, Al was the only one in the office. The phone rang, and he answered it on the first ring.

"Bylas Police, Sergeant Victor speaking."

"Sergeant Victor, this is Helen Dane, State Department. We met in Safford in connection with the Wesley murder."

"Yes. I remember you. How can I help you Miss Dane?"

"The Republic of Turkmenistan has sent formal apologies to the United States, the San Carlos Apache Tribe, and the Wesley family for the behavior of Mr. Abdulov, who acted on his own and outside the interests and the laws of Turkmenistan.

"They also have offered recompense to the tribe and the Wesley family for their loss and have asked the State Department to provide an equitable amount to be paid to both the tribe and the family. I have been assigned that task.

"I would like you to assist me in meeting with the proper tribal officials to determine how much recompense should be paid. You can connect me to the right legal people regarding compensation—this afternoon if possible. Then, with the guidance of these people, I would like to present the letter and the compensation plan we devise to the tribal chairman and council, as soon after that as possible."

Al thought for a few seconds. "I think I can get time this afternoon to meet with a tribal judge and prosecutor. They should be able to help determine equitable compensation. Could you be at San Carlos by one o'clock? I will meet you at Apache Gold Casino. Would you like to let State wine and dine four to six people? It might set up a more relaxed environment. If not, I'll escort you the rest of the way into San Carlos."

"Yes. Let's do a private dining room meeting at the Casino, but no more than six guests. That is my limit without prior approval."

"I will call the cell phone number on your card to let you know the particulars, but I'm pretty sure there won't be a problem getting the people we need there."

Al knew that Judge Calvin Lowe scheduled personal work time on Tuesday and would always make time for Al. The court secretary said Judge Lowe was in chambers and could not be disturbed.

"Not even for me, Suzie Q?"

"Oh. Hi, Al. I'll put you through."

The Judge picked up, and Al explained the meeting and asked the judge to invite people to represent the prosecutor's office, a tribal attorney for the family, and maybe Linda Kenton, the mental health director.

"No problem," the Judge laughed. "If they are too busy, I'll order them to come! I have Ed Prosser from the prosecutor's office and the young attorney Evan Sneezy scheduled for one o'clock. I'll just change the venue. And if Linda can't come, I'll have her send a representative. After all, it's not every day you get invited to a 'State' dinner."

Al texted Helen Dane. "It's a go. One p.m., Apache Gold Casino. Judge Calvin Lowe, Prosecutor Ed Prosser, family attorney Evan Sneezy, and a representative from the mental health department. See you there."

Chapter 27

One of the ways that Marco Olvera spent free time in Miami was researching in the local library. George Simmons had recommended he go see the librarian Delvan at the Miami Memorial Library. He hunted up the library—a huge block and concrete building stuck inexplicably on a residential street up one of Miami's canyons. The inside was full of book stacks, specialty rooms, and study tables. It included a Miami High School hall of fame. The place itself was as interesting as a museum and a treasure trove of old and new books.

Delvan Hayward was a very personable and energetic lady, who Manny thought was older, but certainly not old. She explained that the building was the old Miami High School Memorial Gymnasium. She pointed out a picture that showed the magnificent old high school on top of the hill above the gym with a concrete ramp connecting the two. She mentioned that she frequently made the trek up and down that path as a student; she had graduated in 1964. Manny quickly calculated that she was over seventy; he had guessed at least ten years younger than that.

She noted in the photo the old Miami Public Library, looking like a modest house just up the street from the current library. She said the old library was marvelous in large part because of the long-time librarian Mrs. Emily Cheves. The contents of the old library were moved into the former gym under the direction of Mrs. Cheves in 1969.

Delvan mentioned that she was soon to retire. She loved working in the library, but now she wanted to get back to her first love, her art.

Manny told her, "You should know . . . librarians, archivists, and teachers are my heroes. I have loved learning all my life because of people like you. Thank you."

"Well, the patrons make it worthwhile."

Upon learning that Manny wanted to learn about Miami History, she helped him select several books, which he sat and looked through. He selected one and began reading. He would visit two or three times a week while working at SWI. It made his solitary time bearable and gave him opportunities for conversation with Delvan and others at the library.

~

Helen Dane drove to her apartment to pack a few things and book a room at Apache Gold. She had been working late for several days and decided she didn't feel like putting in another long day with a two-and-one-half hour trip home to boot. As she pulled into her parking lot, she got the text from Sergeant Victor telling her who was coming to the meeting. She was surprised that the sergeant could get those people arranged for so quickly. She made her reservation, stuffed necessities in her overnight bag, grabbed a hanger with pants and a blouse on it, and took a bottle of water from the refrigerator. She drove to Oracle Road, then entered her trip into GPS and was on her way.

Helen had never been North on Oracle road past Oro Valley. She was happy to leave the traffic of the Tucson metro area. She left Canyon Del Oro and the Catalina Foothills where the homes and businesses were less dense, and she could enjoy the view of the rocky Pusch Ridge and the lush north side of the Catalina Mountains. She was not as happy when the four-lane highway of Arizona 77 became two lanes with no divider.

The countryside was familiar saguaro forest and high chaparral until she reached the town of Oracle, where she was surprised to see a few miles of lush chaparral, oak, and pinion. The greenery quickly retreated in her mirror as she descended into the San Pedro River Valley. She was back in lowland saguaro and palo verde, with a long narrow riparian forest up the river valley that would continue for fifty miles until she reached the Gila River at Winkelman.

Driving north on the San Pedro, Helen saw the Aravaipa Creek sign and was excited because she had heard of the beauty of the creek, but she was quickly disappointed that it was just a wide expanse of dry river bed at that point.

As she crossed the Gila River Bridge, she could see she was heading into some steep and rugged mountains and felt some trepidation. The road proved to be tame enough for her, and she was fascinated by the steep layers of limestone dotted with saguaros and desert brush on the mountains, and the thick cottonwood and willow forest along the river channel. Here and there she caught a glimpse of the river, which was a much larger flow than other rivers she had seen in Arizona.

She crossed Dripping Springs Wash and began climbing quickly into the higher mountains. She saw a herd of javelina run across the road, through a wide pullout and then west into the canyon, so she pulled over and managed to get one photo of them. It felt good to stand a bit, so she walked around enjoying the surrounding mountains. A white cross on the point of a craggy hill to the east caught her eye. She quickly realized why it was there when she saw that the rugged cliff profile looked like the face of Christ from the famous Hofmann *Prayer in the Garden* painting. She took a photo of that as well and resumed her trip.

As she gained elevation, the juniper-oak forest appeared followed by ponderosa pine forest, and there were even a few patches of snow on the shaded side of the deeper canyons. These were impressive mountains with cliffs and canyons deep enough that she couldn't see the bottom. A sign said she was going through El Capitan Pass. From there she dropped quickly down to the valley and US Highway 70 a short distance west of Apache Gold.

Helen was an hour and a half early when she arrived at the hotel, so she hung her clothes in the closet and unpacked her bag. She spent about an hour studying the file on the Wesley murder and the Turkmenistan apologies and offer. She was hoping the tribe would suggest a lower settlement, so she could encourage them to ask for more. If their suggestion seemed too high, it would be hard to moderate it.

This would be a real opportunity to do something good for the tribe, but she had no idea what they would come up with. She was encouraged by the inclusion of the mental health director in the meeting, because that might indicate they were thinking about some facilities or professional services. That would be more appropriate than a new boat dock or something similar.

She got a text from the sergeant: "It's about thirty minutes to the meeting. How far out are you?"

"I'm here. I got a room for the night."

"We are in private dining. Tell the hostess *Apache Tribal Court Luncheon.*"

"I'll be right there."

The hostess gave Helen a stick-on nametag, Helen Dane, US Department of State, and led her to the room. Helen asked her what the process was for ordering meals.

The hostess said, "Sergeant said to give you a few minutes to introduce yourself, then pass the menus and take orders. He'd like to meet until the plates are delivered and then as long as necessary after eating."

"Thank you. That sounds excellent. The bill will come to me. When I start my introduction go ahead and bring the menus."

"Yes, ma'am."

Al and Evan Sneezy had already arrived. Attorney Sneezy looked to be about eighteen years old, a handsome and fit young Apache.

Helen thought, "I must be getting old."

Al introduced each attendee to Helen as they came in. Helen paid special attention to their name tags. Linda Kenton, MAC, BCD, was the Director Mental Services a forty-fivish strong, attractive native. Edwin Prosser, JD, Apache Prosecutor, was a chubby, graying man—maybe Apache, maybe Asian. Helen wondered what MAC, BCD meant, but knew it must be important.

Judge Calvin Lowe, Apache Supreme Court, was a husky, balding white man of 6'8" height. He arrived at two minutes to one, went to one end of the table, and said, "Let's all be seated." The Judge was obviously in charge of this meeting . . . and probably everything else he was involved in. Helen decided she needed to change that dynamic.

Everyone took a seat, leaving the end opposite the Judge for Helen. Helen walked to her seat but remained standing and placed her file on the table.

Then, uninvited, she spoke. "Your honor and distinguished officials, I want to thank you for taking time to meet with me. I appreciate Sergeant Victor for his valuable assistance in making this happen so quickly. I have been designated by the Secretary of State of the United States to meet with you in seeking justice for the death of Mr. Wesley of your tribe at the hands of a diplomat of Turkmenistan.

"The order of the meeting is to first order our meals, after which I can present the offer. We can then begin to discuss what is best for your tribe and the Wesley family. When the meals arrive, we will enjoy a pleasant meal and afterward get down to business. The goal is for me to have an agreed-upon demand for recompense by the end of the meeting."

The hostess and two servers were standing at the door. Helen placed he folder on the credenza, nodded to the hostess, and sat down. They quickly set the table and passed out menu cards with a choice of three entrees: filet, salmon, or an antipasto chef salad. The orders were quickly taken, and the hotel staff left the room.

Helen took the top sheet from her folder and gave a digest of the murder and the problem with diplomatic immunity. She then summarized the Turkmenistan apology and their desire to fairly compensate both the family and the tribe. She then asked, "Judge Lowe, we will get into minute detail later, but are there any questions on what I've presented so far?"

"No," the Judge replied. "Your summary addressed all my immediate questions. I take it you need us to come up with a recommendation that will meet the approval of the Tribal Council and not just the Tribal Court. Is that correct?"

"Yes. I'm to recommend to the Turkmen a monetary payment for the wrongful loss of a tribal member to the tribe, and the loss of a family member to the Wesley family. While I don't have any desire to guide the decision on compensation, I do hope that it will actually make something better for the tribe as a whole and replace Mr. Wesley's earning power and loss of love and comfort—without doing more harm than good. Often an infusion of a lot of money to a poor family ends up causing them more problems than they had. The plan should address those concerns. I'm looking to you as a group to provide that kind of solution."

Judge Lowe said, "May I suggest that, since this group is basically providing consulting to you, we work as an informal team of experts with each person's view given equal weight, including the sergeant's? He is an expert on tribal history and culture as well as having an intimate knowledge of the crime. May we use first names?"

"Certainly."

"Could we have Linda address your points of making the settlement meaningful and how to best help Mrs. Wesley and family?"

Linda, the Director of Mental Services, nodded and said, "I think that is a very wise approach; for example, if we all of a sudden hand Mrs. Wesley one-hundred thousand dollars, she would most likely buy things she doesn't need and never wanted, and she would give money to her children and grandchildren. So, the money would be gone; she would have more stuff she couldn't afford to maintain; and she could have lost more family members to addiction. I think by thoughtful effort we could avoid that and actually help that family. May I give an example of something I thought of as Helen was explaining the problem?"

Everybody nodded.

Linda continued, "They just had a traditional wake for Gato. They spent all the money the family had, plus donations, and took loans to pay for the funeral costs, the food for the wake, the music and singers, and other costs incidental to an Apache burial. That could easily run to twenty-thousand dollars. Even though he was an alcoholic, Gato provided income to his aged mother by working at the store and taking odd jobs when available. That income needs replaced. I've seen her house; it needs serious work. But if we just give her enough money to pay the costs, replace the lost income going forward, and repair her house, most of that will not be done; the money would likely be misspent.

"Whatever the settlement amount ends up being, say it's five-hundred thousand, I think it should go into a small working account and a Wesley trust, both administered by a fiduciary working with Mrs. Wesley to take care of all that stuff. The interest from the trust can be used to actually help her and her family. The small account could pay off the funeral debts, repair her home, and take care of immediate household budget needs. The trust interest can be used to provide long-term supplemental income for Mrs. Wesley and help for her family for such things as medical needs, alcohol treatment, education costs, and even occasional nice vacations. But in all things, it would be carefully managed for their good, not their harm."

Helen said, "I'm stunned. That is a wonderful approach. I don't think we could improve that plan. What do you think, Cal?"

"I agree. Does anyone see a problem with Linda's idea? Or have further thoughts?"

Helen said, "I think from all the bobbing heads that we have consensus on how to handle the family compensation. Since that worked so well, Linda, what about the tribal payment? We are talking a considerably larger amount. How best to help the tribal members?"

"Well, believe me, tribal politics is not my area of expertise," Linda said wryly. "But since Gato was, to a large extent, a victim of alcohol, I would like to see a good portion of the payment go to adding a modern rehab and counseling center and a trust-funded anti-addiction foundation. After that, it would be nice to fund something in Bylas, Gato's hometown, which the community really needs. I'm afraid that's about the best I can offer."

Ed said, "What we don't want is mismanagement, nepotism, money laundering, and corruption. I don't know how the tribe would react to a managed account to avoid those negatives. I don't even know if that's possible."

"I think it is possible," Evan injected. "If the Turkmen specified that the monies be overseen by a board of trustees from both the tribe and the federal government, it would have the effect of a fiduciary account."

Al chuckled. "Now that I like! It's an excellent solution. The irony in it is getting the Turkmen to specify protections against corruption; according to the CIA Fact Book, they are considered the third most corrupt country in the world!"

That struck Cal as hilarious. "Let's not mention that little factoid to the Council! They might see it as calling the red pot black."

Linda was horrified by this topic. "We need to really keep that information confined to this room. While it's true, it's an unnecessary complicating PR factor. However, if we can agree to have the Turkmen place controlling specifications on the tribal compensation, it is worth doing. It should never become public knowledge that we asked for it. In fact, we would all be politically prudent to keep this meeting confidential."

They all agreed and decided that the stated purpose of the meeting was to determine how to legally receive the payment from a foreign government and determine the size of the compensation.

After two more hours of discussion, the group reached consensus on the amounts to be paid and the method to be used in control of the accounts.

The Wesley Family Foundation would receive 1.1 million dollars into two funded accounts, a one-hundred-thousand-dollar operating account for immediate use, and one million in the main account. Evan would be the fiduciary of both accounts, reporting to the Judge.

The San Carlos Apache Gato Wesley Foundation would receive a ten-million-dollar settlement. The Tribal Foundation board would include a representative of the Wesley Family, a representative of the bank, a federal representative, the Tribal Chairman or designee, a judge, and two members elected by the tribe at large.

They also decided that the trusts and foundation should be set up immediately, so that when the funds were received they could go directly into their designated accounts. The judge and attorneys would incorporate the foundation and see that accounts were set up for all three.

Helen explained that the Turkmen could reject the plan or ask for changes, but she thought they would accept it. She promised to keep them informed and hoped to formally present the apologies and restitution to the Tribal Council and the family in the same meeting, hopefully, very soon.

Chapter 28

Though Abdulov did not know it, his replacement on EurMino was Dr. Mary Garay, Dean of Graduate Students at the Turkman Technical Institute. She was on a one-year sabbatical, specifically for this assignment at EurMino to assure that the graduate students received the most from their experience.

By flying in a Turkmenistan government plane, they could fly non-stop from Ashgabat to Davis Monthan Air Force Base in Tucson. It was a horrific twenty hours in the air, made possible by a huge fuel module and a crew lounge with relief pilots.

The Republic of Turkmenistan A-2 aircraft was actually a highly-modified USSR-era Antonov An-72. It was equipped with higher-efficiency jets and was modified such that it could be used for anything from pure cargo to paratroop transport to luxury airliner or any combination of the three by simply plugging modular sections into the cavernous hull.

For this flight, it was equipped for luxury travel, and the normal twelve-passenger first-class module was configured with only four comfortable seats that fully reclined. Each had personal blackout privacy curtains and massaging leg rests. In addition to the passenger and crew cabins, the plane had a small lounge area, a work desk with full internet and communications, television and movies, and a stationary bicycle to keep blood flow balanced. The food and drink were excellent, and the first-class attendant had few to take care of, so service was also excellent.

The plane arrived at the base on schedule, was given priority landing, and taxied to a VIP terminal. Helen Dane, Meret Mulikow, Agent Gabe Garcia, and Air Force security personnel welcomed Dr. Mary Garay to the United States. The crew members would be housed in base officer housing and appropriately entertained until their return trip to carry Abdulov back to Turkmenistan.

Dr. Garay would be kept far from Abdulov until two days before his scheduled departure, when her arrival would be faked for

Abdulov's sake. Helen Dane would provide a detailed briefing of the current EurMino operations and on the assignments and status of each of the visiting supervisors and students.

A comfortable suite at the Starr Pass Resort, would be Dr. Garay's quarters for her first week until the cottage being vacated by Abdulov was refurbished and ready for her use. Helen accompanied her and made sure she had everything she would need. They agreed to meet for dinner followed by the first of a series of meetings.

Dr. Garay said, "I know that I must keep my presence here confidential for a few days, but I would really like to call and visit with my student Diana. She would keep my presence confidential until the public announcement is made. May I do that?"

"As long as you are positive she can keep the confidence. She is home from work about five o'clock." Helen wrote the number on the phone pad and left her own card beside it on the desk. "I'll pick you up for dinner at six tonight."

Dr. Garay set her phone alarm to go off at four and took a nap. At four, she dressed and prepared her hair and make-up. At five, she called Diana.

"Diana, this is Dr. Garay. How are you doing in America?"

"Oh, what a nice surprise! It's so good to hear your voice. I'm really enjoying the work here. The people are very generous."

"That's wonderful. I wanted to share some news with you, but you must keep it completely confidential. I am going to be replacing Abdulov at EurMino, so I will be working closely with you again."

"I am dreaming! This is too good to be true. I will not acknowledge your presence to anyone until you tell me."

"I just wanted to share this news with you. I will get hold of you again in a few days."

~

Kiko Peralta called Lee Gallo, the SWI chief chemist, and asked him to have Diana Niyazov and Cathy Winn meet him at the research lab in half an hour. He explained that he just needed some clarification on some of the tests.

Lee walked out to the lab and told the two technicians to cover their samples and meet Mr. Peralta at the research lab. Cathy wasn't surprised. Bren had warned her to simply state that she did not do anything with the files before yesterday, which was the truth.

Diana, on the other hand, looked apprehensive as she walked with Cathy to the meeting. "I hope Mr. Peralta hasn't found out; it could spoil everything; Abdulov would not get the false files, and my family would be in danger."

Cathy said, "I don't think it would have to spoil your plan. Even if he did find out, just tell the truth about coercion and giving them fake data. I think he would see the logic."

"Yes. There is no other option. But I hope he doesn't know."

Kiko was sitting at the table in the lab's small conference room. He motioned to the chairs across the table. "Please, have a seat."

After they were seated, Kiko took the accordion file from his lap and laid it on the table. Diana's face drained of color and Cathy was worried that she would faint, so she put her hand on Diana's shoulder to steady her.

Kiko asked, "Cathy, did you remove this file from the lab?"

"No."

Kiko said, "Do you want to explain why you took it, Diana?"

Tears welled in Diana's eyes and began to run down her face. Once she gained her breath, the story gushed from her. She told the complete story, hardly taking a breath.

She finished with, "I decided that I could create a fake file that had all false data and show that the process does not work at all. No one would know that is not our actual test data. Any scientist who reviewed it would say it is a worthless failed experiment. This way my family will be safe, and the data will not only be safe, but will cause a complete lack of interest in it. I'm sorry, Mr. Peralta. Everyone here has been so kind to me, and I've betrayed you all. I'm so sorry."

"To be honest, I would have done the same thing to protect my family; and the false data is a brilliant idea." Kiko rose and walked to the work station on the desk. "Show me the file you created."

As Kiko examined the data, he thought, "The file is convincingly authentic, but the data show that the best process results they've gotten are terrible and the worst process results are bad, but not as bad as the best."

"This is great," Kiko said. "When he makes contact, tell him you have it on a flash drive—that SWI secured the paper files too well to remove anything now. Let me know when and where you are to give him the file."

"So, am I fired now?"

"No, you were coerced. Your work is excellent, and I trust you to do the right thing now. Give the flash drive to him and let him pass it on."

He stood and warmly took Diana by the hand. "You are a good employee and a good person. You two take a break, and let Diana regain her composure; then you better get back to work."

~

Another cold front had come in overnight with a light rain. Then, with the temperature dropping below freezing, it had been snowing lightly for a couple of hours. The mud on the road turned to ice and slush.

As Marco drove toward his small office at the tankhouse, he caught up with George Simmons's scrap truck heading to exchange bins. It looked like the wheels on George's truck were smoking; but as he got closer, he could see that George was having to use his sand spreader to provide traction on the slick road. The "smoke" was dust from the dry sand. The sander worked well, even made the road better for Marco. He followed George as far as the office, and George continued to the lower level of the tankhouse.

The office was freezing, so Marco turned on the two electric space heaters and went over to the shop office across the road. In the break room, he made a large cup of hot chocolate and stood at the back window watching the snow blow around. The scrap truck was pulling up the little hill with a full bin of copper on its way to the weigh scale. George had it in low gear and was slowly moving up the hill with the spreaders laying down sand in front of the drive wheels.

Marco thought, "It wouldn't make it at all without that sand."

After visiting with some of the electricians for a while, Marco fixed another tall cup of hot cocoa and went back to his office. The heaters were doing the job; the inside temperature was up to fifty degrees. He would be comfortable enough with his coat and hat on.

He worked until lunchtime on his observations of processes and their industrial hygiene and safety implications. He had fifteen suggested improvements listed in the last section. He completed it and e-mailed it to EcoAnthro.

He walked over to the shop and ate his sack lunch and talked with the workers. Returning to his office he started organizing his similar work on contractors. After a while, he decided to stand and get his circulation going.

He sat back down and leaned back as far as the desk chair would go and watched out the window as the powdery snow, like fine sand, eddied near his window. It suddenly hit him. Sand! Sand in the spreader bins was weighed in before a four-to-five-mile round trip from the scale to the tankhouse, during which it was regularly unloaded on the road.

He grabbed his phone and called Bren, telling him what he had observed. "We've had ice and occasional snow on that part of the road almost every day since October. Whether he knows it or not, George has been trading sand for copper!"

~

Lymie Crockett delivered the four boxes containing Jenny Sanchez's and Candy Dosela's lesson plans and personal belongings to the Klondyke School on Wednesday. He said that delivery was the last work that had to be done inside the building, so it was all theirs to get organized and decorated. The ladies decided to have lunch at Jenny's house, then spend the afternoon preparing for Monday's first day of class.

Cowboy agreed to help them by watching the kids. "It will be my take-your-kids-to-work day."

Candy watched as Cowboy loaded the Polaris Ranger with water, sodas, and the lunches she had made. He also took his usual tool supply kit, binoculars, and Winchester .3030.

"The kids love to go to work with you," she said. "Six sections of grazing land in the Santa Teresa Mountains is a lot more fun than an office. They get to see the cattle, doctor injured cattle, clean around springs, and shoot any predators you come across. The kids love these trips with you."

"Yep, and I enjoy teaching them about nature and cattle. I couldn't do this every day, but I'm glad when I can."

Cowboy headed west to the range, and Candy headed east to meet with Jenny at the school.

The PTA had tilled, fertilized, and leveled the hard dirt in front of the school and seeded it with a mix of winter rye and Bermuda grass. They were working on a bigger plot in back for a playground.

The school had been transformed with fresh paint, the now-gleaming antique maple floor, new Venetian blinds, and large framed prints of American historic events. Even the old 1960s-style student desks' wood laminate and gray-painted metal shined like new. A large American flag hung above the blackboard. Lymie cleaned the antique alphabet displayed in print and cursive above the blackboard. The student computers, spaced by bookshelves, stood along the west wall.

"What a wonderful mix of the old and new!" Jenny exclaimed. "This is perfect."

Candy added, "Yes! And the heater is working."

It was a cloudy day, and the outside temperature was fifty degrees, practically freezing to a desert dweller.

The ladies filed the papers as appropriate in the two desks and the filing cabinet and arranged their desk items. They formed the student desks into a two-row arc, arranged with the small desks for the first and second graders on the east side, the sixth graders in the center, and the third graders to the west. Lymie had left two of each-sized desk stacked to one side in the storeroom *just in case*, and the remaining desks were stored in the shed.

They wrote a welcome note on the blackboard in chalk, along with their names. It would be something new for the kids to see an actual blackboard in use. Jenny was very excited to begin this new teaching experience.

~

George Simmons received the following e-mail from Dave Willis:
George, I have thoroughly examined our books and discussed the scrap process with all participants but can find nothing wrong with the process. I talked with the controller, and she said that something is obviously wrong and that we need to keep working on identifying what it is. She also said to reassure you that we

won't hold you liable for the difference, unless of course it turns out you were deliberately stealing. So, if you find the problem, let us know. If we find it, we'll let you know.

George shook his head. "This is as bewildering to them as it is to me."

~

Mergen Abdulov felt much better. The doctor said the infection that had made him so sick was cleared up and that most of the slash wound had healed. He just had three deeper spots on his right breast and down near the hip that were still not quite grown back together, but they were healing well.

Abdulov told Mulikow that he was tired of being indoors, so he would drive up to the mine at Miami and visit with the student working there.

"I don't think it's a good idea to go back to the area where you had your difficulties," Mulikow told him.

"Of course not. Miami is 150 kilometers from Safford where the incident happened. Besides, I will probably just have a scenic drive and dine with the student, get a report on her activities, and drive back. It may be six hours at the most, and I need an outing."

As he left Tucson, he laughed that Mulikow did not want him to go out. Gutless Mulikow was afraid to order him to stay.

Mulikow is frightened of me. And he should be. I would take pleasure in breaking his neck with my bare hands. I hate bureaucrats who have never served their country.

Abdulov called Diana and told her to save the file to a thumb drive and bring it to him at the Italian place where they ate before.

Diana answered, "It's already on a drive. The restaurant is De Marco's in Globe. Do you remember where it's located?"

"Yes. I will see you at six."

Abdulov then sent an encrypted message to his Russian handler, saying that the file would be delivered that night.

He thought, "It's nice to be back on the job, building up my retirement account."

~

Diana called Mr. Peralta's cell phone. "Abdulov just called to arrange to pick up the file. I'm to meet him at six o'clock at De Marcos to give it to him."

"Okay. Don't do anything different than we discussed."

At six o'clock she entered De Marco's and, seeing Abdulov seated with a drink, she went to the table, placed the thumb drive by his plate, and sat down.

"Well, thank you," Abdulov said in Turkmen. "A bit clumsy for espionage, but then you've had no training. Let's order dinner. While we wait, I will fill out your quarterly student evaluation card. That way we can eat, and I can travel back to Tucson. The trip has tired me more than I expected."

Diana disguised a moment of panic when she saw Marco Olvera who had reviewed the lab processes and discussed industrial hygiene with them. He was seated across the room with a tall Indian in western dress, but they apparently didn't see her.

Abdulov gave her good marks on her student evaluation card. As they ate, he asked if she had any news from home. She avoided any reference to her parents' work, politics, or economics. She mentioned that her brother had been nominated to the National Military Institute because he was the top student and a high school football all-star goalie. This seemed to please him; he told her that a country's greatest citizens are soldiers.

They finished, and Diana was happy to be in her car going home.

~

From across the street, Deputy Haley saw Diana drive away from the restaurant. Abdulov went to his car and immediately placed a laptop on his dashboard and started typing. She used binoculars and saw him insert a thumb drive. She smiled.

He didn't wait to get home to save the contents of the drive. He'll probably e-mail them to his boss using the restaurant WAN. Pretty sloppy work, Abdulov.

She was relieved to see Diana leave by herself, heading toward Miami. Abdulov didn't follow her. Abdulov left driving toward Globe, no doubt heading back to Tucson. She saw Al follow at a distance. A text from Al to her and Manny said, "Abdulov turned south on AZ 77." The plan had worked flawlessly.

~

Back at the hotel in Tucson, Meret greeted Abdulov as he came in. "So how was the trip?"

Abdulov handed him the evaluation card and said, "I overestimated my physical condition. I'm exhausted. I must go to bed."

"There are a few things we must discuss first. I received notice that in order to smooth over the situation with the man who attacked you, they are promoting you to Auditor of Quarries and Mines. Your replacement will arrive in two days to be briefed by you. Then you will return by government plane."

"A promotion is a good thing," he said on his way to his room. He took off his jacket and shoes, lay on the bed, and was immediately asleep.

~

Dr. Mary Garay received a call from Diana Niyazov asking if she could arrange a visit with her right away. It was an urgent matter of personal importance. Dr. Garay asked for a bit more information and determined that if it was something important enough to Diana, she should act on it immediately. She arranged to travel to Globe in the morning.

Dr. Garay enjoyed the drive through the mountains to Globe. She arrived at nine and was escorted to the lab where she was welcomed by a receptionist, who introduced her to Dr. Lee Gallo.

Dr. Gallo invited Dr. Garay into his office. Dr. Garay explained her new position at EurMino and that she was Diana's master's advisor at the Technical University.

"How is she performing in her work?"

"She's excellent. Other than her initial orientation on our work and lab operational culture, she required no training; she is very strong in all the technical and chemical processes. She has a wonderful attitude about the work and has befriended everyone she works with. I'm only sorry that her time in the program is half over. I will be very sad to have her leave."

Dr. Garay asked, "If it is not too disruptive to your work schedule, could I meet with her for an interview?"

"Of course. In fact, this is probably an excellent time. Her samples are in the digestion process, so she is in an idle half hour or so. You may use the conference room across the hall from this office. I'll take you to her work area now." Lee handed her safety glasses and a lab coat. "Follow me, please."

Dr. Garay watched for a moment as Diana checked her sample beakers and adjusted the heat on the hot plate. When the younger woman saw her mentor, her face lit in a bright smile. The doctor walked to her and gave her a brief hug.

Dr. Gallo said, "Diana, take a break and go with Dr. Garay to the conference room. I'll keep an eye on your samples until you return."

Dr. Garay closed the door and sat near Diana at the conference table. "I felt you had an urgent need, so here I am. Tell me what is troubling you."

Diana explained in detail Abdulov's coercion of her and her feeling of remorse for betraying the trust of her hosts.

Dr. Garay said, "Nobody can fault you for your unwilling cooperation. I would certainly have done what you did. I have learned that Abdulov was acting against orders and lied to trick you into cooperating. But you and I both know that such coercion is common in our country."

"Yes, I certainly understand that. There is more that I cannot tell to just anyone; but I feel I can trust you, and I need you to know. I also tricked Abdulov. I replaced the data with completely false information. He did not get the confidential files, but meaningless garbage. In reality, I didn't betray the trust of SWI and Lee Gallo."

Dr. Garay burst out laughing. "I'm sorry, Diana. I know this is serious, but what you did is perfect justice. Now you cannot let anyone know this, but Abdulov is a traitor and sold your meaningless garbage to the Russians!"

~

Sheriff Bobby Bitters had left messages, but Kiko was on an underground tour of the new Resolution Copper Mine near Superior with the Arizona Society of Mining Engineers. When the tour and the wrap-up meeting was over, Kiko turned his phone back on and returned Bear's call.

"I have good news, Kiko. It looks like my deputy has figured out who is stealing your copper."

"Are you going to keep me in suspense?"

"It's your scrap dealer, George Simmons."

"I don't believe that. I don't think he would steal."

"You may very well be right. It could be inadvertent. Manny, your man Marco, noticed that with the cold weather and slick road conditions, Simmons has been regularly using the sand spreader on his truck to provide traction. When the truck is weighed in, the weight of the sand is included, but from the scale to the tankhouse and back, he is using the spreader. The weight of the sand is coming off the tare weight of the truck. Ergo, more copper is going out than the difference in the weight shows.

"As my daughter says, SMH! That's *smack my head*."

"Yep. It's just like that!" Bear laughed. "Marco is going to have George weigh in empty, sand all the way to the tankhouse and back empty, then take a new weight. It will show how many pounds of sand have been exchanged for copper per trip."

"When is Marco going to do the test? Tell him I want to be there for it. Never mind. I'll call him. Thanks for the news, Bear."

Marco answered on the first ring.

Kiko said, "Marco, when is the test of George's sand spreader going to take place?"

"Probably in an half-hour. He's filling the sand bins at his yard in Miami, then coming over."

Kiko ordered, "I'm on my way there. Don't start without me."

"Okay, you aren't the only one we're waiting for. George had me call Dave Willis and invite him. Dave said that a lady named Serendipity wanted to see it, too."

"Serendipity?"

"I think she's his supervisor."

Kiko laughed, "That's Sarah Reditti! She's our Controller."

Marco was first to arrive at the scale. He waited in his Jeep for the others to arrive. Next was Kiko. He got out of his truck, so Marco joined him.

Kiko said, "I passed George at Burch, so he's probably about five minutes behind me."

Marco added, "Dave said he and Sarah will come out when George arrives."

Five minutes later, George pulled up on the scale, waited for the green light to move off the scale, and took the weigh-ticket from the print slot. He stopped to talk with Kiko and the others. Dave and Sarah were just walking up, so Kiko said, "Marco is a consultant with EcoAnthro. This is Dave Willis, Metallurgical Accounting, and Serendipity, our Controller."

Marco flushed a bit and shook hands, "Nice to meet you, Dave and Sarah."

"I'm sorry," Kiko grinned. "Marco thought Dave said *Serendipity* was coming with him. I thought it was kind of funny. It does sound like that."

Sarah looked challengingly at Marco and asked, "So you have trouble with Latin names?" This drew another laugh from Kiko.

George said, "Latin? Sounds like some kinda furren name to me."

"Okay, George," Marco said. "Let's get down to business. Did you fill the sand bins?"

"Yep, they are at capacity."

"Now, run the spreader down to the tankhouse, turn around, and run it back. Turn it off before you get to the scale, though."

Kiko said, "I'm riding with George."

The round-trip difference in weight was 982 pounds.

"So, the maximum difference in weight is almost half a ton," George said. "However, it will normally be less that that because I usually only run sand going uphill unless the whole road is slick. I've been getting just about a ton too much copper every two weeks all winter long. I probably owe you fifteen- to twenty-thousand dollars."

Kiko said, "We're not going to worry about water already under the bridge, George. I appreciate you calling it to Dave's attention. But going forward, you will need to tell the scale man how much to adjust for lost tare weight. Dave and George, I want you and the scale boss to decide how you are going to do that. And implement it immediately. Marco, thanks for figuring this out. It was driving me crazy."

~

Back in her room in Tucson, Dr. Garay called the cell phone of Adelya Isaev, the lead steward on the Turkmen flight crew. Adelya fit the stereotype of a beautiful and personable flight attendant, but she was much more than that.

She answered the phone in Turkic. "This is Adelya."

Dr. Garay addressed her differently. "Commander Isaev, I have visited my student Diana as you recommended, and she freely admits that she was coerced by Abdulov under threat to her family to provide confidential files to him; the same files that your agency discovered he sold to the Russians.

"That's unfortunate. She had a lot of promise, but this will probably untrack her career."

"But, there is more," Dr. Garay continued. "She did not give him the actual files; instead, she made a dummy file with all false data in it. What he sold to the Russians was pure garbage. Once a metallurgist looks at it, they will be convinced the Americans are on a fool's mission with their research."

"Ha! That is delicious irony! As it turns out, Diana handled a terrible situation with extreme intelligence. I will clear her of any suspicion, and no further action will be taken. I'm glad this worked out. Women in our country have a lot of lost ground to regain."

~

Billy Benson was returning from the quick afternoon run to Morenci to deliver the Greyhound package when he heard Allred on the police scanner tell dispatch he would be in a meeting and out of touch for an hour or so. Billy drove to the motorcycle shop and rented the Harley Street Glide with attached sidecar and drove it to the storage locker.

He pulled into the storage facility and changed into his deputy uniform. He covered the uniform with a jacket, effectively hiding the shirt from view. He secured the baby bag, child seat, and helmet in the sidecar and drove to Bren's sister's house.

As he arrived, he saw Ann sitting outside watching Layton play on a jungle gym in the front yard. He pulled into the driveway. Layton immediately ran to the fence next to the cycle. Billy took off the helmet and put on his deputy cap and unzipped the jacket to reveal his uniform, as Ann walked over near Layton.

"Hi, Layton! How do you like my motorcycle?"

"It's big! I like it a lot!"

Billy chuckled and said to Ann, "You must be Ann. I'm Deputy Perry. Bren thought Layton would get a kick out of it."

"Oh, he sure does. Nothing could thrill him more."

Billy stepped closer and plunged the needle in, pumping the Ketamine into her shoulder. Ann was startled and confused and immediately began to feel dizzy.

"Oh, I'm sorry. You better sit down," Billy said as he half carried her to the plastic lawn chair and settled her into it.

"Auntie Ann said it will be okay if I take you for a ride. Would you like that?"

"Yes!"

He lifted Layton into the safety seat, strapped him in, and put the helmet on him. The boy thoroughly enjoyed the ride as they drove to Nanna Beth's house.

As he lifted Layton out of the sidecar, Billy told him, "Daddy said for me to let you play at Nanna Beth's house for a while, then to come back and give you a ride home."

"Okay."

He handed the diaper bag to Beth. "Layton, this nice lady is Nanna Beth. You play nice with the other kids like Daddy said, and I'll be back to give you another ride on the motorcycle."

As he drove off, Layton was running to join the other children.

Chapter 29

Dr. Garay's staged official arrival day included a brief flight in the Antonov so the official greeting party could observe the arrival. Agent Garcia drove Ms. Dane, Meret Mulikow, and Mergen Abdulov in the deluxe Lincoln Navigator to Davis Monthan in time to see the Turkmenistan jet land and to welcome Dr. Mary Garay to America.

With Helen Dane's agreement, Agent Garcia was security and driver for the party for the next two days until Abdulov was airborne. Garcia wanted to be sure the murderer left the country. Gabe was present everywhere that Abdulov went, and with the help of the NSA, was monitoring Abdulov's cell phone, tracking both his communications and his travel. Gabe was either present for, or electronically heard, everything the Turkman heard, said, or sent by electronic communication.

They all loaded into the blacked-out FBI Navigator, and Gabe, for the fun of it, drove them with emergency lights through Tucson to the Hacienda del Sol.

Dr. Garay spoke to Abdulov. "I was able to rest well on the plane. I'm sure you will find it very comfortable as well, but I would like to take a shower and a short nap before we meet."

Abdulov replied, "I'm not back to my normal stamina yet, so I will nap as well. I believe Meret has arranged for us to meet at two p.m. in his casita."

They met as scheduled. Abdulov provided Dr. Garay with the evaluation cards on all seventeen of the students, and he told a bit about each student and where they were assigned. Gabe knew Abdulov did not realize that he was leaving under a cloud of suspicion, so he was in a jovial mode and on best behavior.

The new appointee and the incumbent discussed the program, and Abdulov told her about places to stay and dine as she visited the students and mentioned the routes he had enjoyed the most. They were finished and back in their own rooms by three-thirty.

The group, now including all seventeen of the students and two visiting officials from other EurMino countries, met in a private dining room for dinner. Entertainment was primarily a mariachi band, supplemented by a floor show of a Tohono O'odham dance group. Five of the EurMino students had instruments and put on a medley of traditional Turkmen music, which ended in a surprisingly enjoyable jam session with the mariachis.

Before dinner was served, Meret Mulikow thanked Abdulov for his work with EurMino and wished his future held "everything that is due you;" he then presented him with two gifts, a copper and turquoise bola tie, with which Mergen immediately replaced his necktie, and a big black Stetson hat, which the honored guest was equally proud to wear.

Dinner consisted of five small plate courses, each from a different culture: Turkmenistan, O'odham, Mexican, American pop, and a small local grass-fed filet mignon, followed by a petit pastry dessert buffet and an open bar, of which Abdulov took full advantage. Gabe managed to add a sizable dose of Benadryl to the last of Abdulov's drinks, which assured that he would sleep deeply, allowing Gabe to also get much needed sleep.

The next afternoon, Gabe drove to Mulikow's casita, where Meret accompanied Abdulov in the Navigator to Davis Monthan. Meret waved as Abdulov boarded the white, green-trimmed plane with the Turkmenistan flag painted on its tail. Meret was truly happy to see this evil man go, as was Gabe. Gabe deliberately stayed at the loading area until he saw the big AN-72 airborne and heading east. Mulikow did not object. Gabe would continue to track Abdulov until he was on the ground in Turkmenistan.

~

Bren finished a meeting with the Globe Police Chief to discuss how the State Antiquities Task Force worked and how they might help with a theft of artifacts from a local museum. As he was walking to his car, dispatch called on the cell phone and told him they got a call from a confidential informant asking that Bren call him immediately.

"Who was this CI?"

"He said he was Billy B. and said it's important that you call the number I just sent by text."

"Okay. Thanks, Jess."

Bren checked Billy's GPS location. He was in Safford on US 70, heading west. Bren then checked Billy's position history and saw that he had been to Ann's house. Bren called her but got no answer, so he called the sheriff.

"Bear, I think it has started. Billy Benson's been to my sister's house where Layton is being babysat. There is no answer on her phone. Please go check on them and let me know what you find out."

"I'm on my way."

Bren dialed the number Billy had left.

"Well, hello, Detective Allred. Nice of you to call."

"What do you want, Benson?"

"I just want to have a little face-to-face chat with you for old time's sake."

"I'm not interested in talking with you."

"You are if you want to see little Layton again. It was nice meeting Ann. She's a nice lady. Pretty, too."

"All right. You have my attention. What's your game?"

"You know where the old Ballard Machine Works is near Ashurst? I want you to meet me there. Where are you?"

"Just leaving Globe."

"Meet me at that old shop in forty minutes. Pick up the cell phone at the door and call the number written in the dust. I'll be waiting. Don't bring backup. This is just between you and me."

"Do you have Layton with you?"

"No, but he's safe for now. Do what I say, and you will get him back. Remember, no back-up or it's all over."

"I'll be there. I'm hanging up so I can concentrate on driving."

Bren called the Sheriff. "Any news?"

"Ann has been drugged, but she's okay. They're taking her to the hospital. Your son is not here."

"After Benson left Ann's he drove to 9845 Highway 191. He was there only a couple of minutes and then left. Go check that address. It may be where he took Layton. Let me know."

"I'll do that, Bren. What's Benson's location right now? I will get a squad on him."

"Don't do that until we know about Layton. Once we know, I'll give you his position."

Bren quickly reviewed Benson's movements after dropping Layton off and was relieved to see the criminal had not been near Lizzie's school or Bren's home; he was apparently heading for the machine shop. He quickly resumed his trip east through Peridot. Bren was running with his emergency lights, topping out over the bumps on the east side of Wildhorse Canyon at 90 miles per hour, when Bear called back.

"Bren, Layton is okay. Benson left him in day care. I have him with me right now. Deputy Lopez was in the area. He surveilled the place and confirmed only the owner and the children were there, and he backed me up as I went for Layton. The sitter had no idea what was going on."

Feeling almost weak with relief, Bren said, "Thanks, Bear. Tell Andy Lopez thanks for me. I can see that Benson is just leaving Pima. Don't stop him, but quiet back up will be good. He's going to meet me in the old Ballard shop building near Ashurst. I think it's best if he thinks his plan is still working."

"Alright, Bren. I'll have Deputy Lopez approach Ashurst from the back way but hang back a ways from the building. I'm on my way on 70."

The sheriff called Al Victor on his cell, explained the situation, and asked him to follow Bren at a distance and wait for further instructions. Al agreed to help.

Bren called again. "Bear, Benson just cut off his GPS ankle bracelet, so we no longer know for sure his exact position. Our best bet is to get him at the rendezvous."

"I called Al Victor," the sheriff said. "He is going to follow you at a distance to the rendezvous."

When Bren arrived at the building, he drove past it and turned at Ashurst Road and spotted a black motorcycle with a side car parked in the brush behind the building. He called Bear with the information as he pulled up to the slightly-open front door. He opened the trunk, put on his vest, and took his rifle with him. He dialed the number and heard it ring inside the building.

Benson said, "Hang up the phone and come on in."

He cautiously pushed the door wide open and stood back, looking first one way and then the other inside the old shop. There was a large press to the right, behind which a person could easily hide. The left was clear. He quickly slipped in and stood against the press, letting his eyes adjust to the gloom. About forty feet away he saw a well-shaven Benson just staring at him.

Bren raised the rifle and took aim. "Give it up, Benson. It's all over." In that instant he noticed something was odd about the light around Benson, it was a darker square than the surroundings.

He sensed movement just to his right at the same time Benson raised a hand gun. Bren fired and understood what was going on as a mirror shattered; he ducked below the body of the press and lobbed a mini-flashbang over the machine, covering his ears and closing his eyes.

The effect was somewhat stunning even to him. He raised his rifle to position and slid around the press to find a quivering Benson with a smoldering pant leg and fire starting in some oily debris next to the press.

He grabbed Benson by the collar and dragged him away from the growing fire, placed a knee on his back and tie-wrapped his wrists, then shoved him out the door in front of a charging Al Victor, who grabbed an arm and pulled the prisoner toward Bren's cruiser.

Bren removed the fire extinguisher from his trunk and sprayed foam on Benson's trouser leg. Then he helped Al frisk the prisoner and lock him in the back of the cruiser before rushing in to attack the flames in the building.

Al got his own extinguisher and rushed to help, as did Andy Lopez and the sheriff, who arrived just moments behind Al. The sheriff noticed a book lying on the bench next to the press and picked it up. It was a journal written by Benson. The fire department arrived and made sure the fire was out, then spread absorbents over the floor to draw up the remaining oil.

Guillermo Benson's parole was immediately revoked, and he was returned that day to ASP-Florence and ordered to complete the terms of his original assault convictions. New charges would eventually be filed against Guillermo Benson for kidnapping, assault against a police officer, simple assault against Ann, impersonating a police officer, and illegal possession of controlled drugs.

Chapter 30

The hostess greeted Abdulov with a smile and placed his cowboy hat carefully in the overhead bin. Abdulov was happy to be going home and happy that the pretty Adelya handed him a large glass of Smirnoff on ice before he even took his seat. He marveled at the mountains and canyons as they flew northeast from Tucson.

He thought, "These Soviet planes are the best. The overhead wings let you see unobstructed views. They are comfortable and roomy, and they can land and take off almost anywhere."

The hostess handed him a menu, and he checked the things he wanted. She handed him another giant vodka when she picked up his menu order. Every item of his mixed Turkmen and Russian meal was superb. They were now flying away from the sunset, toward darkness. He was feeling relaxed and drowsy, and his wound was aching a bit. He had taken the last of his pain reliever before he left. The hostess brought him two pills and another vodka.

"Sir, we are going to be flying through the night, mostly over water. It is the ideal time to sleep."

"Thank you." He took the pills with the vodka. Within ten minutes, he was beginning to feel the effect. He decided he better finish his drink, so he slugged it down and felt himself drift off.

~

Bren was joyfully reunited with Layton. The boy was excited about today's motorcycle ride and getting to ride with the sheriff; he had enjoyed a great day. The only trauma was Bren's. Bren delivered Layton to his mother-in-law's house and explained that Ann was feeling sick.

I don't know what to tell Monica. She worries enough about my job when things are normal, and with her present mercurial emotions this will be hard on her.

He returned to be officially interviewed by his fellow officers. Bear Bitters, Andy Lopez, and Al Victor worked on making a report of the incident and gathered and filed evidence from the scenes at Ann's house, the Ashurst Shop, Benson's storage locker and hotel room, the Just-N-Time truck, and the motorcycle.

Pinal County Sheriff's Detective Danny Tomkins served a search warrant on Benson's room at the halfway house in Apache Junction, removing all his personal belongings and impounding his car.

Bren told Sheriff Bitters, "I can't figure out what Benson was trying to accomplish. How was attempting to ambush me in the shop going to cast me in a bad light?"

Bear replied, "Billy Boy had a handwritten journal that covered the period of time from his release up to the meeting today. In it he lists almost daily threatening phone calls from you in which you are trying to shake him down for drugs and money under threat of framing him on false charges, sending him back to prison.

"He even has his cell phone record showing the time and duration of each of these calls from a burner phone he says you used. It's the one you picked up at the door, so it has your fingerprints on it. He was hoping to get roughed up by you, then make his charges against you. He mentioned your harassment to his parole officer last night."

Bren said, "So his scheme was police corruption and brutality against a vulnerable parolee. If his plan worked, I would be dishonored and go to prison, and he would be the star witness against me."

"Yes, but he wasn't nearly as smart as he thought. By coordinating his GPS position during the supposed calls from you, he was always out and about in Safford. The GPS record on the phones show his phone was in the hotel room and 'your' phone was exactly where his ankle bracelet shows him to have been. So, he was using the burner phone and calling his phone, and letting it go to voice mail, which he would hold open a while to create minutes of 'connected time'."

Bren shook his head. "He didn't know we knew every move he made . . . or that my day log would not align with the times and places of the calls he made to his own phone. Thus, we expose his setting up his fake call record and fake diary from two different sources.

Bear added, "Without that advantage, the only serious witness against him would be Ann. But from the dose of Ketamine she received, it's unlikely she will remember anything that happened that day."

Bren nodded, "That loss of memory is what makes it a preferred date rape drug. The victim doesn't remember what happened."

Bear continued, "The day care lady could only describe the 'father' who interviewed her as a bearded working-class man and was surprised it was a deputy that actually dropped the boy off. She doesn't remember much about the deputy, not even his name. She didn't recognize that they were the same person. So, he actually had a pretty good frame up on you, if we had not been on to him from the start. I've called the DPS Investigations Division to conduct the formal investigation, and I will handle the case from our end. We'll call you in for interviews as necessary."

"That sounds good to me. Thanks for standing by me through all this."

~

When they were mid-Atlantic, the copilot walked into the crew lounge. "Ma'am, we are leveled at one-thousand feet and going at minimum speed. We are depressurized. Time to put the traitor to bed."

Adelya unsnapped the two levers holding the seat in place. "Wait a minute," she said. She took the hat from the bin and jammed it on Abdulov's head.

They rolled the seat through the baggage room and the fuel tank passage into the vast empty cargo space and sat it on one of the roller tracks. She instructed her assistant to snap on his lifeline, as she did hers, before she pressed the button on the wall. The ramp lowered, opening a gaping hole in the back of the plane. The roar of the air and the jets was nearly deafening. She pressed a second button that started the rollers, and the seat quickly carried Abdulov to a long freefall and a sudden impact with the ocean. The heavy seat with no floatation was a perfect anchor. Abdulov was no more.

Adelya pressed the "close" button and the big ramp came up and sealed the cabin shut. "Tell the pilot to resume the normal flight path."

"Yes, Ma'am."

As they walked back to the now-empty passenger module, the copilot said to the hostess, "Well, Commander, at least he died doing what he loved."

Adelya smiled. "Yes, drinking and jumping from airplanes."

Fourteen hours later, Lazaros Coreas, on his forty-six-foot trawler out of the Azores, spotted something odd in the water and scooped it up. It was a big black cowboy hat. He handed it to his net master, saying, "O mar dá presentes estranjos." *The sea gives strange gifts.*

Jack Locke was asked to schedule his shift two hours later, since the lab was holding a mandatory "all hands" meeting at eight o'clock. He had told Emma that he would stay and have supper with her before driving up for his eight o'clock start, but that would mean he would have a shorter time with her the next day.

He enjoyed the dinner because Emma had finished this cycle of chemo, and she had regained some appetite. It was the most "normal" thing they had done for weeks. It did infringe on his meager workday sleep schedule, but the lighter, happier time together was well worth it.

He finished up cleaning and securing the platinum room, washed and re-racked his glassware, and had everything ready for his next shift by 7:30. All of the day shift people were there, busily preparing their day's work prior to the start of the meeting. Most of them had found a minute to visit with Jack, which he enjoyed. He had many friends among his coworkers, and his odd schedule kept him from seeing most of them.

At eight, they all gathered in the wide east aisle and the outer edges of the several work stations. Jack sat on his lab stool where he had a good view of the proceedings. Lee called the meeting to order. There was a little uneasiness among them because these kinds of meetings often announced cutbacks in production and temporary layoffs, or other unpopular changes. This feeling of unrest was heightened by the presence of Mr. Peralta, the Executive VP, along with the operations manager and a few other random department heads.

"First, thank you for adjusting your arrival times or postponing your departure," Lee said. "Let me assure you we are not gathered to give you bad news, but to recognize a fellow employee." He introduced the dignitaries, the last of whom was a nice-looking lady in a business suit and heels, looking a little odd with a red SWI guest hard hat on her well-coifed hair.

Lee continued, "Our main lab ware supplier is North American Science Outfitters, and Ms. Alma Himmel is their Vice President of Customer Relations. She would like to make a presentation at this time."

"Thank you, Mr. Gallo. I would like Mr. Jack Locke to come forward." As the crowed parted to let Jack through, she continued, "Our company erroneously marked as back ordered a shipment of platinum that was actually buried in peanuts deep in the crate. It caused a major investigation and a lot of damage to the morale of our shipping employees. It didn't make our insurance company very happy, either, since the lost material was worth almost $83,000." She explained what had happened to create the problem and that the platinum could have been taken without anyone ever knowing.

"But when Jack recently put the remaining items from the crate into service and made sure only peanuts were in the crate, he found the missing platinum. Rather than keep it, he reported it, saving our company considerable loss and an increase in our insurance premiums. Therefore, our board of directors has ordered that Jack receive the gratitude of our company for his honesty, and we have cut a check to him for the standard finder's fee. So, Jack, it is with gratitude and joy that we present you with a check in the amount of $8,300 dollars."

There was applause and cheering as Jack sheepishly accepted the check, and almost every individual congratulated him.

The big wigs all departed through the office, and Lee told Jack, "Kiko Peralta would like to visit with you in the office."

Kiko shook Jack's hand and congratulated him. "You have been with the company in various places for a long time and always done a yeoman's job. I know you are in hard times with Emma's medical costs now, and I want you to know that when you need time off to tend to her or to business related to her illness, you can have the time you need with no adjustment to your salary and no counting days. Lee agrees with me on that, and if necessary, he will personally run your assays."

"I appreciate that more than you know. I was really tempted to keep that platinum, but in the end, I couldn't do it . . . in part because of how good this company has been to me."

"I wish the company could do more in helping with your costs, but we can't take on that kind of expense for our employees and stay in business." Kiko handed Jack a business card. "However, I have ordered a company attorney to take charge of dealing with the insurance company, providers, and facilities to negotiate lower rates and keep them from hounding you.

"So, send all bills to her and make any payments through her. If somebody contacts you about medical costs, have them contact her. It won't stop the medical expenses, but it can regulate the amount and the rate of payment and keep you from having the aggravation and worry. I've told her to meet or talk with you by phone each week and to send correspondence timely to the need. I think Emma's going to get well, and you shouldn't lose everything in the process."

~

At the end of the work day, Kiko Peralta drove down to look at drill sites that had been pioneered by a dozer around the old Giacomo mines and was happy to see they were ready. The drillers were due to set up for boring the first hole the next day. As he drove back toward the plant, the sun had set and the clouds were blazing tones of yellow and red, causing the landscape to have a golden glow. He turned on his lights.

As he drove by the tankhouse, he saw Marco's Jeep sitting by the small, portable office. The lights were on. Kiko pulled over and stepped inside. "Working late tonight, Marco? I thought since you solved the theft, you would be heading home."

"I just want to get the rest of my report for EcoAnthro completed, so I'm finished with my part of the work. This is my last day on this job."

"Well, be sure to include this in your billable hours. Your work as a consultant in environmental, industrial hygiene, and security has been excellent. You deserve every penny you are being paid. In fact, I would hire you, if you ever decide to leave law enforcement."

"I've enjoyed working for you, and I've learned so much. Of course, we will only benefit from the pay to the extent that we expense it for living and travel costs. The rest of it will go to the sheriff's office general funds."

"I will be giving a glowing report to the sheriff on your work for us. I hope we can work with you again sometime."

Kiko thought about the work Marco, Cathy, and Al had done for him, and it didn't seem right that they wouldn't be properly compensated for it. So, he called the sheriff.

"Say, Bear, I wanted to thank you for the great work your two undercover officers and Sergeant Victor did for me. We have successfully resolved both problems."

"Yes, they are really good at what they do. I appreciate your acknowledgement of them."

"We need to send out the W-2 forms to Cathy, and EcoAnthro will be sending 1099s to the other two. We will be changing their employee names to their correct names in our payroll records."

"You won't need to do that, because what they don't use for expenses all goes into our general fund. It is a long-standing policy that officers can't take pay from outside the department."

Kiko said, "We pay for off-duty officers frequently to provide security at special events, and I know the schools and businesses like Walmart do the same thing. Those officers get to keep the pay."

"Well, even in that, you actually pay into kind of an agent fund in our office, and the officers are then paid out of that."

Kiko countered, "Well, these people did real work for us exactly the same and of as high or higher quality than our regular employees. It is not ethically right to not compensate them for that labor. When I left tonight, Marco was working to finish up the reports he was doing for us. Not only that but they were away from their family and their home and community responsibilities. And our payroll records have to show that we took taxes and social security out of the pay."

Kiko added, "They were not paid for police work but for actual added-value production work they performed for us. Don't be stubborn on this thing. Figure out a way for them to receive their due for the work they did for us—work that had absolutely nothing to do with the great police work they also did. If you need, I can send one of our tax lawyers to help you figure out how to do this. It's only right, Bobby."

"Alright, I'll take you up on that. Send the lawyer up this week, and he can look at the law and the policies. If he can show me how to legally do that, I will gladly do it."

Chapter 31

It was nearing the end of his day shift at the store, and DeVon Goode was in the stock room getting it organized and cleaned up.

The manager, Harold Kite, walked in. "Hey, DeVon. The place looks great. You know that Merlinda is getting married in two weeks?"

"Yeah, to some white guy."

"They're going to move to Flagstaff, so I need to replace her as stock supervisor. Now that you are sober all the time, do you want that job? You already know how to do everything."

"You trust me to do that?"

"You aren't going to drink anymore, are you?"

"I don't think so; but I guess I will always be an alcoholic."

"Me, too. But I didn't drink for twelve years already. I can see you are doing good now."

"Yes. I will like that job. Thanks, boss."

"You better clock out now. I don't want to pay no overtime."

DeVon walked home. Going inside, he saw Ma cutting up potatoes.

She said, "I'm going to fry up some potatoes and sausage for dinner. It will be ready pretty soon. Why don't you wash up and set plates on the table? Did you see the Talking Woman at the Health Center this morning?"

"Yes. She is helping me. I've been sober now for five weeks,"

"That makes me happy, DeVon. You're doing good."

"Harold wants me to be stock supervisor when Merlinda moves away. I told him I won't drink no more."

"That's a good thing. I'm proud of you."

"Talking Woman told me I don't drink to hurt no one; but drinking hurts a lot of people, not just the drinker. I think she is right. I'm sorry I hurt you."

"My son, I know she is right. Alcohol has taken everyone but you away from me. I don't want it to take you. Now go wash your hands. I will put the food on the table."

~

Agent Garcia of the FBI called and asked for a half-hour meeting about the Wesley murder. Sheriff Bitters sent a text to Bren and Al asking if they could meet at his office at eleven in the morning.

They met as planned, and Gabe first asked, "I suppose that Sergeant Victor told you that the Republic of Turkmenistan extended an official apology and offer of compensation to the Tribe and the Wesley family?"

Bitters answered, "Yes. That's good."

"No law officer, including me, is happy when diplomatic immunity allows a murderer to walk free. Yet, it is the only way to keep corrupt governments from executing our own diplomats, so it is a necessity. I know it burns in your gut, because it does mine; so, I'm going to tell you something that has to be completely off the record, completely confidential, because it is need-to-know information. You do not need to know, but you deserve to know. If you can't provide complete deniability that this meeting ever happened, then I will leave now without further discussion."

Bitters said, "I agree to those terms. If either of you don't, please leave."

Bren glanced at Al. "We accept the terms as well."

Gabe said, "The Turkmen recalled Abdulov home. They sent a replacement, and Abdulov left two days ago. We had surveillance of the trip, satellite monitoring of the entire flight, as well as the internal communications of the Turkmen intelligence services. The plane was equipped with four first-class seats when it departed Davis-Monthan. Over the mid-Atlantic the plane slowed, dropped down to one-thousand feet altitude, and dropped an object out the rear cargo ramp into the ocean. It was dark, and the satellite image of the object is not great, but it appears to be an occupied first-class seat.

"The plane increased to normal cruising speed and altitude and flew nonstop to Ashgabat. On arrival, there were no passengers, but eight crew members, none of them Abdulov. There were only three first-class seats remaining on the plane. Intercepted communications say that not only did Abdulov commit murder and put the EurMino deal in jeopardy, but he had sold stolen intelligence taken against government orders to a known Russian handler, so his execution was sanctioned."

Gabe finished, "We didn't get to administer justice, but it has been administered."

~

Since they owed Turkmenistan assurance that the funds were used properly, the State Department insisted that a representative from the department be included on the Board of Directors of the Tribal Foundation, and that Helen Dane was to be the first appointee.

Mulikow sent the suggested settlement for wrongful death to his superior in Ashgabat, who quickly responded to accept those terms. They would arrange for the payment through the US State Department as quickly as possible.

The ad hoc committee established by Apache Judge Lowe had acted quickly to incorporate the foundations, establish the boards, and opened trust accounts with a bank. Judge Lowe appointed Attorney Evan Sneezy fiduciary to the two Wesley accounts. So, when Helen Dane was notified by State that they had received the Turkman funds, she provided the account numbers and the amount to be deposited into each account.

In just over one week from the first proposal, the meeting convened with the Tribal Council, all members of the new foundation boards, several members of the Wesley family, a good number of curious tribal members, and all the local press in attendance.

Helen Dane invited Gabe Garcia to attend with her and asked Sergeants Victor and Allred to sit with her on the stand. Helen had hoped Mulikow would at least attend the meeting, but he simply refused.

Later, when Helen and Dr. Garay were alone, Dr. Garay explained, "For a public official to stand and make such an apology, though it is the right thing to do, is politically dangerous. If the decision falls out of political favor with a change in administration, it could be career-ending to have such an embarrassing thing on your record. So Mulikow has wisely kept his name off every correspondence and is not shown anywhere as an approver or recommender. I would love to present the apology and compensation, but that would be especially bad since I'm a female and should not be doing such prestigious things. Women have lost a lot of ground in my country since the fall of the Soviet Union."

Earlier, to lessen the tension for the Wesley family, Al met with them and told them that the Turkmen government had arrested the killer, and he had it on good authority that the man would never breathe free air again.

Helen read both apologies, the one to the family first. She explained, "The Turkmen were very upset that a person they entrusted to represent them had behaved so badly. He has been removed in disgrace and dealt with by his country's laws, which are harsher than our own. They know they can never replace the victim, but they wish to use his name to do good things for the family and the tribe. They understand this better than most, because the Turkmen are themselves tribesmen, and their country is home to five tribes. They want only good for the Apache people."

It was well received, and there were several speeches about their friends, the Turkmen. Helen realized she had oversold the goodness of the dictatorial, vengeful, and corrupt government but consoled herself that the Turkmen people were generally good but oppressed.

~

Harvey Richards had benefitted from both the addiction meetings and the grief support group that Wilma had first told him about. He attended their sessions each week. He had recently become a sponsor to help a new member of the addiction group.

He became involved in a community service organization that used retired volunteers to work a couple of days after school with children from single-parent homes. They helped them with homework, encouraged them to participate in sports and other activities, and in general treated them like grandchildren.

He continued his can and trash collecting a couple of days a week, and he had greatly increased the time he spent on his photography; he even won ribbons for his photos at the county fair. The result of all this was that he didn't spend so much solitary time looking at the four walls of his motor home or watching television: he was with people, he was helping others, and he was doing things he enjoyed.

Wilma Dillard had also continued her participation in the support groups and was now actively working in her church, teaching a monthly class in Relief Society and visiting three ladies as a ministering sister. She forced herself to attend the social activities held by the church: dinners, work meetings, and even those put on by the teenagers and children.

Harvey had mentioned in a meeting that he and his wife had always danced, been in dance clubs, and taught square dancing. He said that he missed that. Wilma invited Harvey to attend the over-forty singles social group of the church. Most of the singles were pretty well all over sixty and almost all women. He attended and became very popular because he was actually an excellent dancer. He enjoyed being in the company of ladies without the awkwardness of romance, though he and Wilma became good friends. His life was back on track, and he intended to keep it that way.

~

Sheriff Bitters had two meetings in his office with one of SWI's labor attorneys: Jillian Bowe, JD, CCP, according to her card. During the first session, Jillian and a student intern spent the day reading the department employee handbook and going through correspondence files dealing with overtime, extra duty pay, use of SO employees and equipment for private security, rules about private part-time work not related to law enforcement, and rules pertaining to conflict of interest.

She also read the county statutes relating to such things. The following day she spent in her Phoenix office writing a case study of the undercover operation and her conclusions on the legality of embedded undercover officers as employees in part of the investigation.

Bowe concluded that none of the federal, state, or county laws, or Sheriff's Department rules prevented deputies from working at a second job, as long as it did not conflict with their duties and loyalty to the department or county. She referred to several instances when deputies were regularly allowed to work for private security in uniform and using county equipment for a fee paid to the county and from which the deputies were paid by the hour for the extra work.

When undercover deputies were paid by a private company for work they were actually doing while they are undercover, either with or without that company's knowledge, it was no different than a second job and it did not conflict with their job as police officers. The pay, Bowe determined, should belong to the deputies and should be reportable income for tax purposes. She noted that they would have to file taxes as on any other income.

Bowe had made an appointment for that afternoon to discuss the question with Miles Autry, a tax law specialist in the Arizona Attorney General's Office. She e-mailed her report to him ahead of their meeting. Autry read the well-researched document and did some research of his own. He agreed with her conclusions and found no conflict or legal issue. He said he would send her a letter to that effect.

Jillian said, "Thanks. I'll put that in the file with my report. However, I'm meeting with my client tomorrow, so for now would you be willing to write a note of agreement on the last page of the report and sign and date it?"

Miles did, and the meeting ended.

The next day, Jillian again met with Sheriff Bitters She gave him a copy of the report and explained it to him and said that the AG's office had reviewed it and agreed with its conclusions. She called his attention to the signature at the end.

Bitters got Pat, Manny, and Al on a conference call and explained about the pay and advised on the tax situation.

"Congratulations for jobs well done," said Bitters. "You deserve the bonus. However, keep in mind that this was a unique situation and future undercover investigations may be handled differently."

~

Deputy Pat Haley, aka Cathy Winn, picked Diana Niyazov up for a steak dinner at the Copper Bistro on Cathy. They placed their orders, and drinks and salads were set on the table.

Cathy said, "Diana, you have become a good friend, and that friendship is genuinely important to me. I will be returning back to my regular job up in Safford, so will no longer be working with you."

"Oh, that makes me sad."

"On the days you come to Pima, let's plan on having lunch together, and when I can, I will visit you in Miami."

"Yes! I will like that."

"I have had a secret that I couldn't tell anyone, but now I can. I'm a sheriff's deputy, a policeman, and I was sent to Miami to find out who was stealing copper from SWI. We solved that mystery, so now I can tell you who I really am."

"I didn't know about stealing copper. Who was doing it?"

Pat explained the situation and how it was discovered. Then Pat said, "So, now I need to introduce the real me to you and hope we still remain good friends. My name is Patricia Haley, but I go by Pat. I really have blonde hair and blue eyes." Pat handed her real driver's license to Diana. "I'm not married, but I have a fiancé, Andy Lopez, who is also a deputy."

"But you are so good as an assay technician."

"I took sciences and chemistry at university and was given task training before I went to work in the lab with you. Other than my name, appearance, and occupation, everything you know about me—the way I think, the things I like and dislike, and my friendship for you—are all real."

"That is good . . . Pat! At least, I will get to see you each week."

~

Diana was at her lab station busy preparing the day's liquid assays when Mr. Peralta came to see her.

"I know that you had to attend the farewell dinner for Abdulov, so you knew he was leaving."

"Yes."

"I talked with Miss Dane of the State Department and thought you would be happy to hear that Mergen Abdulov had been removed from the US and arrested by his own government, and you will never have to worry about him threatening you again. Miss Lane said, 'He will never breathe free air again.' She also said you would know his replacement. It is Dr. Mary Garay."

"Thank you. I always worried because of him. I'm glad he is facing justice." She smiled. "But I'm very happy about Dr. Garay. She is my graduate dean at university, and I also spent time with her at Abdulov's farewell dinner."

~

Al was at the substation trying to get the shift reports e-mailed to San Carlos, when his cell phone rang. It was Bonnie.

"I'm going to take the kids to Joe's science fair. Are you going to be able to make it?"

"Yes. Go ahead and get them there, and I will come as soon as I get this stuff e-mailed to San Carlos. I should be there before anything starts. I know he's eager to see how the judges graded him. I'll be there a couple of minutes behind you."

"Good. Run with lights and siren if you have to," she laughed.

Al had invited the Allreds to come, and they arrived at the same time as Bonnie and the kids. The kids all went into the school activity center together. Bonnie saw Al driving up in his police SUV, so the adults waited for Al who, as a joke for Bonnie, turned on his emergency lights for a few seconds.

They were all delighted to see that Joe's display had three ribbons on it, third grade grand prize, all school third prize, and a blue ribbon for "Best Use of Art." Joe's teacher was as proud as Joe. Pictures were taken, and everyone congratulated the boy.

For his project, Joe researched the Gila monster. The three panels on his folding display included his drawings of the animal, including ancient symbols. It was titled *The Science of Gila Monsters: Nah-shunt-tun-neh*. The first panel, "Anthropology," was about Southwest Native belief that Gila monster was the first medicine man so could heal. The second panel, "Zoology," emphasized that they could go for months without eating yet maintain normal blood sugar. The third panel, "Medicine," told of Byetta, made from Gila monster saliva for controlling blood sugar. In front of the display he had made two Gila monsters of clay, and a clear jar contained Gila monster scat found near Bylas, all resting on a drawing of habitat.

Afterwards, they all went to the Victor home were Al barbecued hamburgers. They sat on the patio watching the sunset turn Mount Turnbull aglow with red. Al thought, "It's wonderful to be back to normal life again."

~

Pat Haley finished her last shift as an assay technician on Wednesday. On her way back to her apartment, she stopped by Walmart and bought two treatments of hair dye remover. She first removed the brown lenses from her eyes and considered throwing them away, but then she decided to clean them and store them. She might need them again sometime.

Pat followed the instructions on the box, and returned her hair, as closely as she could, to its natural color. She packed her things, loaded them into her car, and headed for home.

When she reached Safford, she texted Andy: "I've completed my out-of-town assignment. I feel like celebrating. How would you feel about taking me to get a big ol' cowboy steak? Anywhere you would like, as long as it's in Safford, my treat."

"Great news! Welcome home. What time should I pick you up?"

"I'm hungry. Make it six."

Pat put on a black sheath dress, stockings and heels, a maroon scarf as neckwear, and her squash blossom Navajo necklace. She decided to carry a light sweater just in case it became too cool out.

Andy semi-dressed up, wearing tan slacks, a maroon turtleneck, and a light tan sports jacket. He knocked on her door and was happily surprised that she looked pretty much like her gorgeous old self. They embraced and kissed.

"Well, look at you! You are such a wonderful sight for these lonely eyes."

Andy drove to the Branding Iron, and they sat at a window overlooking the valley. They decided to each get a Porterhouse and the fixings and take what they couldn't eat home.

After finishing, Pat said, "Guess there's no place to go dancing on a Wednesday, is there?"

"There *are* some drawbacks to Safford," Andy said. "But first, I need to tell you how bad I've felt being away from you so much over the last few weeks. I think it's time we did something more permanent, maybe time for some actual commitment from me."

He placed a small black velvet box in front of her. She opened it to see a beautiful emerald-cut diamond that had to be way out of Andy's pay range. She gasped.

Andy took her hand. "I want to spend every day of the rest of my life with you. Patricia Haley, please say you will marry me."

~

Manny packed his single bag and loaded it and a few items of clothing on hangers in the Jeep. He stopped at a barber shop for a short haircut and to have the beard shaved off, then headed for home. He knew that school would be in its last two hours when he reached the house, so he parked the Jeep in back, out of sight of the school. He put away his clothes and bag and waited until the students' parents showed up to pick up their kids. Then he walked over to the school and walked in.

Jenny and Candy were getting some papers ready for the next day's classes, so he stood behind Jenny without saying anything. Candy noticed him and smiled in surprise. Jenny turned to see what was going on and was amazed to see her husband. She grabbed him and almost made him lose his balance.

"Surprise! I'm back. No more out of town work!"

~

Monica Allred told Bren that she felt ten months pregnant, so she didn't care if the baby would decide it was time now. She was eight days from her official due date. She frequently experienced cravings, and she really felt like some spicy Italian food.

She said, "I've been wanting Italian food all day long."

"Well, we wouldn't mind Italian, would we kids?"

"I want it," Lizzy said.

"Me too, me too," agreed Layton.

Bren said, "Why don't you get started on it then?"

Monica punched him in the arm.

Lizzie said, "You better watch it, Bucko. You're going to make her mad!"

"You're getting to sound too much like your mom. But, you may be right. Why don't we go to Toni's instead?"

As they drove to the restaurant, Monica asked, "So what has happened at work? You haven't been this relaxed in weeks."

"I feel like a ton of worries has been lifted off me. We successfully ended a long undercover operation. We found out that a really bad guy that we could not touch because he was a diplomat was arrested by his own country. My favorite aunt is recovered. I have my two best deputies back home. The love of my life is all clear for landing a new baby, and it feels like the universe is back in balance again."

You will also enjoy the new editions of the other books in this prize-winning series from Aakenbaaken & Kent:

The Wham Curse
Deputy Allred and Apache Officer Victor - Book 1

An inexplicable murder of a young Apache boy draws Deputy Bren Allred and Apache Tribal Policeman Victor into a mystery that can be solved only when they tie the murder to a century-old robbery of Army Paymaster Major Wham. Set in both the old West and today's ranch country, the story explores the natural and cultural history, and people of the contemporary rural southwest.

Saints and Sinners
Deputy Allred and Apache Officer Victor - Book 2

Intrigue and murder along the US/Mexico Border. Seventeen-year-old Mariana Villalobos' mystic gift creates a sensation in northern Mexico as hundreds of people undergo a personal religious epiphany. Even gangsters reject crime. Seeing revenues tumble in the drug trade, the Liones cartel issues a hit order on the girl. The Mexican police hide Mariana in the Gila Valley of Arizona while they work with a defector and international law enforcement to dismantle the gang. Graham County Deputies Bren Allred and Manny Sanchez join forces with San Carlos Apache Tribal Policeman Al Victor to identify assassins and protect Mariana. It's a race against time for agents of the DEA, ICE, Spanish Policia National, and the Mexican Policia Judicial. Can they bring the Liones cartel to justice before the girl is harmed?

The Baleful Owl
Deputy Allred and Apache Officer Victor - Book 3

The murder of an archeology student and attempted murder of a second pull Apache Tribal Officer Al Victor into what seems to him a senseless killing. The Arizona Antiquities Task Force brings Deputies Bren Allred and Manny Sanchez into the case. They find themselves investigating a sophisticated high dollar artifact theft ring centered around the unique Baleful Owl effigy. The ruthless ring leader is not motivated by greed, but vengeance for imagined wrongs. Before the case is solved, one of the officers will be the unwitting target of the skilled assassin. The Baleful Owl joins The Wham Curse and Saints & Sinners as the third mystery in Virgil Alexander's rural cop series. Mixed with the main story line is the natural and human history of the Southwest. The cultures of the native tribes, the rural ranchers and farmers, and Hispanic traditions are woven into the unique fabric of the contemporary West.

Acknowledgements

Lois, my teenage sweetheart and forever wife who always assists and encourages me with my writing. I would be lost without her.

Thanks to Mike Orenduff, Publisher at Aakenbaaken & Kent for republishing my first three mysteries and for publishing *Murder in Copper*.

Also, to Billie Johnson who passed away in October 2018. She was the owner of Oak Tree Press. I am grateful to her and her staff for taking a chance on my earlier books.

To Robert Shank who provided geological expertise for this story.

To Sandra of Udall Editorial Services for her excellent editing, good advice, and patience.

The gorgeous Sleeping Beauty sunset on the cover is the work of Globe Photographer Kenneth Chan.
http://www.kennethphotography.com

CPSIA information can be obtained
at www.ICGtesting.com
Printed in the USA
LVHW091537210222
711634LV00012B/78